WANDERING
WILD

WANDERING
WILD

JESSICA TAYLOR

Sky Pony Press
New York

For my parents, for giving me the opportunity to
pursue my dreams.

First Edition

This is a work of fiction. Names, characters, places, and incidents are either the product of the
author's imagination or used fictitiously.

Sky Pony Press books may be purchased in bulk at special discounts for sales promotion, corpora
gifts, fund-raising, or educational purposes. Special editions can also be created to specifications. F
details, contact the Special Sales Department,
Sky Pony Press, 307 West 36th Street, 11th Floor, New York, NY 10018 or
info@skyhorsepublishing.com.

Sky Pony® is a registered trademark of Skyhorse Publishing, Inc®, a Delaware corporation.

Excerpt from PLAYER PIANO: A NOVEL by Kurt Vonnegut, copyright © 1952, 1980 by Kur
Vonnegut, Jr. Used by permission of Dell Publishing, an imprint of Random House, a division o
Penguin Random House LLC. All rights reserved.

Visit our website at skyponypress.com.
jessicataylorwrites.com

10 9 8 7 6 5 4 3 2 1

LIBRARY OF CONGRESS CATALOGING-IN-PUBLICATION DATA
Names: Taylor, Jessica, 1985- author.
Title: Wandering wild / Jessica Taylor.
Description: New York : Sky Pony Press, [2016] | Summary: A teenage girl from a family of Wanderers must choose between the
hustling, rambling way of life she has always known and the townie boy for whom she falls.
Identifiers: LCCN 2015025638| ISBN 9781510704008 (hardback) |
ISBN 9781510704022 (ebook)
Subjects: | CYAC: Swindlers and swindling—Fiction. | Love—Fiction. | BISAC:
JUVENILE FICTION / Fantasy & Magic. | JUVENILE FICTION / Love & Romance. |
JUVENILE FICTION / Family / Siblings. | JUVENILE FICTION / Animals / Birds.
Classification: LCC PZ7.1.T39 Wan 2016 | DDC [Fic]--dc23
LC record available at http://lccn.loc.gov/2015025638

Jacket design by Sarah Brody
Jacket photograph © Margie Hurwich / Arcangel Images

Printed in the United State of America

"I want to stand as close to the edge as I can without going over. Out on the edge you see all kinds of things you can't see from the center."

—Kurt Vonnegut, *Player Piano*

CHAPTER 1

I'M IN LOVE WITH THE SOUND OF TURNING WHEELS. My brother, Wen, says I'm crazy. He hears only the gravel kicking up on the battered doors of our Chevy. Nothing else. He doesn't hear what I do. To me, wheels sound like new places, unknown riches.

They sound like possibility.

I didn't realize that not all people wandered until I was five or six years old. The idea of some people staying put seemed silly, what with all the world to see.

Wen gives me a little grin as he steers the Chevy. He's still a year shy of his license, but the age of fifteen hasn't stopped Boss from putting my brother behind the wheel. Not that a real state-issued driver's license is something I earned on my sixteenth birthday—or something we'd care to earn at all.

The foot tucked under my hip tingles and throbs from being cramped for hours. I uncoil my limbs, unstick my skin from the vinyl seat, and let my toes wiggle the AC vents up and down.

Wen cuts his eyes at me over the top of his sunglasses. "How ladylike."

"Ladylike?" I glare across the truck, winning a smile. "How boring."

My feet aren't like other girls', I know. They're browned from sun and dirt, toenails painted the brightest shade of drugstore red I could steal.

His smile fades as he turns his attention back to the road. He hates this part of our life. Says these trips create an aching inside his chest, like he's always leaving part of himself somewhere else. He told me once that he imagines little pieces of our hearts scattered all over the South, and he wonders if those pieces can ever grow back or if our broken-up hearts find a way to compensate, pumping a little harder.

He doesn't dare share those foolish, heartsick thoughts with anyone but me. And my dreams—those are secrets I don't voice at all.

I rest my head against the seat, careful not to catch my hair in the sticky spots where the duct tape is peeling away from the cracked vinyl. Wen thinks I'm drifting off to sleep, I'm sure.

With my eyes closed, I pretend we're not driving through the South Carolina wild. I'm somewhere I've only seen in our encyclopedias, riding through the Sahara in a safari Jeep with the top off, sand stinging my skin.

Wen soon cranks down the manual window, inviting the heat and humidity inside, swallowing my daydreams of arid climates.

He cracks his knuckles and groans. "My new shirt."

Blood trickles from a gash that's opened on his knuckle, and a crimson spot blooms under the paisley cotton sleeve of his shirt. A few drops are nothing. He's lost too much good clothing to stains we scrubbed and scrubbed and couldn't remove.

I shimmy lower in my seat and squeeze my eyes shut again. "Better than spilling your blood in the dirt."

"Thanks for the input, Talia."

To anyone who knows me at all, I'm Tal. Wen calls me Talia, the way our mother does—did—only when I've gotten under his skin. We haven't seen Mom since parole confined her to the state of Ohio.

I'd rather not argue with my brother, so I listen to the hum of tires carrying us far away from places we're ready to leave behind. The names of the towns all melt together, their flavor the same. Every one of them tastes like an orange we've sucked dry.

We pull into a little town called Pike, sharing nothing more than twenty-two dollars and the hunger for a mark. Through the thin Chevy windows, I catch the sounds of civilized life: the purrs of lawn mowers and the voices of trusting people who haven't learned better yet.

We have almost an hour to use to our advantage before we'll meet up with the rest of the caravan and hit the road again. For now, it's just my brother and me adrift, checking out our prospects, the best place to hook a mark.

There's a Denny's by the gas station at the edge of town. Wen flicks his eyes toward me, and I can practically see the possibilities turning in his head.

"You're thinking toureys?"

"Read my mind," he says.

Something about scamming tourists makes me queasy. A quick gas-up and a belly full of greasy pancakes, and those families are on their way to the beach or an amusement park or wherever the hell tourists take their kids for their end-of-summer getaways.

"Let's explore first," I say.

Cruising down the main drag, Wen slows the truck and points to a run-down local joint with a dilapidated sign. "Chicken and . . ." He drops his sunglasses to the tip of his nose and pushes them back into place. ". . . something."

Those great big burned-out letters spell out a word that makes me beam inside. "Billiards. Chicken and Billiards. Interesting."

"Your pool game is rusty."

"So I'll warm up."

"I vote for Denny's," he says. "We need a tourey, not a local."

A tourist means we can run a scam in this town again because after we're through, our victim will be on his way. But I'm not in the mood for a scam or a trick or a sleight of hand. I'm craving a hustle—a little not-so-friendly game I'm sure to win.

"There's a spot around the side." I point to a stretch of curb that's long enough to park our Chevy and the tent trailer it's dragging. "Ours for the taking."

Wen whistles long and low. "I don't like it, Tal." But he does a U-turn on Main Street and slides us into the parking space.

Rona turned the Chevy and tent trailer over to us when I turned fourteen—old enough to pass for sixteen, my real age now. And the age on my fake ID. Living off the grid, without real birth certificates and social security numbers, we couldn't get legal driver's licenses anyway. We don't even have last names.

The air conditioner dies, making the humidity glue my white tank top to my rib cage and my jeans to my thighs. As Wen slides from the cab, the sun highlights the purple smudge beneath his left eye.

"Wait. You look like a bum." I fish around in the glove box, fingers dancing through a collection of counterfeit insurance papers and registrations, until I hook a tube of concealer.

"I am a bum, Tal, and I hate that shit."

"We have to hand over fifty to Boss. That's it. We'll get pizza with the rest of the money. Okay?" I say.

The promise of food usually breaks through his pesky moral code, and I'm not above manipulating him with a doughy, greasy wheel of cheese. A luxury.

He slips back inside the truck's cabin.

I grab Wen's smooth chin between my fingers and dab a glob of concealer over the bruise. Before he can answer, I start blending. He winces each time my fingertips touch his skin.

Inches away, I look at my little brother in a way I haven't in months. His dark hair is cropped too short. From a distance, he's a man—a small man by most people's yardstick, but still a man. This close, he's almost pretty with his long lashes and lips that are fuller than mine. Bare-knuckle fights have cracked open those lips more times than I can count.

Not tonight. Not as long as I'm successful.

Outside, the sun sears the road. The smell of gasoline and dust hangs in the September air. On these civilized streets, we don't fit in, though we've trained all our lives to do just that. The crisp scent of the forest is a memory, one I already miss.

Through the glass of a dress shop, a woman stares

after us, and I can no longer shake the feeling we're con-spicuous. My white tank top is startling against my skin. I'm tanned—not that rich-kid, I-spent-the-summer-in-Saint-Tropez kind of tanned. Tanned in the way of something that belongs in the wild. Not the ideal look for a hustler trying to blend in with the townies.

Wen blows out a long breath as we near the front door. "I have a bad feeling about this place."

My hand poised over the door handle, I turn back.

"Wen," I say. "Fortune favors the bold."

CHAPTER 2

I PUSH MY SUNGLASSES ON TOP OF MY HEAD AS WE make our entrance. While I'd love to survey the prospects—the five or so people eating fried chicken or throwing back a cold one—I leave that job to Wen.

He struts his way to the bar, faking confidence that only I know he's lacking.

Road signs, license plates, and assorted tacky memorabilia hang from the walls of Chicken and Billiards. The place is gritty like a great big welcome home. That is, until I see the Confederate flag hanging from the ceiling behind the bar.

These people wouldn't accept us if they knew the truth—that we're a couple of Wanderers in their root-planting world. I envision the word forming on the tongues of the townies, hissing from between their front teeth: *gypsies.*

Wen props his elbows onto the counter. "Two Cokes, please."

"Y'all are from out of town, aren't you?" asks the

guy working the beer tap.

"Yeah, our parents are taking care of this real estate thing nearby. My sister and I got bored and came downtown."

I walk around the perimeter of the room, all the way to the pool table, where I run my fingers over the watermarked mahogany rib. The royal blue bed is faded, and some of those cue sticks are obviously warped, but I *oooh* and *ahhh* as if I'm mesmerized by this mysterious game. At least, that's what I want these people to think.

Wen comes back holding two old-fashioned bottles of Coke.

"Options, please," I whisper as a Coke slips from his hand to mine.

He eyes the flag. "I think we should take off. I still have that bad feeling."

"Wen, run it down. Coordinates. Give them to me."

He presses his battered knuckles to his mouth, holding my stone-cold stare, then sighs. "Okay. Old guy by the window keeps looking at your ass. There's a waitress—"

"No waitresses." Waitresses are wives or mothers or students. They might go for the scam but not out of greed. Out of desperation. Desperate markies are something I don't do. We all have a line, and that's mine.

"Fine. There's a white-bread guy by the counter about your age. Rich as Croesus, no doubt."

My brother's chock-full of useless knowledge, like who the hell Croesus is, but I prefer my information to be of the useful variety.

I glance around Wen to the plaid-shirted back at the lunch counter. A dark head is bent over an open textbook. Book smart is the easiest kind of mark. They think they're untrickable, and even when they've been outwitted, they won't admit it because then they wouldn't be untrickable. It's a vicious cycle—one I feed off in every town.

"Perfect." The Coke is ice cold as I tip it back and let it glug down my throat. I come up for air and throw my voice. "So, this is pool?"

"Yes, sister dear," says Wen. I don't allow myself to smile, though I love it when he does his sarcastic act.

"What's the object of the game?"

Wen talks a little louder than me. "You claim a suit—stripes or solids—then you pocket all of them. To win, you pocket all the balls in your suit and pocket the eight ball last."

I point around the edges of the table. "Does that mean you knock the balls into those holes there?"

"Exactly."

"Teach me how to play."

"Ah. Come on, Amy." *Amy.* We hadn't even agreed on aliases. My brother's not bad at rolling with the flow of a con.

"Please."

"Only if we make it interesting."

"Fine," I huff. "Twenty bucks on the game."

House cues are hung from the wall beside the table. Wen rolls each one between his palms, a casual gesture to anyone else. Truth is, he's making sure they're not too warped. Mine is low quality, but straight as a pin.

Wen racks the balls and breaks them, and the show is on. He makes a real production of giving me tips, talking about *precise aim* and *fluid strokes*. I line up perfect shots one after another, only to tilt the cue and miss them all.

The boy at the lunch counter looks back at us every few plays.

It's not long until Wen calls, "Eight ball, corner pocket!" He sinks it, and the game is done.

"Is that it?" I ask.

"Fast game. Don't forget you owe me twenty bucks, Amy."

I hop up on the edge of the pool table, crossing my legs and uncrossing them. Markie boy's watching me. He lingers on the torn knees of my jeans, where tanned skin peeks through the denim, before I draw his gaze to mine. For a moment, I think he'll try to look away, and that's when I smirk. He gives me back a sheepish smile. *Yahtzee.*

He closes his textbook and swaggers over to us. "Wasn't really a fair game if you ask me."

I twirl the cue stick between my fingers. "I couldn't agree more."

With his shirtsleeves rolled up to his elbows, he's right out of the pages of some sleepy-Southern-town courtroom drama, but he's a couple of graduations shy of being the protagonist, the young hotshot lawyer hell-bent on setting the town on its ear.

"Hey, man, I'm Joel," Wen says. He steps between us and clasps the guy's shoulder. "This is my sister, Amy."

"Spencer Sway." He shakes Wen's hand, all manners and orthodontics and naïveté, and then reaches for mine. Our palms meet; this is the part where I usually hang on to the mark a little too long. This time, it's Spencer who keeps my hand inside his, running his thumb across the back of my hand until my skin tingles. And I can't help it—I'm intrigued.

A smile tugs at the corner of his mouth before he lets go and turns back to my brother. "You want to play another game?"

"Twenty bucks okay with you?" says Wen.

He thinks he's challenging Wen, but it's me who will be playing Spencer Sway—in more ways than one. Spencer reaches into his pocket and riffles through his wallet, where there's a substantial amount of green inside. He presses a twenty onto the corner of the table.

My heartbeat quickens with the anticipation of that money becoming mine.

Now it's time to make the switch from Wen to me. If Spencer refuses to play me, then we'll have to take our chances with Wen, who's only a fair player.

I have a good feeling about Spencer, though. He'll play me. Or I should say: let me play him.

I pull two tens from my pocket, all I've got on me, set them atop Spencer's bill, and take the cue from Wen.

Hair hangs over Spencer's right eye as he glances up from racking the balls. He's still wearing that smile. "We really don't have to play for cash."

"You're insulting me, Spencer. It's fine."

I close in on the table, and he pushes the hair from his eyes, those unruly strands the only thing out of place on him.

Spencer Sway was no doubt born right here in Pike and is destined to die here, too, with his kind, light brown eyes, jeans a dark indigo like they've never been washed, and plaid shirt that's all perpendicular lines and starch.

I almost feel sorry for him. Every few months, I wake up somewhere new, with the forest, the river, or the ocean right outside the windows of my tent trailer. He's trapped in this finite, small-town world while I have infinity at my fingertips. While the world is mine.

"Would you like to break?" I say.

Spencer chalks his cue stick. "Do you want me to?"

"Oh, I think I can manage." I brush my hand across his upper back as I navigate around him. His shirt feels stiff against my fingertips. Most of our clothes are threadbare and worn in a way that makes them so deliciously soft against our skin. Except Wen's. He never keeps anything around too long. He prefers the finest buttondowns we can swipe from department store shelves.

The balls explode outward from my sharp break, two stripes disappearing in a corner pocket. It's murderous and beautiful and everything I love about the game of pool.

It kills me to have to miss the next shot, but it's necessary.

I line up my cue, strike, and the ball barely rolls a few inches down the bed.

"Don't worry about it," says Spencer. "That was really good for a beginner." He takes his turn, sinking a solid. "So you're in town for a real estate thing. What kind of a transaction?"

"You're just full of questions, aren't you?"

"Guess so." A cocky little smile spreads across his lips. "And I have a feeling you're full of secrets."

I rest my elbows on the edge of the table, cradling my cheek in my hand while I look him up and down. "Our parents are transferring some property, if you must know. One of their old summer homes they're sick and tired of." I nod to the silver watch wrapped around his wrist like an expensive handcuff. "I'm sure you know a thing or two about discarding unwanted toys."

The cue pauses between his fingers. "Ouch." Right then, Spencer makes a combo bank shot. This game is turning disastrous fast.

"You're breaking my heart, Spencer Sway."

He grins, lining up his next shot. I hold my breath, willing him to miss. He does.

"Watch your weight distribution this time." Spencer steps behind me, his boat shoe nudging my left foot backward. "Keep your left foot about two feet behind your right."

I take a long drink from my Coke, wipe my mouth on the back of my hand, and kick my shoes off. "Thanks for the tip."

Wen meets my eyes. I'm forgetting myself, caring more about the win than discretion. Letting my rules become a casualty of this game.

"Fourteen ball, corner pocket," I say.

Wen shakes his head slightly. The key to hustling is to avoid pocketing too many impressive shots, or the mark knows he's being had; at least that's what I'm always telling Wen. Breaking my own rules isn't wise.

"That's a difficult shot, Amy." Spencer actually sounds a little concerned I'm getting myself in a pickle. He's right about it being tricky. It's one most players would miss. One a novice shouldn't even attempt.

What Spencer doesn't know is that I am no novice.

I blow the hair clear from my eyes as I bring the cue in line. Wen gives me a look sharp as glass. I ignore him and shoot the fourteen ball into the corner pocket.

Spencer slides his hands deep inside his pockets and grins. "Impressive."

Wen stands away from the table with his arms crossed. "Beginner's luck."

It takes every drop of restraint to miss the next shot.

Spencer lifts up his cue, aims, and one after another, sinks the last of the solids. "Eight ball, side pocket," he calls.

All the blood drains from my face as the ball disappears from sight.

If I had forty more dollars, I'd snap my fingers and say, "Double or nothing." But I'm broke, and I'm honestly not sure I'd win anyway.

He's living proof I can be conquered.

Collecting the cash from the edge of the table, I fold our money in half—his and mine—and walk to him, the crisp bills as good as disintegrating in my palm. I plant one hand on his chest and, with the other, drop the money into his shirt pocket.

"Good game."

His cheeks darken as he retrieves the bills. "Take your money, please."

Wen's words are hurried. "That's really nice of you—"

"You take it," I interrupt, pushing Spencer's winnings away. "It's yours."

"No, really, I was just having fun. Been playing pool with my dad since I could see over the table." He arches closer and brings his mouth beside my ear as he whispers, "I didn't mean to hustle you."

The words pour over me, seeping into all the places where embarrassment settles and never lets go.

I *didn't mean to hustle* you.

"Spencer." I squeeze my hand around his, making his fist swallow up the money inside. "I insist."

As my brother and I step onto the dusty sidewalk outside, dazed and squinting against the sun, clarity washes over me like ice water. There won't be any pizza tonight or any winnings to take to camp or any explanation that will satisfy Boss.

I failed, and I've offered up my little brother as sacrifice.

CHAPTER 3

IT'S JUST ON THE OTHER SIDE OF THE FOREST, THAT place where our existence bleeds into theirs. That's where our new home always is, though the whole caravan is sweaty and road sick and dying for me to pick the exact spot.

We're parked a few miles outside of Pike, Wen and me and the rest of our Wanderer camp. Wen's at the wheel, and I'm gooping another coat of red polish onto my toes.

Lando, Boss's son, stands beside me at the Chevy's passenger window, baking under the summer sun in his crisp pin-striped wool. He dresses like his dad is dead and he's been made Boss already, strutting around the dusty camp in his fine suits.

"My temper's getting hotter than a two-dollar pistol," Lando says. "I do believe your talent is waning, Talia, and so is your usefulness."

Wen's grip is nervous on the wheel, one hand squeezing tight and the other stroking the scabs on his knuckles.

I twirl the ring on my finger, this oversized faux thing I stole from a secondhand store near Montgomery. "Does Boss think my talent is fading?"

Lando ducks out of the sunlight and under the shadow of our truck. He isn't much older than me, but he looks it—living out in the open has aged him at least ten years past his twenty-something.

"You listen to me." Lando stabs his finger through the air. "What my father thinks is none of your concern."

I've hit a sore spot, bringing up the idea that Boss might trust me more than he does his own son.

"I'll take that as a no. So I suppose I'm still your compass, and I suppose I'll let you know when we've arrived."

A compass. It's the only lie I've ever told that's become unmanageable.

Why Boss lets me choose our new destination—why he calls me his compass—I don't exactly know. I am our camp's compass simply because Boss proclaimed it. And because Boss says it's so, I am.

I was seven the first time I chose the camp's direction. We drove and drove until the light gray sky turned black and then light gray again. Rona was behind the wheel of

Mom's Chevy, with me balanced on top of a small ice chest in the passenger seat, clinging to the handles for dear life, and Wen low in the middle between us.

It was some time after Mom got put away. I know it, because Rona, who was—and I guess still is—our mom's best friend, was in charge of us by then. It could have been two years or two days after; I couldn't say. Maybe childhood memories are that way for everyone—markies and Wanderers the same. But for Wanderers, I suppose, those memories are even more vague. When nothing is the same from day to day, there's no anchor, only ambiguous, timeless, placeless years that flow together.

All I remember is the trees rushing past our windows, their branches interlocking and turning the road into a tunnel. Wen ducked low as our truck passed beneath them, like the trees might smack him in the head.

I was tired of driving, of staring at the taillights of an RV. The more restless I became, the less I worried about causing a ruckus. At the fork in the road, Rona came to a stop and cranked the wheel hard left.

"Stop!" I shrieked. "Stop! Stop! Stop!"

Rona slowed, and while her tires were still spinning, I pulled on the door handle and rolled off the ice chest and onto the road.

It was a stupid thing to do—a childish fit—but I was

a child.

I took off, running over the edge of the asphalt, between trees and over brush until the tantrum inside me calmed to a quiet still.

The whole caravan had come to a halt when I jumped out, all of them filing from their vehicles and searching past the boundless line of trees. All looking for me.

Lando was the one to find me. He grabbed a handful of my hair and wrenched me by my roots all the way to the Chevy. I fought him the whole distance with nails and teeth and swift kicks to his shins.

Rona was hysterical, pleading with him to let me go.

Lando froze when we heard Boss's wheezing—this was back when he could still talk—through the open window of his air-conditioned RV.

"Let me speak to the girl," he said. Boss's legs had long since gone out, so Rona lifted me up to reach him. I clung to the frame of the window while his soft hand covered mine. "What's the problem, child? Do you have some reason you feel we should be here?"

"Uh-huh," I said. It was a lie, though.

"What did it feel like?"

"Like—like I just had to get out of the truck."

"Ah, yes. A tugging from within you, telling us we should camp here?"

I nodded.

"And so we shall." He looked past my shoulder, scanning across the bank where I'd been standing. "The Spirit of the Falconer," he said with reverence. "He's revealed your talents. You are our compass. From now on, we won't find our luck, Talia. Our luck will find you."

From that day forward, I became our compass, building lies around this fictional tugging inside me that took us to lucky places. Not everyone in camp believed right away. No, that took time. Time, and another lie. But now everyone calls me their compass. Everyone except Lando. I'm not sure he's ever believed in me.

I take the camp wherever I claim that feeling inside me tugs. North, east, south, or west. What nobody knows—not even Wen—is that I'm the one doing the picking.

My talent is a lie. And there's nothing I do as well as lying.

"We're close," says Wen to Lando, arching across me and speaking in his confident mid-con way. "Don't you think we're close, Tal?"

Lando leans deeper inside our truck when I don't answer. "You said we were close back 'round the other side of McClellanville, Talia."

"Well, now we're a hell of a lot closer."

He kicks at a patch of ground, sending up a dirt

cloud around his black pants, and points a finger at me. "You better take a shine to somewhere before night-fall."

He walks off toward the fourteen vehicles idling on the side of road—RVs, campers, and trucks—our whole caravan.

Wen starts the engine. "You like getting a rise out of him. It's no good, Tal. No good."

Soon everything will be Lando's, us included. When that happens, I don't know how we'll keep going, how we'll keep our wheels on the road. The only change scarier than Lando in control is sitting still.

In the side mirror, I watch the rest of camp trickle into line behind us. We could settle here. That was my plan all along—to pick a spot near Pike. Now I'm dead set on getting far away from this town. I can't chance ever coming across Spencer Sway again.

We drive another hour or so, toward the wide blue sky, with me whispering a few vague directions at Wen.

"Am I on the right track?" he asks.

I open one eye. "North for three more miles."

When my "gift" made its miraculous appearance, Wen was five years old, a kid who might not hold my secret so close to his heart. I'd tell him now—how the aching, the tingling, they're figments of my imag-ination—if I didn't know he'd be hurt by years of my deception.

I pick a place a short distance ahead, a dirt road leading off the mountain into a patch of trees. That's the spot I'll tell Wen to turn.

I wonder what would happen if I claimed we were supposed to be on the other side of the world. What would they say if that fraudulent feeling took me where our wheels couldn't travel?

In the rearview mirror, Rona guides her Mazda truck behind us.

Wen catches me looking and says, "I think you need to stop giving Rona the silent treatment."

"And I think you need to pay attention to the road." I notice Wen isn't braking for our turn at the same time I realize I never told him to make it. "Hey, hey, slow down. Left here."

He brakes so hard the tires screech, and the tent trailer we're hauling gallops.

The truck ambles down the road to the place where cement ends and dirt road begins. Wen steers us around potholes as best he can. The seat bucks under my hips as he yanks the wheel straight.

"Up there." I point to a clearing.

Wen slows the truck under the cover of high-up branches.

They come. The last of the trucks and RVs and cars fall in behind us. Eleven families—thirty-eight of us, in all—circle up vehicles and trickle into the woods.

The sun dips low in the sky, and we keep our hide-away aglow with lantern light to finish settling in. Wanderers carry baskets and boxes, building a home beneath the shadow of trees.

"It's a lovely day for moving," says Wen.

"Yes," I say. "Yes, it is."

CHAPTER 4

IN THE CLEARING, A FEW MILES NORTH OF A TOWN called Cedar Falls, we're safe from discovery. It's a curious thing how nobody finds us, with us parked right beneath the great big sky, in the stretches of wilderness sprawling between markie homes.

I suppose I'm the only one who lies in the dark at night half asleep and prepared for that moment when an outsider stumbles into our camp. It wouldn't take much: a crop duster flying overhead, a lost troop of Boy Scouts peeking through the pines.

Everyone in camp is sure it won't happen—just as certain that no outsider will plant one toe inside our camp as they know the sun will come up tomorrow. They believe we're protected—that the Spirit of the Falconer protects us. No matter how hard I try, I can only stretch my beliefs so far before they get so thin they disintegrate.

We sit around the fire at the heart of camp, ice chests for chairs and no ceiling except the night sky. Smoke burns my throat while we eat a dinner of barbecue and iced tea.

Through the flames of the campfire, Sonia's stare catches me. Her eyes are blurs of smudged eyeliner and mascara. There's a longing there, in her eyes and inside my chest.

For most of my life, I thought Sonia was my best friend. Now something's shifted. I want to find a way to glue those pieces back together, but there's nothing I can do to make them fit, especially now that she's pregnant.

Wen balances his paper plate on his knees as he mops up barbecue sauce with his napkin. "To think, we could have had pizza tonight."

"He won the game," I whisper. "It was only right he keep the money."

"When did your moral code make an appearance?"

I silently sip the last of my iced tea because I'm all out of answers, and his questions are limitless.

While my dinner is still digesting, I lose Wen to a pack of whooping boys.

His words linger.

I'm not sure when my moral code showed up or if it was always there, under the surface like a disease, waiting for the day when some markie would actually beat me fair and square. If that's true, I'm in desperate need of a cure.

Rona crooks her finger for me. I pretend I don't see her and play with the strands of leather that have come unbound from my bracelet.

It isn't long before the blanket shifts, and she crouches beside me. I tuck my legs to my chest, resting my chin in the dip between my knees. We haven't spoken since we left Greenville—that was four days ago. In a way, we haven't spoken in months.

"Wen told me what really happened today," she says. "About that markie giving you the runaround, getting the best of you. Damn if I can't believe he beat you."

When it was time to hand in our offerings to the family bank, we had to give an explanation for our empty pockets. We didn't tell the truth.

"Yeah, even a blind squirrel finds an acorn every now and then."

Her fingers comb through my hair and catch on the tangles the rolled-down windows made. "Honey, I won't tell nobody."

I nod a little, tapping my chin against my kneecaps.

"Your hair is so long now. And dark. Much darker than Greta's at your age." That name steals my breath. It's been years since I've heard my mother's name pass anyone's lips. "You haven't let me cut it since Kentucky."

Gathering my hair up in one hand, I pull it over my shoulder and outside her reach. "I like it long."

When we were children, Rona would tuck us into our sleeping bags and paint the history of our people in pretty words. "Where the sky's a little bluer," she'd say, "the trees a little greener, that's where we'll live until our toes begin to tingle, our feet ache to travel, and we're sick for the urge to wander again."

Sometimes, if we were good, which was almost never, in her storytelling voice she'd reveal secrets from her youth, the scams she and Mom ran when they were best friends growing up in the camp together. Every night, Rona would promise Mom would come back soon. She doesn't promise that anymore.

I can't think about the past too long or how Rona's sitting beside me full of unsaid words, because Wen appears from behind a tent, barefoot and wearing his old, blood-stained jeans and no shirt.

The deadly games are about to begin.

Bare-knuckle fighting is entertainment as much as it's a thriving business inside camp. There aren't many rules, just knuckles against skin and cartilage and sometimes bone.

Everyone's got bits of money tucked away that they don't mind betting on an opponent. Lando takes a small cut of each bet, regardless of the outcome, so while everyone else sometimes loses, Lando is always a winner. Most everyone throws money into the game—out of sport or greed or fear of Lando. No matter the reason, their bets keep Wen's knuckles raw and the camp bank full of cash.

It's a family event, too. When we were kids, we'd sit between Mom and Rona for every fight. Wen would bury his face inside his shirt, even after the last punches were thrown. But me, I couldn't tear my eyes from the blood and carnage.

We're not too different from the markies. They host fights for the world to watch on great big TVs. We hold our fights in secret.

Lando rolls Boss's wheelchair down his RV ramp. We all look to Boss now.

His legs haven't worked since before I was alive, but it was only a few years back when a stroke stole his ability to speak. Now his voice is nothing more than a little blackboard and a package of chalk. Lando's the one to execute whatever demands Boss scratches out, trying to be something to Boss that he'll never quite manage. Trying to become Boss.

The screech of chalk digging into his slate makes my flesh crawl, even before I see the glaring white letters: *Wen fights Horatio.*

At the opposite end of our circle, Horatio emerges from the shadows of Boss's RV. He's got the body of a pit bull packed into a seventeen-year-old boy. Wen's never had to fight anyone as large as him.

Crawling to my knees, I'll do close to anything to

put an end to this. "You can't make Wen fight him!"

Rona grabs my arm, anchoring me to the ground.

Between our old winter blankets, in the high cabinets of the trailer, Wen and I have a Cool Whip tub stowed away. It's full of bills we've skimmed off Boss's take. No matter how low things get, we abide by one rule: Money goes in and doesn't ever come out. I wouldn't say it's for a rainy day—more for a hurricane. Tonight might be that perfect storm.

Against my ear, Rona says, "It's not worth you making a fuss. There's not a thing you can do to stop it. Besides, Wen agreed. Because of the money y'all didn't bring in from the hustle."

Lando leaves Boss with a bell and the chalkboard in his lap, and cups his hands around his mouth. "Listen up!" Everyone falls silent. "Three-minute rounds with ten-second breaks. No hitting below the belt. No biting."

Though the night is cool and the fire is small, sweat drips down Wen's back. He'd never admit it to anyone in the camp, not even me, but I know he's shaking inside.

Slowly, we all turn to Boss. He lifts his feeble hand and rings the bell. It's a small sound, a jingle more than a true ring, but enough to signal the fight has begun.

Horatio swings, and Wen ducks the punch before bouncing straight up and outside Horatio's reach.

Wen's not that large, and he's not particularly strong, but he's light on his feet. He never wins, but he can

31

delay the punches for longer than most. These fights are another kind of con: my brother keeping the game rolling long enough to make everyone believe, if only for a few minutes, that the game is equally matched. He's a trick, too. The illusion of a fighter.

Horatio rears back and aims for Wen's rib cage. The sensation hits—I can feel my own ribs splintering—but Wen turns his body to the side, narrowing Horatio's target and dodging the fist.

"Time!" calls Lando.

Wen and Horatio both retreat to the sidelines.

Rona eases back on her blanket. Six or seven seasons ago, when Wen had his first match, Rona tried acting like fighting was another rite of passage, but I hadn't sat too far from her. With every punch thrown, her fists clenched and her teeth ground together. After she caught me watching, she guarded her gestures more carefully.

Emil gives Wen some water and a towel and claps him on the shoulder a couple of times. But Emil's reassuring grin is a lie.

The game starts back up, and Horatio slams his fist toward Wen. Again, Wen ducks. Horatio stumbles forward, losing his footing. Wen thinks he has him now—I can see it in his smirk. He advances on Horatio, gaining on him with each step. He swings and clocks Horatio's chin.

I'm midcheer as a sly smile creeps across Horatio's face. Wen's leaning forward, all the weight of him off balance, a horrible position to dodge a punch. Horatio's fist crashes into Wen's cheek. The campfire hisses as a shower of blood hits the flames.

Wen falls to the ground and lies perfectly still for a second too long. Then his back heaves, so I know he's still breathing. I'm able to breathe again myself.

The rules forbid striking a downed opponent, and for one hopeful second, I think Wen's about to forfeit.

Don't get up. Don't get up. Rona glances at me—I was whispering it out loud.

Wen's ribs twist under his sweaty skin as he pushes up on his forearms. He plants one foot solidly into the ground as Horatio swings.

His fist explodes against Wen's skull, leaving my brother a heap of limbs on the ground, inhaling the dry summer dirt.

Boss rings the bell. It's done.

A group of boys descends on Wen's unmoving body, slapping at his back and splashing water on his face.

"Tal!" yells Emil across the circle. He loops Wen's arm around his shoulder, lifting my brother to a standing position. "We're taking him back to your trailer."

Rona's hand lingers on my arm as I rise.

I freeze. "Not now."

"Tal, please. Let's talk," she says. "I stand by what I

did. No good would have come from me telling you."

In that moment, those last bits of affection I have for Rona slip away. I hate her for starting this now—when Wen needs me—after there's been nothing but silence between us for months.

She sighs. "Someday, we're gonna have to talk."

I pretend I didn't hear her and head into the shadows between the RVs.

On the lit-up porch of Lando's trailer glows a half-empty fifth of Jack Daniel's. My feet should keep moving. My hands should stay buried in my pockets. But my body's never been any good at doing what it's supposed to do.

I take a quick look around and slip the bottle beneath the waistband of my jeans.

CHAPTER 5

THE BOYS OF CAMP ALL CROWD AROUND THE DOOR of my tent trailer, laughing and blowing smoke rings into the night air. They've dumped Wen inside, and now they're happy to revel in the carnage for a few minutes longer.

"Don't you guys have anything better to do?"

They take one look at me, tapping my foot in the dirt, and the cigarettes hanging from their lips go still. One by one, they part down the middle. They head up the dirt road, slinking around bumpers or slipping between trees, leaving a cloud of smoke in their wake.

I find Wen sitting up in his bed.

The trailer is perfect for only us. We each have our own nooks, the places where mesh netting extends past the base of the trailer, tucking two twin beds onto the ledges at opposite ends. The mesh sides keep a steady stream of air flowing over us as we sleep. There's no plumbing to the kitchen, so bottled water's as good as gold, and there's no bathroom, so we make use of the

RVs around us or, occasionally, the forest. The trailer sleeps six people, floor space included, but only if the dining table is collapsed and converted into a bed.

A halo from Wen's book light circles him. We were fresh out of batteries. He must have robbed a couple from one of the flashlights.

I sink the side of my hip into the Formica tabletop. "What are you reading?"

"*D.*" He flashes me the spine of his encyclopedia as he holds a wad of paper towels against his bleeding cheek.

We have a little more than a half set of encyclopedias, *A* through *N*. Mom and Rona hot-wired some markie's car when we were kids; the encyclopedias were in the trunk. Rona wanted us to toss them, said they weighed us down and wasted too much gas, but Wen wouldn't have it.

Sometimes, I wonder if he thinks he can find the answers to all his questions inside those encyclopedias. The answers to all the magic our people build our existence around. Answers to my supposed gift. I hope there are things that live and breathe outside his books, things people can't explain. I hope.

He lodges his finger between the pages to hold his spot. "So, when you get these feelings about where we're supposed to go next, what's it like?"

Every time we make camp in a new town, it's

become our ritual for me to tell him again. A sad kind of fairy tale. I give my rehearsed answer as I search for antiseptic and bandages. "Like an aching in my arms and legs. It tugs at me, pulling me in the right direction."

"Dowsing's real, you know?" he says. "I read it."

"It's nothing like dowsing. I find places I think will be lucky."

"Well, it's close." He thumbs through *D* and starts reading. "Dowsing is a form of divination in which one locates water, oil, underground metals, gems—"

"It's a good thing I'm not telepathic. We don't have *T*."

The paper towels on his face are now blooming with blood.

"Okay," I say. "Put the book down and come here, will you?"

There was a time when I loved that he read, knowing he wasn't becoming like the other buffoons in camp. The encyclopedias were a distraction then, and not an obsession. Now those books give Wen funny ideas about markie life, ideas I worry will end with him planted in one place, leaving me to wander the world alone.

Rona doesn't like him reading them, either, though she's never said a word about Sonia's paperback romance habit. I guess Wen knowing about the real world scares Rona more than Sonia's made-up ones.

He jerks as I dab an antiseptic-soaked cotton ball against his cheek. Taking his face between my palms, I blow on the cut to take the sting away the way our mother used to. Blood still oozes down his cheek, but the cut's shallow. He won't need stitches.

"Hold this on it. Hard." I press his hand over the fresh paper towel. "Lots of pressure until the bleeding stops."

"Where were you after dinner?" he asks.

"Talking to Rona."

"I was going to tell you the fight was against Horatio."

"Doubtful. You'd have told me it was Horatio, and I would've cleaned out every bit"—I drop to a whisper—"of our savings to get you out of it. Now that, *that*, is the reason you didn't find me."

"You should have taken our money back from that markie. Then I wouldn't have had to fight. You're too prideful, Tal."

He's right. About a lot of things. I'd put my pride ahead of him when I pushed the money into Spencer Sway's hand. That's why Wen got beaten. It's the kind of thing my mother would have done.

"Said the pot to the kettle. You hit the damn ground out there. But you had to get back up, didn't you?"

"That's honor. Honor's different." Wen moves the paper towel off his eyes and looks at me. "Did you talk to Rona, or did Rona talk to you?"

I don't have the patience for speaking in code. "We're not doing this again."

"I don't know what happened between you, but you gotta let it go. When it comes time to marry Felix, you'll want her on your side. We need her—"

"We don't need her," I say.

Felix, his parents, and his brothers and sisters—six kids in all—live with a northeast-bound caravan, and have since I was a kid. He's a faceless, bodiless myth of a boy who Boss has fixed me to.

Ensuring we end up married to our own kind keeps our existence afloat, Boss used to say. Marriages unite us with other caravans that have power and money and connections. Boss'll find other good families, people we'll be compatible with, who we can build lives beside. Passion fades, but family connections can grow into love. Or something deeper that's less fleeting.

Arranged marriages are the lifeblood of the Wanderer community. But living in a society that buys and sells girls doesn't feel right to me and Wen.

He's wearing his saddest of frowns.

"Hey," I say, "I've got fifteen months until I'm eighteen. More than a year to figure things out." Fifteen months to get a scheme into place that gives my future back to the person it should belong to—me.

Wen shakes his head. "When Boss fixes you with someone, there's no breaking free."

The night breeze drifting through the screens makes goose bumps rise on my bare arms. I grab one of Wen's old flannels—one he thinks he's too good to wear now that he's stolen a few nicer shirts—and slip it over my arms. "You know how my mind works, Wen. Give me enough time, and I'll con my way out of this marriage."

He opens his mouth and pauses. I think my reasoning has chipped away at his fears. Until he blurts, "It's one of the old ways. They don't screw with the old ways, and you know it. Besides, it might not be Boss's decision anymore. . . ."

My fingers go still for only a second. I secure the last few buttons, pretending a future with Lando in control doesn't scare me.

Through the screen windows, the blur of a white sundress moves through the dark.

Across the dirt road already beaten down by Wanderer feet, Sonia's smoky eyes watch me from between the trailers. Her hand lifts in a small wave, but I drop my eyes to the floor.

Emil and Sonia are the perfect endorsement for the practice of arranging marriages. When they were born, Boss proclaimed—when he could proclaim instead of scratch out—that Emil and Sonia were betrothed. So they grew up feeling like one of them was the sun and the other the moon.

She's living proof these arranged marriages mean losing a part of yourself. I plan on keeping all of me.

Wen leans forward and stares out the screen door. Sonia's already long gone.

"I've got something that'll make all this up to you." From under the waistband of my jeans, I retrieve the fifth of whiskey.

"And from whom did you procure that?"

"From Lando."

"He gave it to you? You don't mind owing him a favor?"

The bottle of whiskey hums as I use my tank top to wipe invisible germs off the lip. I pass him the bottle.

His fingers pause inches away, and he stares at me. "You didn't."

"Don't worry about Lando."

"He's going to murder us in our sleep!"

"If he finds out," I say, "I'll make sure I'm the only one to blame."

Wen sips and shudders, shaking fat tears down his cheeks. "That's what I worry about."

I tip the bottle back and gulp. Heat spreads from my tongue, over my throat, and deep in my stomach. It's enough of a distraction, for him and for me.

"Take it easy, Tal."

I come up for air with the lantern lights swirling and my body already unwinding from the booze.

As I wipe the back of my hand across my mouth, Wen says, "Sometimes you scare me."

The last couple of swallows slosh inside the bottle as I tilt it to Wen. He holds up his hands, so I knock it back and finish off every drop.

He groans and kills the light.

I climb into my bed, and Wen's voice cuts through the dark.

"Good night, Tal. Good night, you thief, you vagabond."

Rona would come by our trailer when we were kids, kiss us both on the foreheads, and say those very words to us, the words she and Mom exchanged every night in the dark. She doesn't say them to anyone anymore. Maybe it's silly, but it's Wen who whispers those words to me every night, unable to let the trappings of childhood die.

The thrill of the drink takes me far away. Even though my body is lightly swaying in my bed, my mind is racing across oceans.

CHAPTER 6

"How much farther is it to the lake, Tal?"

"Very close. I think."

Behind me, Wen trips over brush and weeds. "I'm not speaking to you all week if we don't find it soon."

I smile. "Promise?"

We're supposed to make ourselves scarce for the afternoon while Rona and some guys from camp set a scam in motion. With me, the compass, and Wen, a bare-knuckle fighter, if there are no cons to run, our days mostly belong to our whims.

We lay off the big cons, Wen and I, at least for now. Too many of our people doing business in town at once is a bottled hurricane waiting to break loose.

"It's like we're walking downhill," he mutters.

"Think of it this way. There's only so far down we can go."

"That's, like, a metaphor for everything you've ever convinced me to do."

Right then, a speck of dark blue glitters in the brush.

A few more steps and the trees give way to a lake that's smooth as glass, water pooling at the bottom of a deep valley like punch in a bowl.

It's early September, and this will probably be our last swim of the summer.

My tank top and cut-offs are a heap on the dock before Wen even drops his sunglasses on the bank. I break the surface, skin stinging as the icy water laps against my calves, my thighs, my waist, before I dive and sink under its weight. The cold knocks the air out of me, so I shoot straight up toward the sunlight.

Wen stands at the edge of the dock, his toes inches from the edge. "Is it cold? It looks cold."

I wring my hair out, holding back my shivers. "Like bathwater."

Wen jumps off the dock and disappears beneath the surface. He comes up shrieking. "My junk shrunk down to nothing!"

I tread farther away from the bank. "Like I want to hear about your junk."

My legs kick hard, harder than they had to last summer at the ocean. The salt makes the water denser and bodies more buoyant—Wen read that in one of his encyclopedias. *B* for *buoyancy*, I guess.

"It's getting warmer," I say.

His teeth chatter. "You're just getting numb."

We both float on our backs and stare up at the fathomless sky. As the waves sway me back and forth, I close my eyes. I'm in a trance or half-asleep when Wen says, "Look at all those houses." He points at the homes dotting the horizon. "That's the life."

"A markie's life. You'd really want to live in one of those prisons?"

His silence is as good as a yes.

After a moment, he says, "We really could leave." His voice is a small, nervous thing using those forbidden words. "Stay put, I mean, when the camp moves on."

Chills stab at me as I right myself. I plunge lower, submerging everything beneath my neck.

Wen swims so close I can see beads of water clinging to his eyelashes. "We could make it. You're street smart. I'm book smart."

Wandering sings to me, maybe too much, and Wen knows it plain as day. Sometimes I think the continental US is too small. I want to see places the Chevy can't go, fly in planes, and cross the limitless ocean. At least wandering keeps us seeing something new every few weeks or months.

We couldn't run our scams, just me and Wen. The camp will protect us if our cons head south. Scamming without camp would mean foster homes for Wen and me both.

But it's more than that keeping me tied to camp. It's living out in the wild, sunrises and sunsets, dancing under the moonlight, and never being tied down to monthly payments or institutionalized learning.

Wen doesn't share those loves.

Before I can stop myself, I say the one thing that might change his mind: "What about Mom?"

He springs away from me like I've bitten him. Instantly, I'm aching with regret.

Mom will be joining us soon. That's the lie we've been telling ourselves for over a year now. She was in prison from the time Wen was five and I was six. Pyramid scheme, a felony.

When they set her free two years ago, the state boundaries of Ohio became her jail. That is, unless she broke parole. Law-breaking is no stranger to us, but according to the judge, if she violated her parole again, her hair would be whiter than snow before he'd let her see daylight.

We said our good-byes, and she got a job as a waitress while her friend from the inside rented her a room in a duplex. Mom couldn't wander, and her friend didn't have room for two kids, so we stayed with the camp under Rona's care, the way things had been for nine years at that point—the three of us waiting.

That was fine by us, until the truth came out last year.

Camp had been silent the night the voices in our heads

started driving us crazy. Wen said we should visit Mom, break away from camp for a few days. We left a few minutes past midnight.

But when we got to Ohio the next afternoon, the duplex was vacant, and the manager of the diner had never even heard of Mom.

Wen didn't say anything the whole way back to the Kansas state line. As I drove, I told him she must have gotten restless, joined up with another camp, and couldn't make it home to us yet. That's what I said, even though I didn't believe it myself.

He stared at the rotted-out floorboard and watched the asphalt passing through the holes between his shoes all the way back.

The lights of camp were twinkling from the way-off road as Wen turned to me. "I don't want to keep rehashing this, Tal. If we keep talking about Mom running off, it's going to become more real, and it's going to consume us, and I want to bury this in a box and forget it ever happened."

"We have to at least ask Rona if she knows something."

"No. Rona will make excuses for Mom, like she always does."

There was nothing truer, so I said, "All right," and, for the love of money, I hoped Wen's acceptance of the whole thing would last. Not two seconds later, I remembered why I didn't believe in wasting my time on hoping.

His lips quivered. "Mom will start to feel bad for what she's done, and then she'll come back."

"Oh, Wen."

"No, she will." His knuckles were white as he gripped the dash. "I know it."

So between us, we let Mom become what she'd been before, someone who was coming back soon, after parole or after a scam or after whatever she was doing. That was the way Wen and I talked, maybe even the way Wen felt. But it wasn't how I felt then, and it's not how I feel now.

Three days later, I realized I couldn't keep my promise to Wen.

After he went to sleep, I crept through the trees, where birches bleached the forest a stark white, all the way to Rona's trailer.

"She's never ever coming back," I said, pacing across the creaking floor while the rest of camp was sound asleep. "Is she?"

Rona sat in her bed with one of her nighttime turbans on her head. "You can't blame her. Greta—your mother—she couldn't be trapped up there—"

"But what about us? Why didn't she come back for *us*?"

"You shouldn't have to know this, but there's no way

around it." Rona wrung her hands and tapped her foot against the trailer floor. "She couldn't stand being held back, by camp or nothing. Even you and Wen, you were anchors to her, and the responsibility became too much."

"You say it like that's normal. We're her kids! You can't make excuses for that." I went for the door, but realization washed over me, and I turned around. "Rona, did you know she was going to run?"

She didn't speak for a long time. Her silence said everything.

"The responsibility of two kids, it would have killed her," she whispered. "She's my best friend. She did the best she could for as long as she could, and you're going to have to accept her for what she was."

That was when I decided Rona had been poison to Mom. She would be poison to me, too—if I was stupid enough to let her.

"Fuck Mom," I said. "And fuck you, too."

It wasn't just a few hateful words that ruined our relationship, but that moment marked a change in the way we looked at each other. The fault line had been there for months, a hairline crack that grew into a ravine and kept spreading until Rona and I were standing on different continents.

I never said a word about it to Wen. To this day, I've stowed it away in the darkest valleys inside me.

The water feels colder. I can't stay stagnant in the lake a moment longer. I look around, and it's not too far to the opposite bank. "Hey, I'll race you!"

Before he has a chance to accept the challenge, I wedge my feet into Wen's stomach and spring off him like he's a diving board. I'm at least twelve feet ahead before I hear him splashing.

My muscles burn, pushing through the water fast enough to keep my lead. First to touch down on the other bank is the winner—always the rules of engagement. Being three inches taller, Wen's got an advantage. I kick, and my foot connects with his shoulder.

Before long, my feet touch a slippery, sludge-covered rock. I stand and yell, "Loser!"

"Cheater!"

"Cheater?" I plant my hands on my hips, right above the waterline, and grin. "You know there aren't any real rules."

Something rustles from behind the trees, followed by the sound of twigs snapping.

Wen opens his mouth, and I say, "Shh."

Two girls pop onto the beach, carrying neon-colored pool noodles and metallic beach bags, wearing sunglasses that are too big for their faces, and speaking in voices that sound like money.

Wen tilts his head toward the far bank. Isolation has become his crutch, and he's not good at casual conversation unless he's scamming someone.

"No, let's stay."

"What's the angle?" he whispers.

"No angle. I'm not going to let a couple of markies run us off."

One of the girls tiptoes close to the water's edge. She wears a one-piece bathing suit, red with navy polka dots and a thin navy belt cinched around her tiny waist.

"You're on your own," Wen says. He swims off into the middle of the lake before the girl even dampens her knees.

"Hey, there!" she calls from the bank. I straighten and run my palms over my tangled, wet hair. She stays planted, so I swim closer. "You're not from around here."

I tell the standard lie we give everyone who asks us for an explanation: "No. We're on vacation with our parents."

"I'm Whitney." For all her interest in me, you'd think I had a mermaid tail instead of two tanned legs, kicking beneath the surface.

"Rachel," I say.

Girls like this are the kind I used to work alongside Sonia. She adored making small talk with markie girls while we stole a twenty or two from their wallets. Sonia said it was as close to markie life as she ever wanted to get, but for an hour or so, she loved walking the tight-wire between our worlds.

Whitney points to the middle of the lake where Wen is floating on his back like a broken starfish. "Who's that?"

"My brother . . ." I run down a list of past aliases. "Elliot."

This pleases Whitney. I can tell by the way her dimples deepen. "You guys want a beer? My cousin bought us some." She winks and adds, "She's in college."

"Elliot," I call. He doesn't open his eyes. "Elliot!" I scream. He sinks into the lake and turns. "You want a beer?"

He shakes his head.

"He's real shy, but I sure wouldn't mind one."

"Ow!" She yelps, and hops on one foot, rubbing the bottom of the other one. "Don't these rocks kill your feet?"

My red toes are splayed on a pile of sharp stones. I never even noticed. "I guess I have tough soles."

"Guess so. I need a pedicure just looking at these rocks. Cozumel this is not."

Cozumel. I file it in my mental list of places to look up in the encyclopedias.

"This is Rachel," she says to a girl with a cell phone pressed against her ear. "That's Nya." The girl with the cell phone lifts her chin.

The can of beer is lukewarm, but I gulp it anyway. Whitney and I sit on the edge of her towel as Nya struts between the trees in search of better reception.

Whitney holds her legs so we're calf to calf, her milky skin next to mine. "Your tan is so pretty. Is it a spray tan?"

"No, it's real." There's no denying that I carry the warmth of the sun on me.

She looks to the other side of the lake where Wen now stands on the dock. "Did you access the lake from that side?"

"We sure did. My brother parked his Beamer on the dirt road."

"I didn't think people still used those old dirt roads."

"Well"—I smile—"we did."

She scans me, from my toes to my bikini and back again. She removes her oversized sunglasses, crinkles her eyes in the sunlight, and grins. "I'm having a party Saturday night." She points to a house at the top of the hill, one with a big wood deck that extends way outward. "Right up there."

"Yeah?"

"It's a back-to-school party. I always throw the best one. Think you can come—you and your brother, I mean?"

Oh, that's an opportunity for moneymaking I can't pass up. "We might be free Saturday night."

She squeezes my hands like we're destined to be the best of friends. These townie kids have been warned against strangers with candy and seedy school janitors, not people like us.

"We've been cordially invited to a party on Saturday night. A markie party. I think you know what that means."

Wen places his hands on his knees to catch his breath. Walking to camp through the brush isn't as easy as it was on the way down. "Saturday night is my show?"

"Damn straight." Saturday night, Wen's in charge of the con. "I'm Rachel," I say, "and you're Elliot."

He rubs his wet hair. "What happened to Amy and Joel? Should have used those names from the Chicken and Billiards hustle back in Pike. Joel and Amy."

"Pike is two hours away." Two hours separating me from that pool hall, and more importantly, me and a boy named Spencer Sway.

"You used to make us cross state lines before switching aliases. You're losing your touch."

My foot catches something, and before my face smacks the dirt, I break my fall against a tree. The piece of plastic between my toes has come free from the socket on my flip-flop. As I try to force the piece inside the hole, I realize Wen's bent over something in the grass.

I hop closer and notice the chocolate-colored feathers. It's dead.

"It's an owl," Wen says like he can't quite believe it.

Our people tell stories of long ago, when a man called the Falconer was the greatest Wanderer huntsman. He and his falcons provided enough prey to feed his camp until the markies started building homes that outright destroyed falcon habitats and hunting grounds. Faced with a starving people, the Falconer trained owls.

When the Falconer passed from this world into the next, the owls came out in droves, flocking across the sky to guide him into the underworld, or that's how the story goes. Now they say the Spirit of the Falconer protects Wanderers, sending owls as warnings. The stories are like oxygen in camp. Everyone believes them and always has. But in my heart of hearts, I don't.

"Shit," he says. "I don't want to leave yet. We just got here."

As soon as we tell others about this owl, they'll throw together our belongings, and we'll all be flying down the road again. I wouldn't mind if it wasn't for Whitney's party—if the seeds of my con hadn't already been planted.

A thought occurs to me, a sinister proposition in the eyes of camp.

"Wen, what if we don't tell?"

"What do you mean don't tell? Someone else will see it."

"Let's bury it. Nobody has to know."

He stares up at me, squinting against the sunlight. Finally, he nods. To agree to be my accomplice in this, he must hate the road more than I ever imagined.

We use broken branches to dig a hole beside a hawthorn tree. Wen lifts the owl into the grave, and, as we're covering it, a weight builds on my chest—the gravity of what we could be hiding. I could be wrong about everything—omens and the Spirit of the Falconer, too. But I don't think I'm wrong.

I step away and let Wen drop the last handful of dirt.

CHAPTER 7

WE'RE IDLING BESIDE SOME MARKIE SCHOOL IN THE middle of town when I notice Wen looking longingly out the passenger window at a group of teenagers swarming from double doors.

When we were kids, we'd drive through big cities and small towns, through the swamplands of Louisiana, through the Rockies, and one sight appeared over and over, no matter the landscape outside the Chevy. Kids our age would be lined up at bus stops or waiting in crowds outside of schools, all loaded down with backpacks. The longing would catch me for a few seconds, and I'd wonder how it would be to spend my mornings standing on the asphalt beside them, spilling gossip, and trading secrets.

That feeling always floated away from me. Not Wen, though. He'd press his small hands against the window, trying to erase every inch of distance between him and them.

"Padding, it's all padding," Rona would say. "That's what those markie school lessons are. Organized day care's all it is. You kids are too smart for those markie schools. Those teachers would waste your time." Then she'd reach over and pat my leg. "And you, Tal, you'd eat those other kids alive."

"Look at these people," Wen says now. "Those backpacks are probably full of books."

"Must get heavy."

His shoes scrape against the rusted-out floorboard.

I dance my fingers against the steering wheel, willing the light to change colors. "You'd miss so much if you stayed in one place, you know?"

So quietly I almost don't hear him, he says, "You don't even think about what we leave in our rearview mirrors."

He read to me once—in *E* for *Earth*—that the world spins at a thousand miles per hour, but we don't even feel a shudder. Sometimes, it seems we're running right along with it. I know what he wants. He wants to sit still for a while and watch things go by—the things we don't stay long enough to notice.

There's a small part of me, the part I try to ignore, that wants to kick back and watch the world carry on around me, too. I almost tell Wen, but the light turns, letting me gun it through downtown and away from the school and all those foolish temptations.

Between the drugstore and the post office, I park the car. "We need batteries. But, first, we need money."

We case the sidewalk from the truck, our clothes sticking to our skin as we wait for a markie—an opportunity—to walk on by. Soon a man wearing a sport coat and starched-and-ironed jeans heads our way.

"I got this one," Wen says.

"Why, thank you."

"Save your gratitude." He spills some bottled water in his hands and runs them through his hair. "The last time you took lead, we lost out on a pizza."

Wen struts down the sidewalk, heading straight toward the man. I lift up on the steering wheel, craning my neck to watch the exchange closely. Especially the critical moment their bodies meet.

Wen never slows his steps, and the man's pockets don't crinkle as Wen lifts his wallet then circles the block before heading back to the Chevy.

He dumps the cash and tosses me the wallet while he counts.

"Eighty-three dollars," he says.

"Not bad." We should save it, but the pizza I promised is waiting, and the movies are calling.

In the shade of the drugstore, I kick the wallet under a bench. Some Good Samaritan's bound to return it to the man, so at least he'll get back his ID and credit cards.

As I look up, I'm struck by the sight.

Great big windows take up the whole face of the drugstore, every inch of them spotless except for painted-on advertisements for back-to-school specials like wide-ruled notebook paper and number two pencils.

There's something about those windows.

Wen glances at the drugstore, the street, then the drugstore again. "What is it?"

"It's nothing," I say. "Nothing."

But there's no denying that these wide windows, with their Palson's Family Drugstore logo, are familiar.

Wen slides down the waxed aisle of the drugstore, wearing a pair of mirrored aviators, the price tag hanging between his eyes. Off the rack, I grab a pair of black sunglasses studded with fake diamonds. I pucker my lips and perch the frames on the end of my nose as I look in the mirror.

My reflection reminds me of the picture of Mom that Wen keeps inside the glove box of the Chevy. Sunglasses cover her clear blue-green eyes as she makes a peace sign at whoever's taking the picture—Rona, no doubt.

I place them back on the rack where they belong.

Wen admires his reflection and fingers the price tag. "I think I'm going to buy these."

"You'll be wasting our money. Every dollar we spend is a dollar we have to steal."

I check the aisle for people and the ceiling for cameras, then slip the glasses from his face and into the bag at my hip, price tag and all.

Wen homes in on a point past my shoulder. My suspicion prickles. We might have to make a run for it.

"Our friend from the pool hall," he whispers. "He's walking this way. Three. Two. One."

I mouth, *shit*, before I whirl around and come face to face with the lazy smile of the only boy to ever get the better of me, a boy I thought belonged two hours down the road in a town called Pike.

I smirk and cross my arms. "If it isn't Spencer Sway, the pool shark."

He ambles closer, wearing a lazy smile. "You know, you've kept me up at night, riddled with guilt over that."

"Oh, Spencer, there's enough losing in life to feel bad about. Never feel bad for winning."

He glances to my hips, where my bag is slung, hiding the shoplifted glasses.

Wen thrusts his hand toward Spencer. "Hey, man."

"I'm sorry," Spencer says as he pumps Wen's hand. "I can't remember your name."

Wen opens his mouth, but nothing comes out.

Spencer's face is frozen with this expression that will only hold so long before it melts into uncertainty. I can't remember, either. This is the moment when you give a name, any name, and hope against all hope

61

that the markie never remembered the first alias you told them.

"Joel," Wen says. He holds up the batteries in his hand and makes his way toward the register. "I'll go pay for our stuff."

I skim over the dark indigo of Spencer's jeans, his buttoned-up linen shirt, searching his arms for something interesting, a package of condoms or a bottle of booze. But there's nothing in front of me other than a white-bread boy who's easy on the eyes—in a way markie girls would like. All he's carrying is a white paper medicine bag and a thick book with the words STONEWALL JACKSON UNIVERSITY FALL CATALOG running down the spine.

"Getting a jump on next year's plans," he says with a weak smile.

I nod like I understand what he's saying, and he slides the book against his hip, so the title's no longer readable.

Behind me, I hear Wen passing money back and forth at the register, changing bills so fast the clerk's getting confused. An old Wanderer trick, which Wen hasn't quite mastered. Sometimes my brother's timing is terrible.

Spencer pivots toward the counter, but I plant my hand in the crook of his elbow and guide him deeper into the store.

"So what are you doing here? I thought you lived

in Pike."

He cringes and leans closer. "Keep it down. I wasn't supposed to be in Pike, and, well, gossip travels quick in this town."

"Oooh," I whisper. "Where *should* you have been?"

"AP chemistry. But my attention span felt a little short that day."

"I can imagine." I flick the white paper bag he's holding. "Picking up your Adderall?"

He smiles and pulls it a few inches out of my reach. "For my little sister. She's got a cold." He cranes his neck to the front of the store where Wen stands. "Hey, are you two okay?"

I swallow. "Perfect."

"It's your brother . . ." He brings a finger to his own cheek—the same spot as Wen's bruise. Spencer's noticed. "That's one hell of a shiner."

"Oh no, he's clumsy as all get out. Fell down and hit his cheek on our family's schooner. High seas. You see, my brother's supposed to wear glasses. Drives our mom up a tree that he won't, but he's vain. Horribly vain."

"Meet you in the truck, *Amy*," yells Wen.

"Why don't your parents get him contacts?"

Smart-ass. "Can't wear 'em. He's got a condition with the shape of his eyes, and the doctors say no contacts."

"Astigmatism?"

"Exactly." Really, I have no idea what he's talking about. I add *astigmatism* to my encyclopedia list. "You probably have things to do, don't you, Spencer?"

"Have you ever considered a career in the military? Because you're an old pro at handing out marching orders."

We step onto the pristine, litter-free Cedar Falls sidewalk. Beside the door, Wen's got one foot propped on the bench, where a little girl is sitting with her ice cream cone. He flips a quarter in the air and slaps it down on his wrist. "See, heads again."

She climbs onto her knees and gapes at the coin. "Wow."

"You ready to go, Mags?" Spencer wiggles his fingers, and the girl comes to his side and takes his hand. "My sister, Margaret."

Her eyes are serious, staring up at Spencer. "That boy can do magic. He throws the coin in the air, and it's always heads."

He was teaching her how to do a controlled toss, a sleight of hand where you toss the coin in the air so it wobbles but never flips. That's how we control the outcome of the coin flip every time. Wen shouldn't be doing it here.

Spencer drops to his knee beside Margaret and dabs at her mouth with a napkin from his pocket. "It's probably a trick coin. Both sides are heads, right, Joel?"

Wen cringes and slips the coin inside his pocket. "Right."

I have to change the subject, so I grab on to my knees and bend to Margaret's eye level. "How old are you, Margaret?"

"Seven," she answers.

"Five," says Spencer. "She lies."

Margaret and I have something in common.

I slump against the front of the Chevy, the metal grate burning through my shirt. "Big age gap. What are you, seventeen, eighteen, forty-five?"

"First guess. She was, uh"—Spencer lowers his voice—"a surprise. In more ways than one." He points to the Italian restaurant beside the drugstore. "We're going to get pizza. You want to come along?"

Wen lurches forward, and it takes all my restraint not to reach forward and haul his pizza-loving ass into the Chevy.

"No, thanks," I say. "Our parents are probably wondering where we got to."

Spencer crosses the dusty sidewalk, leaving a few feet to separate us. "Maybe I'll see you around town."

"Stranger things have happened." Squinting at the sun, I reach up and brush that one stubborn piece of hair free from his eyes. A compulsion, a reflex to fix the one out-of-sorts thing about him.

Both Spencer and Margaret trail off down the sidewalk as our engine turns over.

Wen digs through my bag for his new glasses and

slides them onto his face, inspecting his reflection in the vanity mirror. "So we're not getting pizza now?"

"We shouldn't be eating with them. And I do believe this is a one-pizza-joint town."

I pull into the road, and the Chevy idles behind a crop of kids in the crosswalk. Out the passenger side, Margaret waves at us through the windows of the pizza shop. Spencer lifts his hand.

There's something more behind Spencer's eyes, some kind of knowing that sets my cucumber-cool nerves on edge.

CHAPTER 8

WE LIE IN OUR BEDS, NOT STILL HUNGRY, BUT NOT satisfied, either. I lay my encyclopedia across my shirt, with my eyes closed, and hug it against my chest. Not even *A*, with its grayscale pictures of sweeping plains and rugged jungles, is enough to calm the stirring inside me.

Our screens do nothing to deaden the sound of the kids yelling outside. It's near midnight, and they're still running around chasing fireflies.

Wen stops thumbing through *G* and rolls over onto his side. "She talked to me first, you know? Said she was bored. How was I supposed to know she was his sister?"

"Doesn't matter."

"She was a kid," he says. "Who's going to listen to her?"

"They're markies, Wen, and that's his little sister. They're different from us. They might listen. And you didn't have to shortchange the clerk."

"Don't give me that. You've shortchanged every

clerk who's waited on you for the last six months." He opens *G* and reads, but his feet rustle through the sheets. "Did you know giraffes can live for months without water? That's longer than a camel."

I press my lips together, holding on to my smile. My brother knows I can't stay angry with him for long.

"No, I didn't know that."

I've read through the half set of encyclopedias once, skipping over most of the topics. Not my brother—Wen's read them all cover to cover at least five times.

Our band of Wanderers values the education they believe we need. We didn't sit in classrooms with sharpened number-two pencils poised, studying grammar on a blackboard. Cons and scams were where Rona focused our young, moldable minds. And we learned by doing.

Wen and I could pick someone clean as soon as we were tall enough to reach their pockets. Rona taught us enough about search-and-seizure law to keep our wrists out of handcuffs. Then there was math—math without infinite numbers, geometry, cosines, and tangents. And at the center of our teaching was cold, hard cash. First, there was dealing out bills until we could count it faster than most markies, fast enough to shortchange a clerk. Next, we learned enough statistics to help us place a bet and win.

Education came in small doses, but those who

wanted to find it within the Wanderer world did. Wen and I did both—wanted it and found it—though we had different reasons. He loved the idea of knowing things, and I just wanted to know them.

He wanted to learn how the world worked, and I wanted to learn how to work the world.

"You're not still thinking about going to that markie party Saturday, are you?" he asks.

"And why wouldn't I be?"

"Are you sure it's a good idea? Our luck's been shit since we got to town."

"One night, Wen. One good night and we're free as birds for at least a month."

"*Free as birds*," he repeats, like he's tasting the words. "Speaking of birds . . . maybe that owl was a warning we shouldn't be doing this. From the Falconer."

The owl we buried is a memory neither of us seems able to shake. For me, the owl is nothing but a reminder that I have no faith. I would tell Wen I don't believe, if only that didn't make me the one to shatter his beliefs.

"You really think it works like that? Because I don't see it that way." I hate the cadence of my voice when I'm manipulating my brother. "If something bad was going to happen, we'd have more than one sign, you know?"

He nods to himself.

"Wen, just give me one night."

He turns off his book light, and I know I've won

69

him over. "Good night, you thief, you vagabond."

"Good night."

My mind is already drifting across oceans as a voice cuts through.

"You kids in there?"

Rona's got her nose pressed against the screen, and she's rattling the door.

"We're sleeping!" I scream.

Wen hops off the bed to let her inside. He hangs a lantern from the tent ceiling and gives me a dirty look as she stops under its light.

Rona's applied a bold ring of red lipstick and sprayed so much hair spray her hair is peppered with flecks of white. All fixed up for some reason. I have a feeling I'm about to learn why.

"Felix is here," she says.

The book on my chest tumbles from my mattress to the floor. "What do you mean, he's here? It's not time. I'm—I'm only sixteen."

Our Formica countertop creaks against her weight as she settles her hips against it. She stares down at the linoleum and then meets my eyes. "Sixteen's not so unheard of. Perfectly marriageable in the eyes of Boss."

Nothing was supposed to happen until I turned eighteen—an adult in every world, even the markies'. My months for planning a way to keep all of me, they've been stolen. I'm a good enough thief to know when I've been swindled.

I expect rage to come screaming out of me, but Rona's words are a noose around my throat.

"Where is he now?" I manage.

"Boss's RV. With Boss and Lando. Lando says you gotta at least say hello."

"I don't want to see him. Fuck this."

"Why you gotta talk like that?" Rona sighs. "This ain't nothing, honey. They won't marry you off tonight."

Wen slides from the kitchen booth and wedges himself between us. "She's not going to marry anyone."

This'll hurt him as much as it will me, and I have to stay strong enough for the both of us. I stand straighter and command those fleeting parts of me to stay put a little longer. Nothing's happened yet, and freedom is still mine to claim.

Rona shakes a finger at him. "Don't you be putting more stubborn ideas in Tal's head. She's got enough of them on her own." She turns to me. "It's only a little greeting. You've gotta say hello."

"There must be a way out," says Wen. His words grow shaky, like he's trying not to cry. "Nothing can be that absolute."

Rona rests her shoulder against the door frame. "If there's a way out of it, I'm hard pressed to find it. Not with Felix's family paying such a high price for Tal."

Money. It makes the world go round, they say.

Felix's family used it once to buy me for him. A bundle of money can buy me back again, for myself this time. How to get my hands on enough cash, I'm not sure.

Tonight Felix is a dozen trailers over, waiting to meet me. I've got to treat this like any other con and fake whatever needs faking until I can pull a plan together. Surprise is always a part of the cons and, therefore, an old friend of mine.

I hop off my mattress, the pads of my feet stinging as they hit the floor. "Let's get this over with."

We head toward the heart of camp, Rona, Wen, and me. In some camps, girls get married as early as fifteen, but Boss and Lando have been lax when it comes to that tradition.

I'm three months away from my seventeenth birthday, and it's been eight months since I watched marriage tear apart everything Sonia was.

Sonia got married alongside the roar of the sea. The Wanderers didn't plan it that way, though the ocean was the place I led them three days before the ceremony.

Rumors abounded that the tugging inside me might have been influenced by Sonia's fantasies of bare feet and sand between her toes. My gift is never compromised by my desires, I swore to everyone.

Not ever.

The night before Sonia's wedding, the two of us crept outside long after the camp dozed off. We sat on the dock, dangling our legs off the edge, and drank wine coolers I'd lifted hours before. When the bottles were empty, our bodies buzzing from liquor and laughter, she grinned and tugged us both into the freezing salt water, clothes and all.

Sonia and Emil took off after their wedding to head around the coast for a week, just the two of them. That night they returned, I didn't have her to myself, not for a minute. People from camp kept her distracted, offering up their congratulations and advice about running cons as a married unit, and Sonia's feet stayed planted at Emil's side.

Late at night, I snuck into the new trailer Emil had bought them, untangled her limbs from his, and coaxed her onto the beach.

The sand stung our faces, and the wind whipped our hair into knots. I tried to talk to her about my latest scam and about Wen spending his time buried in his encyclopedias. Sonia barely listened, flicking her eyes in the direction of camp every few minutes like she was afraid Emil would find her outside of their bed.

"Let's jump in," I said, squeezing her hands inside mine.

"Are you joking? It's freezing."

"You've never cared about anything like that before."

She moved her front teeth along her bottom lip and whispered—whispered even though not a soul was around and the wind drowned out her voice—"Emil wouldn't like it." She pulled away from me and balled up the bottom of her sweatshirt in her hands. "I can't be tearing off with you all hours of the night anymore."

I knew those weren't Sonia's words. They were Emil's through and through.

"Marriage isn't going to change you, Sonia."

But we both knew—it already had.

Marriage will wreck me, too. I can't belong to someone when I've only ever been accountable to myself and to the Wen-and-Tal version of the world. Rona said Sonia grew up. But it was so much more than that. She stopped wishing and dreaming and wanting for herself.

"Tal." Rona backs me into a shadowed spot between trailers.

Wen keeps some distance and pretends to give us privacy. He's looking at something. A brand-spanking-new RV I've never seen before is parked beside Boss's. It must belong to Felix's folks.

"You are so smart you scare me sometimes," says Rona. "I know you can spin this any way you want.

This boy can be controlled if you play it right."

"Okay." The word is so cold, I'm surprised she doesn't shiver. I don't want to control or be controlled. I want to be left alone.

I follow her up the steps to Boss's RV, Wen close behind me.

"Finally," says Lando, offering his arm to me as I stand in the doorway. "Our bride."

A boy gets to his feet. He's broad and fair skinned, with slicked-back hair. Felix, I assume.

"You must be Talia," he says. "You're prettier than they said."

I stare back, expecting Wen to laugh behind me, but all I hear is the generator running and the oscillating fan rustling an old magazine.

"That was a compliment." Felix winks. "I mean, I'm glad you're pretty."

Rona digs her knuckle into my lower back. "Say *thank you*."

I say it, but my voice sounds distant and far away.

They sit me down on the sofa. Felix sits so close he might as well be sitting on top of me.

Boss is propped up in his wheelchair, wheezing into the clear tubes under his nostrils. My strength slips away, and I almost beg him to stop this. There was a time when he would've listened, a time when he adored me. A little bit of me loved him, too. All that changed when Lando got hold of the family bank.

Felix knits his fingers together. "My parents are roving for a while. They sent me here with the last of the bride-price for Boss and to meet you, Talia."

"Tal," I correct.

He twiddles his thumbs in his lap. "But *Talia*'s a much prettier name. It's more . . ."

That's when I zone out. He keeps talking with his hands, moving them in front of my face, widening his legs so his knee rubs against mine. I feel like I'll never have any personal space again. I certainly won't have my name.

Everything becomes too much: Felix's thigh hot against mine through his jeans. Wen blending in beside Lando. This is a con that's spun out of my control.

I stand and the room falls silent.

The screen door creaks as I bust through it.

Rona's voice is distant as I run. "With the heat and all, she's not feeling too great tonight. . . ."

Everything whirls around me as I cut between the trees, all the dark leaves and bright spaces where the moonlight trickles between branches. The forest has to hide me and hide me well, at least until I can get my conning face back on.

I slide my back down the rough bark of a tree and bury my face between my knees.

Someone touches my shoulder. I jerk, but it's

only Wen.

"I told the rest of them to stay. They listened." He lowers into the leaves, his elbows balanced on his knees. "You can't marry that jackass. He's going to water down our genes."

Wen elbows me in the ribs, but I can't smile.

"We'll leave," he says.

"Leave?" I laugh as I wipe away a runaway tear. "We don't even have last names."

"We'll get them. Me and you'll pick one out and get all socially secured. Together."

"Now you're talking crazy."

The road of the Wanderer is too wide, too dangerous for two to travel alone. The only way out is to settle somewhere. Thinking of my brother and me trapped in a small town like Cedar Falls makes me claustrophobic.

"Tal, they won't make you marry him until you turn eighteen."

But I'm not so sure. The fifteen months between now and my eighteenth birthday were my crutch, my time to get a plan together that would help keep all of me.

"You'll think of something," Wen says. "You always do."

I don't know about that. All I know is everything is going to change soon. That change isn't going to be me marrying Felix.

CHAPTER 9

LANDO FINDS ME TWO DAYS LATER WHILE I'M TRANS-ferring jugs of water from the bed of the truck into our tent trailer.

"We need to have a little chat, Talia," he says.

Everything inside me twists on itself. "There's nothing to say."

He grabs my wrist so hard I drop one of the plastic jugs. It cracks open, emptying water in loud glugs onto the pine-needled ground. "Sit."

A group of women two trailers down are loading baskets of laundry into the back of their truck. They cut their eyes at us but never stop working.

I take a seat on the tailgate beside him, not because he's hurting me—which he is—or because I have to—which I don't—but because it's easier to comply than fight about something as petty as him forcing a conversation. I'll save my fight for when I need it most.

Wen swore he didn't tell a soul about my hustle going south in Pike. He swore nobody in camp knew.

There's only one reason Lando's come around.

Last night, when Felix came to my door carrying a twenty-four-count box of chocolate bars lifted from a convenience store, I shook my head.

"Thanks, but I'm allergic to chocolate," I said, though I'm sure he'd seen me eating s'mores around the campfire hours before.

He turned a deep shade of red and muttered something about not knowing people could be allergic to chocolate.

Wen bent beside me and watched Felix disappear between the trailers. "What'd you do that for?"

"I'd rather starve than eat his chocolate."

Wen sighed in a mopey way that no other grown boy could pull off. "But *I* could have eaten the chocolate."

"Then get your own suitor."

Felix spent the rest of the night in his fancy, air-conditioned RV, playing electronic games that beeped louder than the crickets.

Two nights he's been in our camp, and I know that won't be his last attempt.

"You've been hurting Felix's feelings," Lando says now.

"Good."

"Talia! That boy is gonna be your husband. You will love and honor him, and he will do the same to you. Marriage needs respect. Mutual respect."

"What if I won't marry him?"

"Your marriage has been contracted for years. They gave good money for you."

They bought me the same way they'd buy a truck, a sandwich, or a dog. "Give it back, then."

"You were barely walking when that boy's parents paid for you. By the next year, it was spent."

A thought occurs to me. Boss won't let me go. He won't lose his compass. I hate to do this, but it's my one card to play, my ace in the hole in a game I'm sure to lose. "They paid for me before."

"Before?"

"Before Boss realized what I am. Surely that makes a difference."

"Oh." Lando rubs through the stubble on his jaw and chuckles. "Our compass. You think you've got everyone fooled, don't you? Well, that little arrangement will die alongside my father."

I glare, but heat flares in my chest, and I break eye contact, giving myself away.

"You want to end the arrangement, Talia, you'll have to pay back the bride-price. And I sure don't think you can raise all that money. Paying us back would mean a lot of Wen's blood spilled in the dirt, a lot of concussions. I'm not sure he'd survive it."

"We'll leave."

"You'd really want to leave this life?"

Of course. Lando's in love with our way of living. Being Boss's son gives him advantages—money and, most importantly, choices.

"You can leave," he says slowly. "The camp isn't a prison. Once you've paid the bride-price, you're free to go wherever the road takes you. You don't pay it, though, and we'll find you, wherever you go. One way or another, you and Wen'll pay it back."

"Exactly how much is my freedom going to cost me?"

"Twenty thousand."

Twenty grand is a fortune. It might not be much to some, but I don't measure it in dollars. Twenty thousand means over a hundred pool-hall hustles. At least four hundred picked pockets. Two thousand short-changed clerks. It's more money than I could ever scheme into my hands.

"You're so damn ungrateful," he says into his collar.

"What'd you say to me?"

"I said you're ungrateful." He leaps off the truck and plants his hands on both sides of my hips, trapping me. "You know what'd happen to you and your brother out in the real world? No daddy? A mama who's run off?" He squeezes his eyes closed, and his voice goes almost sad. "Look, we've given you a family. We've given you the whole world. This is a good life. You don't know how good you've got it. All I ask in return is a contribution every now and then, a little fighting for entertainment, and none of your smart mouth. You'd do fine to make things work with Felix." He removes his hands and rubs them together to brush the dirt from his skin. "You understand me, Talia?"

It takes an immeasurable amount of restraint, but I say, "I think I do."

"Good girl."

The wheels of my mind turn ninety to nothing as Lando saunters between trailers. Now there's no way I'm simply walking away from Felix, not without paying back the bride-price. It's going to take more money than I've ever seen in one place and a scam so big it'll come close to cracking my world open.

But even if I die trying, I will buy my soul back.

An hour after the last light fades, Wen and I creep out of our beds. Camp's always been early to bed, early to rise. When power's a limited resource, there isn't much reason to get out of sync with the sun's rhythm.

That markie party's probably only now starting to roar.

In the dark, I fumble to open the cabinets, searching between blankets. Finally, I hook the smooth plastic.

"You think Rona's asleep yet?" asks Wen.

"She's got to be."

Earning every bit of the bride-price isn't going to be easy with Rona keeping her gaze glued to us.

We slide down to the linoleum floor and click on a dim flashlight. Wen opens the Cool Whip container, and together we dig into the money we've been stockpiling since I was thirteen and Wen was twelve. A ten here, a one or a five there, and the occasional twenty. We iron the bills against our pant legs, piling them in neat stacks until the tub is empty.

I count first, flipping the dollars like a blackjack dealer with a deck of cards. As the last green bill falls, I groan. "Seven thousand, four hundred, and eighty-two dollars."

It's not enough money, not for all the years we've been saving.

"Well, that can't be right," Wen whispers.

He counts after me, coming up with the same number. A little over seven grand. That's all we have to show for enough scams to bring a blush to the cheeks of the most seasoned markie criminals.

"There's still the party," he says.

"We'll make five hundred at most."

"Not if I push it. One good night and I could clear a thousand."

Pushing it's risky, though, and Wen can't get caught. Not again. "I don't know. Remember Augusta?"

There's no way either of us will forget our stay in Augusta, Georgia. The camp had decided to head to

Memphis to scalp fake tickets at a music festival where there was bound to be a ton of toureys. But Wen wanted to see the Grand Canyon.

We left on our own journey before the sun came up. For two days, we felt freer than ever before—until the truck broke down, Wen tried to hot-wire the wrong car, and he ended up behind bars.

"I'll be smart about it, Tal. You work the room. Give me a signal if it starts getting hot."

Even if we do pull a thousand, there are still so many thousands to go. A fortune to Lando—and a bargain in exchange for me. Not that I'm conceited. My value's got nothing to do with long hair or curves or full lips; it's the simple fact I have a talent for the cons.

Tonight, I need that talent more than ever, and the money, too.

The combination of those needs is the surest way for a con to go to hell.

CHAPTER 10

WE STEP THROUGH THE FRONT DOOR OF WHITNEY'S home, under a high foyer ceiling full of nothing but unused space. The wastefulness unsettles me, but Wen finds the bookshelves lining the hallway, and his eyes are heartsick. He's in love.

He runs his fingers along the spines. "Look at all these."

I give Wen a little shove toward the pulsing music inside. "You've got a job to do."

The glass coffee table is a sea of bottles, ashtrays, and bongs. Vodka, peach schnapps, weed, or cough syrup — it's a pick-your-poison kind of affair. Whitney's curled up on an L-shaped couch in the middle of the room, surrounded by a couple of girls and a pack of boys.

"You came!" she yells, clapping her hands together. She leaps over the back of the couch in a short lilac dress with silver beads sewn along the bodice in a diamond pattern. "I didn't think you'd come!"

"Wouldn't miss it," I say.

Even though Whitney and I spoke only for minutes, she hugs me. She pulls away and collects my hands into hers.

"You look so pretty," she coos.

With dark waves swinging low on my back, my hair is perpetually tangled. Tonight I've gathered some pieces from around my face and secured them with bobby pins. Whitney homes in on my bracelet, silver poured in the shape of leaves linking together into a circle, and spins it around my tanned wrist. Wen and I saw it in the window of an antiques shop before my fifteenth birthday. I'm certain he bought it for me, which annoyed me, but to this day he swears he stole it.

"Everyone, this is Rachel." Whitney points around the party, calling off names I immediately forget, before she weaves her fingers with mine and guides me away from the couch. For nothing more than an instant, I'm a normal girl. "Drinks and snacks are in the kitchen. Bathroom's down the hall. Oh, and poker's in the den. If you play."

Oh, do I ever. But, no. I can't let myself get distracted.

"Now," she says, "introduce me to that gorgeous brother of yours."

"This is my brother, Elliot." I tilt my head, and Wen comes to my side. "Elliot, this is Whitney."

Wen leads Whitney away, like we'd planned, leaving me to work the room alone. This is Wen's scam. I'm only along for support.

There used to be three or four of us scamming a group of markies, sometimes Sonia, and sometimes Emil, too. Now that they're married, Emil would prefer to have her mop his floor than run his cons.

I miss her at my side.

How with one glance across a crowded room, Sonia'd see in my eyes that the plan had to change. How she never strayed far from Wen if things got hot. Most of all, I miss her wild laughter as we pulled away from the scene of the crime.

"For you." A boy wearing a white visor with a little green alligator appears at my side with an open bottle of beer hanging limply from his hand. "I'm Craig."

"Rachel. I'll get my own beer if it's all the same to you." Last thing I need is for Wen to put the brakes on the scam so he can cart my roofied ass back to camp.

Over the hum of the music, he says, "Um, sure thing. Kitchen's this way."

It's my job to insert myself into the group, to become one of them, or make them think I'm just like them for a few hours. Craig is my ticket to the inner ranks.

I collect a beer from the ice chest and head to the living room, where Wen already has Whitney and a few other girls crowded around him. With my back against the living room wall, I watch the scam unfold.

Wen's got that forbidden-fruit look in his eyes as he reaches inside his pocket. I read his lips: "You girls want to party?"

"Isn't that what we're doing?" someone asks.

"No, *party*-party." It isn't long before he utters the magic words: "You want some ecstasy? I'll give you my special price."

This is how the ecstasy scam always goes down. Devious and delectable.

Of course it's not real ecstasy Wen's pushing. If we were pushing drugs, we'd be dealers. Not that my delicate scruples would be offended. But if they were real drugs, there would be no scam, and if there's no scam, there's no rush. Plus, real ecstasy is expensive to buy and tricky as hell to make. And that would seriously cut into our time and bottom line.

Wen passes the little baggies to the girls first. The green transfers from their sleek, manicured fingers into Wen's shirt pocket. Others find their way to the couch to score—at least sixty people by my count. And, once again, we're invincible.

I run numbers in my head. If he sells it all, we're one giant step closer to buying my life back. My body aches to walk over and count the money, make sure he's not getting stiffed, but I can't be a part of these transactions.

It would be too suspicious.

One of the girls presses her hand to his cheek. Wen isn't exactly smooth when it comes to girls, but he gives her a small smile, a cute one. He's coming up in the world, putting the *con* in *confidence* tonight. Most people don't know that the *con* in *con man* comes from the term *confidence man*. It's not that Wen is—confident, I mean—but he's quite the actor when he needs to be.

Craig reappears at my side. "Your brother's the life of the party."

I smile and rest my fingertips on his bicep. "He should be careful. We hardly know you people."

"We're cool. We're cool," says Craig. "So y'all cook it up yourselves?"

"Of course not. What do I look like?" I take a sip of my beer. "A chemist?"

With Craig close behind me, I walk out onto the deck.

It's crowded with people: flashes of skin, blurs of letterman jackets, stiff fabrics with labels reading, DRY CLEAN ONLY.

I set my beer on the railing and lean over the edge. My stomach leaps into my throat as I look down. The house is built on the side of the hill, making the front one story and the back, two. The deck wraps around the upper level, stopping halfway up the trees here, and it's far, far down to the ground.

"What a nice little canter you have," he says.

In a shadowed area of the deck, Craig's hands paw over my hips and slide around to my ass.

"Craig, stop." I arch away and shove at his chin.

"Fresh meat," yells one of the letterman jackets, followed by, "Hey, girl, I'm Jeremy."

I smell booze—something hard—as Craig releases me. I turn to find a blond jock staring at me like I'm edible and he's spent a month stranded on a desert island.

"Has anyone ever said you have a way with words, Jeremy?" I say. He stares at me, blank–faced and drunk, his eyes glassy as marbles. "Nope, didn't think so."

Craig chuckles and socks Jeremy in the shoulder. "I'd be nice to her, Jer. Her brother brought the fun."

"You boys need to go tell my brother, Elliot, that you're my new friends." I wink. "He'll give you his special price."

The party goes on for another half an hour before the air starts stirring. It's getting riskier with each minute we stay, what with people popping pills that aren't getting them high.

I catch Wen's eyes through the sliding glass door, but he's not reading the urgency in my stare. He's an animal tonight, pushing the product hard. It's all about me, helping me buy myself back from Felix.

Jeremy says something about "sugar pills," and my heart beats faster. It's time to get Wen. Cash out before you pass out.

I get Wen's attention and rub my fingertip across my bottom lip, our emergency signal. He makes excuses to the girls before meeting me outside, all the money tucked away in his shirt.

I tug him close and whisper, "It's getting hot in here."

He freezes, recognizing the phrase I haven't used since the night he ended up behind bars. "Okay."

Jeremy steps onto the deck, blocking our path inside the house. He grabs Wen's collar and throws him against the house. "What'd you sell us? The fuck did you sell us? I'm not feeling a fucking thing."

"You ha-have to wait a little while for the high to kick in," Wen says.

"I took it half an hour ago, bro. Now give me my money back."

"Why?" Wen asks. "You gonna beat the shit out of me?"

"The beating-the-shit-out-of-you part isn't negotiable."

"Come on, Jeremy." I level my voice and tug on the sleeve of his T-shirt, but his grip doesn't loosen. "Let him go. You're high, and you're about to make a huge mistake."

"No, the problem is I'm not high. And that's *his* huge mistake." Jeremy shakes Wen harder and rakes his eyes over me. "Hey, you in on this with him, bitch?"

Two of his gorilla friends close in. Hands sink into my skin as someone slams the sliding glass door shut, drowning the music and trapping us on the deck. They could do anything to me.

Worse than that, they could do anything to Wen.

There's a faint chime, one I first think I've imagined. Bodies go still, and someone cuts the music. In the silence, it's louder this time—the ring of the doorbell. A girl says the one word guaranteed to make this party spread: *cops.*

Someone throws open the front door. Jeremy takes off running through the house. He may not be high on ecstasy, but I guess he's not interested in the cops escorting him home to Mommy and Daddy for underage drinking.

Things aren't looking up much for Wen and me yet. *It wasn't real ecstasy* isn't the greatest legal defense.

A few people on the deck scatter, but most are stunned. A boy and girl concealed by the eaves of the patio don't even break their lip-lock.

"Hey, Occifer," I hear a girl slur. "Those people are selling drugs out there. But they're not really drugs— they don't even work."

What the hell?

Wen groans. "I told you this place was bad luck."

I grab him by his shoulders and dart toward the railing.

I glance over the edge. To the plummeting drop to the forest floor. It's too far to jump. Wen points at one of the trash bins leaned against the deck posts below. It should break our fall.

"It may not be safe." Wen swings his leg over. "I'll go first."

His other leg comes around, and he lets go before I can tell him no.

He crashes, and I lean over the railing. The plastic trash can is cracked through the lid, my escape route destroyed. Officers scramble out of the house and onto the deck as I hide in the shadows.

"Amy?" I hear behind me.

I whirl around and collide with the chest of Spencer Sway, who's wearing the most surprised smile. "Just what are you doing here?" I ask.

"Cleaning up at poker. What are *you* doing here? Stalking me? Your timing is damn near impeccable."

"Tal!" Wen whisper-yells from below.

"Tal?" asks Spencer.

"I'll explain later." I bend close to a knothole in the deck floor. The time Wen did in juvie means he can't take a pinch, but I can. "Wen, you gotta go."

"No." He flips the busted trash can onto its lid. It shimmies as he shakes it, rickety as hell. "You're not throwing yourself on the grenade. Hop over."

Footsteps draw closer. "I'll be okay. Go, Wen. Please go."

There's shuffling in the dry leaves below—he doesn't want to leave, I'm sure—but finally I hear the slap of his feet through the pine needles.

Spencer gives me a crooked smile. "So he called you Tal, and you called him Wen? I'm eagerly awaiting my explanation."

"Not now."

I need to get lost, and there's only one way to do it: I have to blend in with the markies. There are too many people here for the cops to arrest us all.

Some pitch full bottles of beer over the railing; some rub the bleariness from their eyes. Still, there's that couple, lost in each other's mouths.

There's no way around it. I do the only thing I can think of.

"Shh." I hold my finger to my lips. I back Spencer up until my hips are pressing into his, pinning him to the side of the house. Against his mouth, I whisper, "Please."

Our eyes meet under the floodlights.

I kiss Spencer Sway.

CHAPTER 11

WE'RE NOTHING MORE THAN A COUPLE MAKING OUT at the party, that's what the cops will think. Everything will go to hell if they don't.

I've kissed boys before—markie boys, all of them—always in the interest of a scam. Kisses I made into something tragic.

I don't think about Spencer's lips against mine, only the way the feet sound behind me, clicking against the deck. Closing in. I don't think about the feel of him, the electricity, not until his hands slide from my shoulders, shimmy up the skin of my neck, and tangle in my hair.

The balance shifts, and he pushes me against the siding instead. I'm not the one kissing him anymore. Spencer is kissing me, and he's slowing it down. Way down. It's softer, easier, rhythmic, pulsing through me.

Footsteps approach. Boots that *stomp, stomp, stomp*. Stop.

"You kids need to break up the tongue bath and go

home." The voice is clear and authoritative—without a doubt, a cop.

Spencer pulls away, his mouth swollen and his eyes intense. I'm conjuring up lies, ready to take the lead as Spencer says, "Sure."

He catches my elbow, skims his fingers down my forearm, before his hand engulfs mine.

We step through the threshold of the glass door, away from the officer and his handcuffs.

A girl with bleeding mascara blocks our path. This, I didn't account for.

"Nooooo," slurs the drunk girl, pointing at my chest. "Selling the drugs. Right here."

Someone grabs my shoulder, turning me around— Officer Goodwin, according to his badge. Red acne scars dot his cheeks, which means he's young. And young cops are the worst kind—they've got something to prove. He slides a flashlight from his pocket and shines it on Spencer. "Kid, everyone's saying you two are selling drugs."

"Not him. The girl," the drunk girl slurs, "and the other guy."

I put on my game face and cross my arms. "What drugs?"

It's a lame play, but if there aren't any drugs, there isn't any proof, and Wen usually watches everyone swallow them before he doles out more.

"Officer, I can assure you I'm not selling drugs."

Spencer laughs. "And neither is my girlfriend, Tal." He tucks his palm against the dip of my back.

The word *girlfriend* ripples through the party like a tidal wave, the last syllable rising higher each time it's repeated.

Goodwin lifts his chin and squints at me. "Tal?"

"Talia."

"Tal?" the drunk girl says. "Whitney said her name was *Rachel*."

Whitney tiptoes around the couch and wraps her arm around the drunk girl's shoulders. "I definitely said Tal." With that, Whitney leads her away.

Goodwin steps forward and gives me a tentative smile. "Mind if I search you?"

I can't let him. I've got two fake IDs in my wallet and no way to stash one. Legally, he can't search me without my consent or without probable cause. He might have a case for probable cause, but he's not getting my consent.

I start to say just that, until Spencer speaks. "Judge Sway wouldn't like this, sir."

Goodwin frowns. My thoughts run rampant. *He's going to haul us to the station, Boss will have to put up the bail, we won't be able to pay him back, and Wen will have to fight until he's dead. He'll die fighting one of these days—he will.*

Spencer whips his wallet from his back pocket, riffles through it, and produces his ID. "I don't mean any disrespect, Officer, but I'm Judge Sway's son."

Goodwin hovers a flashlight over the ID. "Spencer Sway. I'll be damned." He gives it back to Spencer. "Okay, then. You kids go home, and don't let me hear about any more trouble tonight."

Spencer brings two fingers to his forehead in salute and snaps them to his side. "You got it, Officer."

He drapes his arms over my shoulders and steers me around the furniture and through the crowd. Some guy says, "Spencer Sway. That figures." More whispers trail behind us as we make our way to the front porch.

Whitney's arms are crossed as a cop questions her in the doorway of the kitchen. She lifts her hand in a half wave as I go by. My almost friend. I actually feel ashamed for the first time in my life, and the evidence is hot across my face.

"Don't worry about Whitney," Spencer whispers into my hair. "Her party will be the talk of the whole school on Monday, thanks to you. Come on."

CHAPTER 12

FLASHING LIGHTS FROM THE PATROL CARS PAINT Whitney's lawn red and blue. I race to the sidewalk. There's a gap along the curb—where we parked the Chevy. Wen's already gone.

A shadow stretches across the sidewalk before me, and Spencer Sway says, "That guy left you?"

"Our truck was parked there." I point to the empty space, between a Volkswagen and a BMW. "Was."

"Is he really your brother? Not your boyfriend or something?"

I shudder at the thought. "Cross my heart, Wen is my brother."

Even though I'm stranded, I can't be anything other than relieved Wen is safe. Still, I've got to get out of here. I give Spencer Sway the once-over. "Are you too wasted to drive?"

He rocks on his heels and smiles. "No, I didn't drink anything."

"Designated driver? Puritan? Prohibitionist?"

"No." He laughs a little. "I like my mind sharp when I'm playing cards."

"Smart."

"And my car isn't here. I walked."

"Shit." I could call a cab, but then the driver would know where we're living, and that's not information we hand to outsiders. I suppose, though, for Spencer, with his Good Samaritan ways, I would have made an exception and let him drive me home.

"So, *Tal* . . ." My name sounds like an allegation on his lips. "I live about eleven or twelve blocks that way." He points down the hill toward the lake—the pricier views of the water. "We have a basement with a pullout couch. I'll take you home in the morning."

I don't know why he'd let me sleep inside his house—him knowing about me hustling in the pool hall in Pike, passing fake drugs to his friends—but he's inviting the danger. It's equal parts sexy and terrifying.

"Couldn't you drive me home tonight instead, once we get to your house?"

Even I don't trust myself to spend a night in his world.

"I would. I really would, but my parents—they're real light sleepers—and I'd have to open the garage door, which is loud. You'd have to spend the night."

There it is—his reason to help me. I know a thing or two about the lies boys tell in the dark. "I'd be sleeping in your basement, and you'd be . . . ?"

"Upstairs, two sets of locked doors between our lonely bodies, I swear. The basement's sort of musty, but the futon's pretty comfortable. That's the best I can do."

Nothing's right about leeching off markies and then accepting their kindness. But I'm something I've never been before: helpless. Tonight, I have to put my pride aside.

We head down the separated sidewalk, and I remember I haven't even thanked him yet. I should, even though he was the one who distracted me from jumping and making a clean getaway.

"You saved my ass back there." That sounded nothing like a thank-you. I try again. "Thanks, really. Thank you."

He shoves his hands deep inside the pockets of his jeans. "So it's Tal? Not Amy or Rachel or Bertha or something else?"

"Talia. But everyone calls me Tal."

"Tal," he repeats carefully. He gives me this sideways look like I'm the most amusing thing that's ever happened to him. I probably am. "I'm still Spencer, like I've always been."

"You a heartbreaker, Still-Spencer? And don't lie to me. I'm practically a human lie detector."

"Not the last time I checked."

"Then why'd that guy at the party say it figured you were taking off with me?"

"I think it had something to do with me lying to the cop about you being my girlfriend. Taking that risk. I'm sort of the fallen angel of the popular crowd."

"You haven't gotten yourself in any trouble by lying to that cop, have you?" I don't know why I'd care about something like that—a little slap on Spencer's wrist—but I do.

"Nah."

After a few more blocks, he turns up the walkway to a two-story brick colonial easily large enough to function as an orphanage or a small hotel. Or, I guess, the home of a judge.

"So your dad gets you out of a lot of trouble?"

"My dad?"

"Judge Sway."

He steals a sidelong glance at me and smiles. "Judge Sway would be my mom. I'm a little disappointed. You seemed like the kind of girl who'd be a lot more progressive."

From under a mat that spells SWAY HOME in cursive letters, he finds a loose key and works the lock. Markies are that way, closing their windows and putting locks on their doors, but keeping a key to all their valuables right under the welcome mat.

"I'm the worst at keeping up with my damn keys," he whispers.

He smuggles me through a maze of hallways and

down the stairs into the basement, where I'm hit with a musty, familiar smell, like Wen's encyclopedias. I want to breathe in deep and hold the air of this place inside me forever.

"My mom thinks basements are one of the few things the North is doing right," he says. "She's always been terrified of tornados. So she insisted the builders blow out the foundation for a real basement."

We wind around a pool table, beside bookshelves stacked with old books—some so high I'd need a ladder to pluck one off the top—all the way to a futon.

He gestures to a closed door with his chin. "Half bath's right through there."

"Spencer?" I sit on the edge of the futon and cross my legs, waiting for him to look at me. "What were you doing with that pool game?"

"Would you believe I was trying to impress you?"

"Oh, I was surely impressed."

He reaches inside an old dresser and tosses me a flashlight. "I'll come back in the morning. If my parents see you, I'm deader than dead. And, hey, since I'm giving you a bed for the night and all, could you promise not to rob us blind?"

"Don't worry." I turn the flashlight on, holding it under my chin like we're sitting around the campfire telling stories about things that scrape and scratch around the forest. "I always case the joint first."

He grins and backs away from the bed, like he suddenly realized he's knee-deep in quicksand and sinking fast.

Spencer leaves, and my eyes adjust to the pitch-black darkness of no stars and no moon. I think of Wen, alone in our trailer. He must be worried as hell.

More worried for me or worried for himself, I'm not sure.

Wen and I haven't been apart for more than a few hours since the day he was born. When he was six, he told me he dreamed we got separated and our world spun out of control. He said the trucks lifted up, the trailers, the Wanderers, everything careened through the atmosphere and came crashing down.

But that was something Wen dreamed up after Rona snuck us into a midnight showing of *The Wizard of Oz*. It was a few weeks after that time I went missing, right after Mom went to prison. Everything for Wen always goes back to then.

They packed up camp—the elders, Rona, everyone—and piled into our cars to head to our new destination.

They traveled for almost an hour before picking a campsite. Wen thought I was sleeping under some old quilts in the back of Rona's trailer. He barely spoke as a child—I was his voice. Wen still isn't much for speaking to people other than me. Nobody noticed I wasn't there. Not even Rona.

It wasn't until they heard Wen's frantic screaming that they realized I was gone. Rona hopped into her truck to find me. She didn't even get the gear into reverse before I stepped from the shadowy woods, dry leaves glued to my feet with mud.

They say I must have walked almost forty-seven miles, that the Spirit of the Falconer guided my feet to the new camp. Those who were unsure about Boss declaring me the compass said it had to be true, that I was something special.

The superstitions, the lore, the magic, they're all as common to us as trees. But the camp's explanation was wrong, and so was their belief in me.

What nobody knew was that I was playing out in the woods when I was supposed to be tucked away in the back of Rona's trailer. I'd been pretending our mother was lost among the pines and it was my job to find her. Hours later, I broke the line of trees and saw nothing but tire tracks and an abandoned camp.

I wandered the forest alone until finally I came to a road. A family pulled over, a husband with a handlebar mustache and a wife with long blonde hair and strawberry-colored lips. They had a couple of kids, too—a baby boy in a car seat and a girl my age. The dad and mom seemed so worried: the dad's brows pushed together, and the mom bent to her knees as they asked me questions about my own parents.

I knew where to find my camp. Boss had talked to Rona about pulling over at a rest stop near Memphis—where they'd let me take over and work my compass magic.

We piled into the car, the mom and dad in the front seat and me sandwiched in the back between the car seat and the girl. I must have seemed strange to them, my hair tangled and my dirty feet pressed against their beige interior. That didn't stop them from following my directions.

An hour or so later, I noticed a mile marker for exit fourteen and told them to drop me off. The mom and dad exchanged a look, but he pulled the car to the shoulder anyway. I told them *thanks* and took off running. They called out after me, but that made my feet go faster.

The sounds of camp trickled to my ears, and I knew my sense of direction was dead on; I'd found my camp.

I walked toward the nearest light, and there was Wen rushing to meet me. The rest of camp wasn't far behind. So, again, I let everyone believe it was true, that the forest was a part of me, and I was a compass.

Now Wen is out there again somewhere, probably on the verge of dying with worry. Maybe it's because we don't have anyone except each other, but I feel his anxiety like a phantom limb.

I squeeze my eyes closed and hear him speak as clearly as if he's beside me: *Good night, you thief, you vagabond.*

Sleeping here is nothing like sleeping in the forest. The forest is beneath my fingernails, caked on my feet, coursing through my veins. No bar of soap could ever scrub away the wilderness.

New sounds drone all around me. The buzzing of the lights and the hum of the freezer.

The house seems like a living, breathing thing with the creaking and cracking of the foundation settling around me. I don't want to close my eyes, not with this beast waiting for me to fall asleep, ready to swallow me whole.

CHAPTER 13

"YOU HAVE TO WAKE UP. WE GOTTA GO."

I blink, and Spencer comes into focus, standing over me with the hood of his jacket pulled low, shading his eyes.

Panic sweeps through me as I leap off the futon. The windowless walls feel like they're closing in around me, and I remember I'm in a markie home, away from camp, and Wen doesn't know where I am.

A burgundy, hooded sweatshirt with navy piping hangs from Spencer's fingers. "It's chilly outside," he says. I give him a look, but he shrugs. "My mom won't miss it."

I take the sweatshirt, even though I don't need it at all. It's a simple thing—Spencer caring that I might get cold in the morning air—but as I slip my arms into the sleeves, I can't help but feel guilty. Again, my conscience has taken human shape in the form of Spencer Sway.

A coursing sound rushes through the walls around

us. "What the hell's that?"

Spencer groans and whips the hood off his head. "Shower. My parents must be awake."

The maze of hallways is less confusing this time around. Bathed in the bright light of morning, pictures line the downstairs walls, a man and a woman and Spencer and his sister.

It's the exotic locales behind their shapes that draw me in.

My feet go still against the hardwood floor.

I don't want to admire the photos, but I can't help myself. All my pictures live in a shoebox in one of the top cabinets of the trailer.

"Door's this way." Spencer reaches for my hand. When I don't take it, he sighs and points to the pictures of only him, his tongue rolling out the names of cities like he's speaking another language. "Barcelona, Sevilla, Madrid." He moves so close I hear him swallow. "I spent junior year in Spain as an exchange student. I want to travel everywhere someday."

Travel, not wander. That's not something I'm sure I understand.

"We really have to leave," he says. "Now."

"What about the other ones?"

He nods to each of the photographs, moving in a counter-clockwise circle. "That's London, Paris, Dubai, Moscow"—and the last one—"and Cape Town."

Cape Town is a name I've run my fingertips across an infinite number of times.

"That's in Africa," I whisper.

"Yeah." His mouth twitches. "That's where they keep Cape Town." I don't even react to his teasing. He shuffles his feet against the floorboards. "Okay, come on."

I bring my hand close to the frames as if there's a way for me to touch the glass and fall into these other worlds. But I stop a few inches short because I can't reach through and because I don't want to smudge the glass and leave behind any more evidence that, for one night, I was a part of Spencer's life.

A door creaking upstairs breaks my trance.

Go, he mouths, pushing the air with his hands.

We make it to the foyer and tiptoe to the front porch.

I creep outside first and hear a man speak from inside. "Where are you headed so early?"

I hug the siding of the house as Spencer, who's still inside, pulls the door against his back. There's an urge to run, but it's not the law or a gun or a fist I'm afraid of, for a change. It's Spencer getting caught. Running won't save me. It will only guarantee his exposure. And I care that my scams are bleeding into his world. I've never given a damn about a markie before.

"Dropping some notes off for George," I hear Spencer say.

"I thought you were having brunch with Bob

McAllister today. Your mom told me to tell you she left your slacks and shirt in the closet under the stairs. She had them dry-cleaned."

"I'll be back in plenty of time."

"Bob's got an in with the admissions committee, Spence. You wouldn't want to be late." After a long pause, the man says, "All right. Hurry back."

"Yeah, 'kay, Dad."

"Don't forget to take some cash for the valet at the club."

"Roger that."

Spencer shuts the front door, and we hop off the porch. Inside the garage sits a silver sedan, a total family car. I would have expected something different from the Sways. People like them usually buy their sons shiny, new cars to race around town.

As we pull into the road, a white-haired man next door scoops something out of the driveway. He balances it on the blade of the shovel, holding whatever he's carrying far away from his body as he moves toward his trash can. I crane my neck. Gray feathers fall from the shovel and into the trash.

My breath hitches. Another owl.

Spencer guns it, and now that we've driven away, it's like a dream. I bury this second owl deep in my subconscious. Because I don't believe. And because the possibility I'm wrong and everything is real—omens and the

Spirit of the Falconer—those are thoughts I can't let haunt me.

"I really need to go home," I say. "My brother's probably on edge."

"Okay. Where's home?"

Home right now is a patch of land in the forest. "Um, we're camping."

We *are* camping, but not in the recreational sense Spencer's probably imagining. I could ask him to take me to our hideaway, but after my night away from camp, there's no telling the chaos I'd drag him through.

"Let me out near a pay phone. I'll call someone to come get me."

There are few people I could call under any circumstances, not only because my calls would start a free-for-all commotion that would have Lando breathing down my neck, but because most of us don't have phones. It's not the Wanderer way. The phones we do own are all prepaid, leaving no paper trail or proof we're anything other than some urban legend.

Without knowing the story Wen spun for the camp, there's only one person I trust to call anyway: Rona. And I'd rather pull out my fingernails with pliers.

"Listen," Spencer says. "Blame it on an overdeveloped sense of chivalry, but there's something not right about setting a girl out by the side of the road. You can use my cell if you really want to call someone. But how 'bout I drive you wherever you need to go instead?"

I give him a few directions, the rest of the way through town, down the highway, and off the paved roads.

Spencer checks his watch. He's gonna be late for his meeting—he must know it.

"I've heard of people dressing for dinner before," I say. "Not brunch."

"What?"

"Your slacks and shirt, all freshly dry-cleaned for that brunch you're about to be late for."

"Oh, um, not usually. This is different, I guess. Some defense attorney my mom knows who can get me into the right college."

"How do you know it's the right college?"

A smile teases at his lips. "In the Sway household, there's only one college. It's Stonewall Jackson University or bust, if you know what I mean."

I don't.

Spencer pulls his sedan under the cover of trees, two miles from camp. It'd be stupid to lead him any farther.

"This is close enough." My hand twists around the door handle as the car slowly rolls to a stop. "I'll walk the rest of the way in."

"Close enough?" he says as I open the door. "Wait. You're camping out here?"

I touch the tip of my sandal to the ground and say, "Thanks for the ride, Spencer Sway." But with the door half open, the car purring beneath us, I double back. Resting one hand against his cheek and the other on the steering wheel, I kiss him.

As I pull away, he rubs his lips together and opens his mouth to speak, but I shut the passenger door and seal all his words inside.

CHAPTER 14

I'M OUT OF BREATH FROM THE TWO-MILE HIKE, TRIP-ping over fallen branches and drying pinecones. Through the line of trees, I watch Wen washing his face in a bowl of water under the shade of our tent trailer's canopy. He's doing it in his neurotic way—dunking the washcloth, wringing it, wiping his face. Repeat. He only does this when he's worried.

The RVs parked on each side of us are cracking with footsteps and creaking with doors swinging open. I silently beg Wen to look up and see me there, so we can steal a few moments to make sure our stories jive. I can't walk into camp like nothing happened, not with-out agreeing on a cover first.

He towels his face, and as we make eye contact, his shoulders relax. He looks around before ducking under a branch and following me into the thicket of trees.

A ways from camp, Wen paces as I sit on the remains of a fallen tree—most of which we've chopped into firewood for our camp. I tell him about how I got free from the cops last night, how I slept over in Spencer's basement, his whole family walls away.

What I don't mention is how I kissed Spencer on the deck of Whitney's house. And I don't dare tell him about the second kiss in Spencer's car. That's the kind of thing I would have shared with Sonia. Since I can't say those things to her now, I guess I want to save that part of the memory for myself.

Wen's pacing stops as I finish my story. "I stashed all the money as soon as I got back."

"How much?"

"Eleven hundred and eighteen."

"Not bad." It puts us closer to the bride-price but not close enough. "Nobody asked where I was?"

"Rona did this morning. I told her you were still sleeping. She thought you were depressed or something, sleeping so late. I think I dislocated my shoulder trying to block her from coming inside." He scrunches his face and rubs at his collarbone. "I can't believe the markie helped you."

My fingertips trace the embroidered letters on the hip of the hooded sweatshirt Spencer loaned me—SJU.

"Well, he's an okay guy." My voice is bold, that mid-con way I speak. It's a drastic understatement—Spencer was nothing short of my savior last night.

Wen cocks his head to the side but doesn't call me out.

He sits beside me and holds his head in his hands. "I was so damn scared, Tal. I stayed up all night and drove to a pay phone first thing this morning and called the police station. When I realized they didn't have you, I— what if you'd never come home?"

"You should have known that wouldn't happen. We always find each other."

I rest my hand on his back, between his shoulder blades, until I feel him take a deep breath.

"Always," he says.

We walk into camp and pass a bunch of kids crowded around a table. Horatio's shuffling three upside-down cups and teaching them a street trick that'll soon line their pockets with money. He waves as I go by, but I keep walking. I can't forgive him for beating my brother yet.

Wen takes off to help Emil fix the water tank on his RV while I head inside our trailer.

Encyclopedias are strewn everywhere, not stored in plastic bins in the bed of the Chevy where I like him to keep them. I'm gathering the books into a stack beside his bed when I notice the *C* volume on top.

Propping the book on Wen's bed, I flip to *Cape Town* and read the whole entry kneeling there with my elbows sunk into his mattress.

As I read, I think about Spencer and his idea of wanting to be someone who travels but doesn't wander.

The sounds of clanging and cussing come up through my screens early in the morning. I shake out my bed head and peek over the seam where the canvas meets the screen. Outside, Felix is taking the tires off our Chevy.

I throw open the screen door and plant my hands on my hips. "Just what the hell do you think you're doing?"

Felix grins and wipes streaks of grease down the thighs of his jeans. "I'm rotating your tires for you."

"Leave them. We like it done a certain way."

Felix steadies the tire between his knees. "Won't take me long to learn the way you like things, Tal. I'm a fast learner."

I push past him. "Don't overestimate yourself."

"Where're you going?"

"Swimming."

"Isn't it a little cold for that?" He jogs to my side. "You want some company?"

Without turning around, I say, "What do you think?"

I skip rocks across the lake, listening to the faraway sounds of the camp while icy lake water drips from my hair.

I could marry Felix. And it wouldn't make me weak. In fact, it might be the strongest thing I ever do.

I'm practical enough to know that love, if it's real, isn't this over-the-moon, can't-sleep-can't-eat adventure they show in the movies.

Wanderers all have to marry, at least once. Rona was married long ago to a Wanderer named August, but he died with my father when the trailer they were pulling jack-knifed and dragged August's truck down an embankment, crushing his head and my father's chest.

That sounds so brutal, but I don't see it that way. There are a lot of things worse than dying and being forced to leave your family behind. Like leaving the way Mom did.

I wish for a thought to burn away the memory of Mom. It comes almost immediately: that kiss Spencer and I shared in the car.

The first kiss was a necessity, a means to furthering the scam. I don't know why I turned back and kissed Spencer that second time, though. There was no purpose to it, other than pure want. I kissed him because I could. To prove to someone—maybe myself—that nobody owns me.

That kiss was a last act of freedom. It didn't have a thing to do with Spencer Sway. That's what I tell myself.

Trees rustle behind me, and a weight builds on my chest. This sense of claustrophobia keeps igniting inside me ever since Felix showed up.

My wet bra has made my T-shirt sheer, so I cross my arms.

It's only Sonia.

"Hey," she says.

"Hey, yourself."

She drops into the leaves beside me and picks at her green glitter polish. "I'm sorry Felix is here. I know it's not what you wanted."

It's a simple thing for her to acknowledge, but it makes my throat swell.

"He's has been hanging around with Emil," she says. "I know he's not as smart as you might want, but he's pretty nice."

I scoot a few inches down the brush. "There's a glowing recommendation for you."

Beside the lake and me, Sonia presses her palm onto her stomach. "Today something happened, Tal, and I wished you were there so I could tell you." She's so desperate; her eyes silently begging me to be the way we were before. "The baby kicked really hard, and, for the first time, Emil felt it, too. I realized this is my purpose, bringing life into the world."

I stand to get some distance from her.

Three little girls from camp are playing on a fresh tree stump at the top of the hill as we walk back. Watching them leaves me with a sadness that's more like emptiness. I'm homesick for a time I can't have back.

When Sonia and I were young, we'd run around the woods barefoot and filthy, climbing trees, making swords from sticks, and slaying imaginary dragons.

Sometimes, I wish things were still that way, when Sonia and I were best friends and when it was easy to destroy the dragons. The dragons aren't easy to see anymore. Sometimes, the people you trust the most are dragons in disguise.

We didn't know it then, but we were already confined by high stone walls—not of a castle—but of our own expectations.

CHAPTER 15

I GRAB THE KEYS OFF THE HOOK BY THE TRAILER
door and creep around to the driver's side of the Chevy.
"Hey," I yell. "I'm taking the truck!"

Wen's down the road, practicing his card-shuffling
skills with Horatio and Emil, but he comes jogging
beside me before I crank the gearshift into reverse.

"You're going into town?" he says. "Let me come
with you."

"We sleep in a five-by-sixteen tin can together. Can't
I have a few hours of alone time?"

He checks over his shoulder and looks back at me.
"Don't think I don't know what you're doing, Tal."

"That's impossible." I tousle my hair in the rearview
mirror. "I don't even know what I'm doing."

"You're meeting up with that markie boy."

It's not true. I'm not going to meet Spencer, but I am
going to find him.

Town's no doubt hot as hell anyway, with the
rumors of the ecstasy con circulating. It's not going to

be easy—between the townies and Lando—running the scams and coming up with the rest of the money before the expiration of my liberty. I might as well have a little fun.

"It's dangerous," Wen says.

"Let me calm your fears. There's not a thing that's dangerous about that boy."

But Wen's hands stay in place, one on the side mirror, the other on the door, and he doesn't appear to be moving them soon.

"Hey, I appreciate the brotherly concern. I'll be careful."

I follow the path cut through the trees all the way to the road, and the looping highway the rest of the way into town. With the wind in my hair and camp a little picture in my rearview mirror, I'm unshackled, even for only a few hours of freedom.

Each turn grows more uncertain once I pass downtown. What I'll do when I get to Spencer's house escapes me. It's not as if I can walk to the door, plant my feet on the Sway family welcome mat, and ring the doorbell.

I don't know why I'm looking for Spencer. Maybe because he helped me when he didn't have to, or maybe because he's a little bit of a liar—that's something I relate to. My curiosity isn't healthy, and the root of my interest isn't anything that will do me any good, but I'd rather not think too hard about that now.

There, up the road, is that brick retaining wall. All my bravery fades away. I decide to drive by the house once, pick up a pizza for Wen, and let Spencer be a memory of our travels—a mental snapshot of a soon-to-be-forgotten, sleepy Southern town.

I drop my speed to a crawl as I pull past the old colonial, ready for my last look.

Spencer sits on the porch in a whitewashed Adirondack chair with a laptop balanced on his knees. With him a short distance away, I realize my mistake. As my foot goes for the accelerator, Spencer glances up. I'm seen, and it's too late to drive on.

He closes his laptop and saunters down the drive. His smile is lazy as he rests his forearms on my open window and tilts into the cab. "You asked me if I was stalking you at Whitney's party. Now the real question is this: are you stalking me?"

"What if I said yes?"

"Then I'd think you were lying."

I press my lips together and try to hold my smile deep inside. "What if I said no?"

"Then I'd know for sure you were lying."

The car idles, and I stare at the unmoving needle

on the speedometer, neither of us disturbing the quiet. Until I do. "So maybe you want to get out of here? That is, if all your homework's done and your bed's made."

Temptation flickers in his eyes, and I can see why. If I had to stay in one place, all I'd want to do is run. But he'll give me some markie excuse, like his mom's got a pot roast in the oven. I'm sure of it.

Spencer glances at his house, and then me, before climbing inside.

"Where to?"

He rubs his knuckle under his chin like he's solving some difficult homework problem. "You like pancakes?"

He gives directions as I wind down the mountain roads and onto the highway.

The diner is at least ten miles from town, a greasy place that smells like french fries and maple syrup. At the back corner, where most of the fluorescent lights are burned out, I find an empty booth. Spencer checks his watch and slides down the vinyl seat across from me.

"So, Spencer Sway, why didn't you throw me to the wolves at that party? You one of those pay-it-forward types?"

He brushes spilled salt off the table's edge. "Those people aren't my friends. Not since last year."

"What'd you do last year? Figure out they're all assholes?"

A corner of his mouth turns up. "That's not so far from the truth."

The waitress flips a white mug right side up on my placemat, filling it to the brim with coffee. I take a sip. Diner coffee is the same wherever you go. Bitter and burned, with a few stray grounds in the bottom of the mug. Maybe that's why I love it—because it's always the same and one of the few things I can depend on from town to town.

I close my menu after deciding on two orders of banana pancakes—one to go. Spencer orders blueberry pancakes with a side of bacon. He pulls back the sleeve of his checkered shirt and looks at his watch again.

"Am I boring you, Spencer?"

"What?"

"Okay, give it over." I lay my hand across the table, palm up. "The watch. Really."

He assesses me as he unhooks the latch. "Am I going to get it back?"

"We'll see about that."

He drops it into my palm, and I wrap the metal band around my own wrist, shivering at the cold against my skin.

The waitress soon sets down our plates and a Styrofoam to-go box. As we eat, I say, "This trouble you got in with your friends, what'd you do?"

"I wouldn't mind having a few secrets. You've obviously got yours."

I steal a piece of Spencer's bacon, and he slides the plate to the middle of the table.

"So, you like to travel?" he says.

"Huh?"

"The pictures in my hallway. You liked them."

Out of all of Spencer's fancy things, Africa is the one thing he's had that I desperately want for my own. "Was Cape Town everything you imagined it to be?"

That wistful look on his face falters. "Oh, that trip was just my parents."

I'm a little relieved nobody at this table has set foot on that continent.

He traces the names carved into the tabletop, names of people like him, who sat in these cracked seats, celebrating homecoming games and graduating from Cedar Falls High with plans to travel the world, only to wind up back here, in some markie home by the lake with a mortgage and kids and a bunch of fading dreams.

"But I want to see Africa someday," he says. "More than anywhere."

So softly I barely even speak, I say, "I want to see it, too."

As soon as the words leave my mouth, I feel a weight lifted and a rush of embarrassment, like I've confessed some dark sin. Africa is my secret, my hope, my fear, and mine for the wanting. Knowing I have to share it with Spencer Sway is a little like jealousy and more like intimacy.

"So you," he says. "There's got to be more to you than pool hustling, shoplifting sunglasses, and dealing fake drugs." He props his elbows on the table and leans closer. "Whatever it is you are."

Every muscle in my body stills.

"Wanderer," I say.

"I wondered." He smiles and settles back in his seat. "Don't worry. I'm good with secrets."

"How come you know so much about all this?"

"This fucking town has a grudge—I guess that's why. Some Wanderers came through here a long time ago. The town can't forget."

All the whispers that we've been here before run through my head. "Don't toy with me, Spencer. What happened?"

"My dad took me to this parade when I was a kid. It was downtown, on Main Street. I don't know; maybe some of my memories are blending together. It was a weird year—we have that same parade every Thanksgiving, but the Wanderers got run out of town, or something."

"What was so special about that year?"

He hesitates and blows out a breath. "Okay, this is crazy, but a kid—one of them—snuck onto a parade float."

Parade. The mystery of this town comes into focus—those wide drugstore windows, the tree on Main

Street, and that sense of *déjà vu* this place keeps conjuring.

I remember balancing myself high in a tree, watching the colors of balloon animals and clowns swirl together with the smells of hot dogs and cotton candy. The town near our campsite was having a parade, and I was a kid trapped between two worlds that kept colliding around me.

Rona had been keeping us for a while, I guess, and Wen and I sweet-talked her into taking us to see the parade. Markie things like that weren't permitted; she could have said no. Maybe she only agreed because we were these motherless things she couldn't handle.

Cops walked the streets, some on horseback, some on foot, down a length of rope that marked the border between the sidewalk and the street. Rona told us not to go anywhere and went off to flirt her way into a bag of blue cotton candy for us all to share.

The parade had a float covered in these white balloons, like a cloud ready to float down the asphalt. I wanted to float, too.

One of the cops guarded the rope that kept the onlookers on the sidewalks and the parade in the street, so I made Wen pretend to fall down and skin his knee. While the officer sat down in the road with Wen, rolling his pant leg to check for bleeding, I slipped behind him, under the rope, and between the clowns and trumpet players, all the way onto the cloud float.

I buried myself deep in the balloons and waited while the music began, trombones and drums accompanied by a marching band wearing red-and-blue headpieces.

Minutes later, the float started to shimmy and shake, rolling down the street.

That's when I popped out like a jack-in-the-box, snarls of my tangled hair blowing in the wind. I lifted my hand to the crowd, showing off the beauty-queen wave I'd seen minutes before from the local high school's homecoming royalty nominees.

I move my gaze up from the diner table, and Spencer's got his face cradled in his hand. He's staring at me like he's trying to figure me out.

I straighten in my seat. "Tell me more."

He squeezes his eyes shut and shakes his head. "I don't know. I don't really remember. They say she ruined the whole parade, but I—I couldn't take my eyes off that girl."

What he doesn't know is that he couldn't take his eyes off me.

Our plates are clean, and my hands are sticky with syrup as Spencer throws two tens on the table. I plant my index finger on one of the bills and slide it toward him. He watches me count my own cash, the little bit I didn't deposit in the Cool Whip container, and lay it on top of his ten.

I drive through Cedar Falls, and as we pass the neighborhood where the party was, I crane my neck. Regret hits me hard when I think about that girl—Whitney—who was only ever kind to me. Who made me feel like I was normal, just like her. Who saved me when the drunk girl almost blew my cover.

As we round the corner onto his street, Spencer says, "Park a few houses down."

I pull the Chevy to a stop two mailboxes shy of the Sway family's brick retaining wall.

"Hey, um," I say, "I've been meaning to ask you—is that girl okay? The one who threw the party." Before I can think to hold back, I add, "I feel a little guilty about her."

"Whitney? You feel guilty about her?" Spencer laughs. "Look, she used you as badly as you used her. If you think she didn't know exactly what you and your brother were, you're not that good a con artist."

"How could she have known?"

"Like I told you, this town holds a grudge. People are smarter here than you're used to."

I'm torn between my growing curiosity and my aching pride. "What was her angle?"

"She had a bet going that she'd throw the most-talked-about senior party of the year. Inviting you and your brother was her ticket."

"What about the cops? Was that her grand finale?"

"Nah, she wouldn't have done that. I take it one of her rivals called them. But after the scene you and I put on, we just about cemented Whitney's win."

You'd think I'd hate her. But I can't hate someone that cunning. Someone like me. If anything, I like Whitney all the more.

Spencer's fingers twist around the door handle. "When can I see you again?"

"When do you want to see me again?"

He clears his throat. "Tomorrow? Could I pick you up out there?"

"I can't do tomorrow."

His face falls.

"Wednesday," I say. "I'll meet you in front of the drugstore at seven."

He smiles. "Wednesday."

"Hey, Spencer." I unwind the watch from my wrist. "You wouldn't want to be late."

He pockets it, leaving his wrist naked except for a

white tan line before he slides down the length of the cab beside me.

He's close enough for the heat of his jeans to seep against my thigh. I want to feel his mouth on mine so bad the blood rushes to my lips.

As he inches closer to me, I know he's going to taste like maple syrup and summer and the tragedy of places I can never go. So I turn away, leaving him only my cheek.

CHAPTER 16

UNDER A MOONLESS SKY, I RETURN TO CAMP. I FIND Wen playing solitaire outside the trailer. Tonight was a birthday celebration for Emil, but I was far away from camp and far away from Boss and Felix and Lando. I was in another world.

I plop into the empty lawn chair beside Wen. "Are you hungry?"

"Not really. Sonia brought me a tin of preacher cookies."

Preacher cookies are the only kind we make in camp because they don't need to be baked and nobody has an oven.

"Oh, I've got something better than those." I push the to-go container and a plastic fork across the collapsible picnic table, to the edge of his cards. "Pancakes."

"Yum." He opens the container and cuts his food with the side of the fork. With his mouth full, he says, "You're eating pancakes with the markie now?"

"Spencer."

Wen's fork pauses midair. "First-name basis. What's the angle?"

"No angle. He saved my ass. He's a friend."

Wen snorts and shovels another forkful into his mouth.

"What?"

"You say it so casually. A friend. Like you've had a ton of friends outside camp before."

I push up from the table. "It's not really any of your business."

Wen catches my arm and rolls his eyes. "I don't mean anything by it. Just curious. Those people at the party, they were all friends."

"Yeah." I'm careful as I lower myself beside him again. I don't like to get Wen started on thinking about how markies live.

He cups his chin in his hand, zoning out into the distance while he chews. "It's interesting how they choose their friends, you know. Our friends are all in camp. We don't have much choice."

"I think they go to school together. They don't have a choice, either."

"Interesting."

That night, Wen props himself up with pillows and a book he bought in town but claims he stole. But me, I lie there, looking up at the cloth ceiling with its duct-tape patches, thinking my nights beneath this roof are numbered. Felix is closer than I ever imagined him being. It's not as if he's moving in here with my brother and me.

I've never been the kind to sit back and let my fate come to me. Defying authority, that's what Rona and Lando called it. When things press down on me, I hit back. Now if only I could hit back to the tune of twenty grand.

Soon Wen turns off his light. He whispers his good-night ritual in a groggy way that tells me his eyes are already closing.

I'm the restless one for a change.

Wen snores softly while someone's generator buzzes outside our windows. My own sounds stir through my mind. And others, too. The click of the second hand on a watch, the hum of a voice. All the sounds of Spencer should be sealed on the other side of Cedar Falls, bricked in and boarded up inside the Sway family home. Here, in my tent trailer, they're unshakable.

I even think I hear a whisper outside my screen. But the things you think you hear in the dark are never real, not even the things you whisper to yourself.

Nothing. That is, until I hear it again.

"Tal."

It comes from behind a tall maple at the edge of camp, catching with the wind so I can't identify the speaker.

I grab my heaviest flashlight from under my mattress and slip my feet into a pair of Wen's boots about five sizes too roomy. I close the screen door behind me, careful the bolts don't creak.

The light from my flashlight is faint as I shine it into the woods.

"It's only me," says Sonia. "I didn't want to wake up Wen." She shifts her sandals in the dry grass. "Would you mind doing me a favor? I gave Emil some real nice cigars for his birthday—well, not real nice—but nice enough. He went to sleep early, and when I was finishing up the last of the dishes, I knocked the last couple into the sink."

A real kitchen with an actual sink was a perk of Sonia's marriage. She got all blushy the first time she showed me the checkered linoleum floor, the sink with running water, and the flushing toilet, like she was embarrassed of having something so fine when Wen and I were still living in squalor. But walking back to my tent trailer that afternoon, that metal siding shone for me—outright sparkled—in a way it hadn't in years.

She rubs her teeth against her lip now. "Emil's asleep still, and I don't want him to know about the cigars."

"You sure you knocked them in the sink?"

She presses her palm to her stomach, and her cheeks turn bright red. "What do you think I did? Smoked them?"

I close the space between us. "Keep your voice down."

Sonia stares over my shoulder.

Rona's there, a robe cinched at her waist and her hair spun into one of her turbans. "What are you girls doing out so late?"

"I'm going for a drive with Sonia."

It's not that I even want to take off with Sonia, but Rona standing in front of me and acting like she won't let me leave makes the desire to go rise up out of nowhere.

Rona glances from me to Sonia and raises an eyebrow. "Can I talk to you, Tal? Alone."

I follow her into the shadows of my tent trailer.

She yawns into her sleeve. "You really are going out with just Sonia?"

"Who else would I be going with?"

"I saw you driving around town the other day. With a boy I didn't know."

That I didn't expect.

I work my hand into my hair, faking casual. "Our ecstasy scam got a little hot."

"You ran your ecstasy scam here?"

"Yeah." I sigh. "That boy helped me out."

She rubs the back of her hand across her sleepy eyes. "I understand, but markie boys can't be trusted. They'll use you and then discard you. Those temptations all end in heartbreak."

Spencer and I, whatever we are, we're not the devious thing she's making us out to be. He's the only person who's ever kissed me and left me feeling like I still belonged to myself.

"And you shouldn't be running around with any boy. You've got a fiancé."

"Are you going to let me go with Sonia, or not?"

I'm pressing my luck now.

Rona's gaze sharpens, but the tension leaves her face just as quickly. "Don't stay out too late. Tomorrow night's the autumnal equinox."

The Chevy is a few miles from camp, past the rolling hills that circle the civilized part of Cedar Falls. We still haven't spoken.

"So you need to get a new pack?"

"Yeah." She flicks her ID between her thumb and forefinger and smiles in the moonlight. "Shouldn't be a problem." Sonia's two whole years older than me. Two years and twelve days that don't mean much, except it's legal for her to buy cigars.

She stows her ID inside her bra. "How are you feeling about Felix now?"

"Don't know." I can't tell her I have no intention of marrying him or that I'm trying to buy my freedom back. I don't trust her to keep my secrets.

"Has anyone said anything about where you'll live after? It's not like they're going to let him take you off anywhere." She flips down the visor mirror and rubs her fingertips under her eyes, smearing away some of the makeup that's settled on her cheekbones. "If I'd married someone from another camp, they'd send me packing. But not you. You're their compass."

"Tried it. Lando says that deal dies with Boss. He believes in me about as much as Wen believes in wearing worn-out clothes."

"That's crazy," she whispers. "Everyone believes in you."

Her limitless faith in me, in the Spirit of the Falconer, it's a curious thing. Believing in something I can't see has never come natural for me. Not since one particular day when I was a kid.

We sat around the campfire, me tucked between Rona and Wen. It was the seventh day of the month, a spiritual day, so we put on the best of our clothes and dragged an ice chest around the pinwheel of RVs into the heart of camp.

We listened to Marius, the camp's spiritual advisor, tell stories of times when horse-drawn carriages kept us wandering. He spoke about the Spirit of the Falconer, too. It wasn't long after the whole compass thing happened.

I'd never recognized a real omen or seen a trace of the invisible Falconer, but I'd lied about the pulling inside me, and they'd believed me. A thought began to snowball: if Marius lied to them about the Falconer, they'd believe it just the same. And maybe, in some other part of the world, some other people were more attuned to the workings of the universe, and maybe they didn't believe in the Falconer.

Right then that doubt lodged itself inside me, and it's stuck with me every day since, something I've never voiced, not even to Wen: *what if* everything *they tell us is wrong?*

Outside the Quick and Easy, I park in the first empty space. I flip through the magazines by the storefront while Sonia selects a package of the nicest cigars the place stocks.

I watch Sonia'a reflection in the convenience store window, the way she flirts through the sale, despite being obviously pregnant. She pays with cash dug out of her bra. It's something I haven't seen her do much of. Pay, that is.

Pretending things are the same between us feels like a scam. I'm not sure who I'm trying to con, Sonia or myself. No longer is our friendship the reincarnation of Rona and Greta's. It's gone. Like my mother.

The clerk drifts to the back of the store as Sonia falls in beside me, holding her cigars. She cocks her head to the ice-cream freezer humming in the corner. The clerk's stocking the beer fridge, not noticing as Sonia reaches into the freezer and pulls out two ice-cream sandwiches I know she doesn't intend to pay for.

"Sonia, no." I grab on to the door she's leaning into and keep her from stepping outside.

Her gaze carries a question I can't answer.

The logical side of me tells me I'm doing this because it's not worth the risk. Every con has to be calculated from now on, a necessity to raise the bride-price. But it's something more than logic stopping me.

"They're, like, a dollar apiece," I say. "It's not worth it."

She knocks her shoulder into the door and breaks my grip. "Being worth it's never mattered to you before."

Sonia's right. Never have I given a second thought to a small item lifted while a salesperson had his back turned. Sonia isn't the only one who's changed.

She climbs into the Chevy with the stolen ice-cream sandwiches in her hands and the cigars under her arm.

I don't follow.

There's no way to reconcile—not to Sonia and not to myself—this shift in me. Stealing two ice-cream sandwiches after narrowly avoiding handcuffs days before feels reckless. I can't. Not after a boy who didn't know

142

me put himself on the line to save me.

I walk to the counter, eyeing the clerk until he makes his way behind the register. In my jeans pocket, I find a buttery soft five-dollar bill and slide it along the counter.

"This is for two ice-cream sandwiches."

CHAPTER 17

WANDERERS MILL THROUGHOUT CAMP, CARRYING jugs of moonshine and baskets filled with bread and grapes, while boys hang lanterns from the trees. It's almost sundown on my favorite night of the year.

Tonight is the autumnal equinox, marking the end of summer and the first night of fall. As much as summer runs through my veins, there's something about the changing of the leaves that will always sing to me.

I hide in the shade of Rona's trailer, the silky, green fabric of my dress slipping between my fingers as I wait for her to leave for the heart of camp. This is how it always is now, when I need something from Rona—even if it's as simple as a shower—I'd rather hide for an hour than share a two-minute sham of a conversation.

The screen door slams, and Rona darts out her door with her black-and-white hair trailing after her.

I close myself inside, take a lukewarm shower, and tug my dress over my head. When Rona found it in a thrift shop two months ago, I told her to forget it. It had no place in our lifestyle, the same as Wen's encyclopedias. We travel light, so it was wasteful to hang on to a dress I didn't need for the last three moves. I didn't want to admit I actually wanted the thing. Still, Rona insisted we make the dress mine.

The sun disappears under the tree line, shrinking through the branches as I go looking for Wen. He isn't inside our trailer, but something else catches my attention. A flash of green sits on top of my pillow. An equinox crown. Rona must have left it for me. It's made of ivy, woven together with strands of tiny burgundy flowers. The crowns take hours to weave. It's obvious Rona spent a lot of time making mine. I can't believe she went to the effort this year.

Wen gives me a lopsided smile as I step outside and into lantern light.

He wears green slacks and a crisp navy button-down shirt with swirls of dark green matching the pants. He's always been vain, and the equinox provides an excuse to indulge.

His face is healing now that we've got some extra cash to keep him from fighting regularly. All our money is supposed to go toward the bride-price, but I can't bear the thought of Wen fighting when we've got enough cash to keep his face unharmed.

He eyes my crown. "You look real nice."

My fingers brush the leaves, and I tug my hand to my side. "I can't believe we're still playing along with all this."

"What does that mean?"

"Dressing up like this. Wearing my crown. We follow all these traditions and pretend camp hasn't sold me."

Wen freezes, an awful look passing over his face as he takes my hands into his. "We'll fix this, Tal—you always fix everything." He lets go and offers his arm. "Don't let it ruin tonight for you."

I put on a dark smile and straighten my crown. *"Carpe diem."*

I take his arm, and we walk, circling the pinwheel instead of cutting through the trailers.

The hum of the music vibrates through me at the heart of camp. A fire is crackling beside a heavy navy blue rug hauled into the dirt to serve as our dance floor. Secretly, I'm dying to dance, to move, to float, to twirl around and around, and forget about the weight bearing down on me.

Boss sits in his wheelchair like it's a throne, wearing a suit that matches Lando's.

Behind them, Felix stands in the dusky light outside Sonia and Emil's RV. Our eyes meet, and he starts toward me.

"Hello, Talia," he says. "You look real good tonight. Always, I mean. Whenever I see you."

"You're a real charmer."

"Thanks." His blank face wobbles into a smile. "The other day, with the tires . . . I'm sorry about that." He lowers his voice. "People've got expectations of me. And of you."

In a lounger at the edge of the dance floor, Rona's long legs are crossed toward Boss, but every so often, she glances at me. I wish I could tell what she's thinking—it must appear like I'm making nice with Felix—and I'd hate it if that's what she thought.

"Maybe I don't care about other people's expectations," I say. "Maybe you shouldn't either."

"No, I'm ready for this. Marriage, I mean. I'm ready to grow up and make my family proud."

He doesn't want me because I'm me. Following through with the arranged marriage will make him a man in the eyes of his camp. It could have been any girl.

"You really think marrying me will make you grow up? Make you a man?"

"This is what we do—"

I fold up my arms. "People around here will tell you lecturing me is a waste of time."

"Look, I'm not real good with words. You should come see my trailer sometime—it's the best money can buy. I think you'll like being married to me."

For the whisper of a moment, I imagine it. A life with Felix, together under the same cloth roof, letting him choose what roads we place before our wheels.

147

That life is no life at all.

We don't eat until the sky is black, and then we devour everything we've all spent days preparing: roasted meats, skillet cornbread, desserts, and candies. We crowd around the campfire and sing the equinox song and pray for a mild fall and winter.

People dart between Felix and me all night, but I feel his gaze burning through their bodies and into my skin. Not once do I laugh or smile when I'm not conscious of his stare.

After we're all full of food or drunk on wine or both, the music strikes up. I want to dance. I want to dance all night, spinning until I'm dizzy.

My mouth goes dry as Lando ambles to my side with Felix in tow. Our three-piece orchestra strikes up a new song. A marriage waltz.

My rib cage strains against the satin fabric. I can't breathe.

I'd like to think my poker face is as much a part of me as my smile or my frown, an easy expression to slip on when the need arises. Tonight, when I need it most, it fails me.

Lando grins—he knows he's rattled me—and takes me by the shoulders. "You'd love a little practice dance before the real wedding, wouldn't you, Tal?"

Practice. It's only practice. My tension drifts away, but I hold my chin high. "The hell I would."

Wen's a few feet away and blurry through the camp-fire smoke. But I know what he's thinking—*Don't do it, Tal.*

"Come on," Felix says, elbowing Lando. "Don't make her."

Lando brings his mouth against my ear. "Make a scene, and Wen will pay for it."

I glance at my brother, in his nicest clothes, with his healing face. "Fine."

The band increases the tempo, and Felix puts his damp hand into mine and leads me to the rug. I'd rather never dance again than be led this once.

We stop in the middle of the crowd of Wanderers all swaying to the wedding waltz, and I drape my arm over Felix's shoulder, keeping a few feet between our bodies.

"Do you really have to look so unhappy?" he says.

None of this is his fault. I almost feel guilty.

His back is stiff as he spins me around the rug. We make two wide turns, and I try not to think about how the thin satin of my dress is the only barrier between his palms and my back.

Wen's sitting at the end of Rona's lounger. They whisper as they watch me. Sonia's on the sidelines, her legs tucked beneath her as she shovels more food onto Emil's plate and refills his wine glass.

Felix hauls me against his chest, and his foot smashes my delicate equinox slipper.

"Ow," I say. A reflex—it barely hurt.

He lets me go and, as he backs away, stumbles over a wrinkle in the rug. He stalks off to the sidelines to a spot beside Boss.

A little smile on my lips, I shrug, toward Lando.

Heading back to my trailer would be so easy, but I'm not letting anyone ruin this night for me.

On equinox, I used to dance with Sonia until the sun came up.

Tonight is still mine for the taking.

I kick off my shoes at the edge of the rug and twirl into the middle of the crowd. This night can make me remember what it used to feel like to be a Wanderer.

I'm twirling around, harder, faster. I catch flashes of Sonia, then Felix, two alternating focal points, two glimpses of my future staring at me. They only make me spin faster.

Dizzy and drunk on adrenaline, I throw my head back. The paper lanterns woven throughout the trees tremble from the music. I'm trying as hard as I can to fall in love with this life I'm living. To fall in love with wandering again. But my thoughts are racing to Cape Town, hot maple syrup, and Spencer Sway.

The sky spins with me as I whirl. Between the strings of the lanterns, something flies across the horizon. It spreads its wings—a barn owl.

My feet freeze on the rug as the owl flies out of my

line of sight. I think of nothing but the Spirit of the Falconer. Even though I'm sure he's imaginary.

The vibration of the lanterns builds into a steady shake. My crown slips off my head and tumbles down my back. I'm the one at the center of it all, surrounded by the dancing camp. They're oblivious. All oblivious.

Until lanterns crash around us.

There's scrambling and screaming as people jump across the flames. The oil from the lamps could burn not only our camp but the forest and the town of Cedar Falls.

A whooshing sound swoops through the camp, sucking up all the flames at once. The air goes still, and if I believed in anything at all, I might think that gust of wind was something magical.

Panic fades, and we all stand silently under the dark night sky.

CHAPTER 18

"I READ SOMETHING IN HERE TODAY." WEN TAPS the book sitting on the edge of the diner table. "It said, 'I can't go back to yesterday because I was a different person then.'" Between his fingers, I can read half of the spine—the name Lewis Carroll.

Wen met the owner of the bookstore the other day, a woman with a bouffant head of white hair named Blanche Fairchild. I hung back in the travel section, thumbing through glossy color pictures in atlases while she spoke to Wen. She said he could read all the books he wanted without paying, as long as he stayed in the store.

"Did you pay our good money for that?"

He runs his fingertips over the embossed cover, not making eye contact. "Stole it."

For a con man, deception isn't his strong suit.

"Liar."

The diner's front door swings open. Wen sinks into his seat, shading his face in the collar of his shirt. The mirror hung above our booth flashes with navy-and-yellow letterman jackets. Jeremy or Craig would probably like nothing better than to finish what they started at Whitney's party.

I lift my chin toward the restaurant's kitchen, silently asking Wen if we need to make a run for it, but he relaxes. It's not them.

"While we're on the subject of paying," he whispers, "are you paying for lunch, or are we going to dine and ditch?"

"Haven't decided."

"I have a feeling you're going to pay."

He's right. The heat from the con isn't what's keeping me honest. It's stupid for me to develop morals now when every dollar we stow away gets us a dollar closer to buying my future back.

"I'm worried about our money," says Wen.

He's got no business being worried, not when it's my freedom on the line. "Don't be."

"When I counted it, the figures from the last con didn't add up."

"I don't know." I shrug. "You must have been off with your first count."

The waiter places a giant pizza in front of us—sausage and mushroom, my brother's favorite—and Wen claps his palms together, grinning for the first time since last night.

I eat all the toppings off my slice first. "Hey, you're okay, aren't you?"

That smile of his shrinks. He lowers his slice back to his plate. "It's just us burying that owl. . . ."

I hadn't even considered what Wen might think. "We didn't cause that."

After the lanterns came crashing down, some Wanderers called for us to leave, saying that the fire was an omen and we were in danger. Some begged for us to stay because it was in this blessed place where the wind extinguished the flames, saving our lives and our livelihoods. We waited for an hour for an answer from Boss, but he didn't lift his chalk, no matter how hard we coaxed.

"You could tell me if you weren't okay," I say. "After last night, I mean."

Wen's eyes are so full of trust and light, when there's nothing inside me except lies and shadows. If he actually came to me with his deep philosophical questions, I don't know what I'd say.

"I know, Tal."

I raise my slice and open my mouth to take a bite.

"But what if you're wrong? What if they're omens? Something could really be wrong with this place."

I want to tell him I don't believe in omens. That nothing the camp's ever told him is real. But my words stay trapped in my throat like a pill I can't swallow.

Wen points to his pizza. "You know I like it like this. It's artisan—that's what they call it. Not with the thick crust." He licks marinara sauce from his hand. "Mom didn't like it this way, I remember. She liked those thick crusts. Maybe someday we could bring her back here."

I must make a face because he flinches. "Sorry," he says. "I know you don't like to talk about when Mom comes back."

Mom's not coming back.

Sometimes I'm so sure Wen knows it, and then he says things like this. We don't talk about our father at all, and I wish Mom could live in the same place inside our memories, not roving the world without us. Of course, he's dead and gone and never coming back. Mom's just stuck in that great in-between.

If lying to himself gets Wen through the days, I won't shatter his illusion.

I set my slice back on my plate. My voice softens to that soothing tone Rona used on us when we were kids, and sometimes still does. "It's not that I don't like to talk about her, Wen. This idea of Mom coming back is doing a number on you, dragging you under barbed wire. Over broken glass. I'd rather tell you an ugly truth than a pretty lie."

He bites off a hunk of crust. "I prefer the pretty lie."

Wen keeps his right hand on the wheel and presses his left against his forehead as he drives toward the drugstore. "Tal, are you sure you don't want to blow off the markie? I could cut my trip to the bookstore short, and we could catch a movie. My popcorn deficiency is becoming a medical condition."

I've convinced him to drop me off in front of the drugstore, where I agreed to meet Spencer. He didn't argue much. He's having his own little markie affair with books.

"I'm going." I reach out the window and tilt the side mirror inward. I apply thick lines of black liquid eyeliner. "Concern yourself with driving straight and not thinking too hard."

"Don't you worry you're getting in over your head with this?"

The wheels strike the reflective lane dividers before he yanks the truck straight.

"Damn it, Wen!" I shake the tube of eyeliner at him. "Why are you driving in Braille? Watch the road!"

"Okay, seriously? You're, like, the absolute worst at changing the subject. This markie boy—"

"Spencer."

"Spencer," he repeats. "He may be in over his head, too. Does he know you're leaving town in a few weeks?"

The question is a knife between my ribs. I don't think I've quite put a definition on what I'm doing with

Spencer and certainly not a time line. "It hasn't come up. And we're just having fun. I would think you of all people would get it."

Between Palson's Family Drugstore and the Cedar Falls Fire Department, Wen brings the truck to a halt. "Be smart, Tal."

"Aren't I always?"

"You're always clever but not always smart. There's a difference."

I shove my eyeliner into my purse and leave all but one of my fake IDs inside the glove box. My brother believes I'm clever, so clever he's not the least bit worried about Felix carrying me away. Clever enough to collect twenty thousand dollars, buy myself some freedom, trade in the Chevy for a yacht, and sail us all the way to Morocco if it strikes my fancy.

At least I'm clever enough to not shatter his illusion.

"One last thing," I say. "Pick up a lottery ticket for me. Numbers seven, thirty-four, fifty, twenty-five, six, seventeen."

"Seven, thirty-four, fifty, twenty-five, six, seventeen. Got it. But why?"

I slam the truck door, rest my elbows on the open window, and lean inside. "All will soon be revealed."

CHAPTER 19

I SPIN A RACK OF CEDAR FALLS POSTCARDS NEXT TO the gumball machine inside Palson's. I pick out a post-card, one with a picture of the lake where we swam, and dig around the bottom of my bag for change.

Through the windows, I see Spencer walk up in a polo shirt and jeans, hair still a little damp from the shower. I pay for the postcard—a first for me—and meet Spencer outside, where the evening sky has faded into tangerine, and streetlights make the sidewalks glow.

"Hello there, Spencer Sway."

He grins and leans his back against the side of his car. "I didn't know if you'd show up."

"I didn't know if I would, either."

I open the passenger door before he can try to open it for me and make this night into something it's not. He climbs in, too, and I kick my sandals onto the dash of Spencer's car, a pair of brown espadrilles made out of leather soft as butter. "Take me to the most amazing place in Cedar Falls, please."

"You get your way a lot, don't you?"

"Always."

He glides through downtown, carrying us away from any sense I have that I'm betraying my world by being near him.

"Are we knocking over a bank or heading for the border?" I say. "Or both?"

He smiles so big it's almost a laugh.

I fish a penny out of his cup holder. "Heads Toronto, tails Tijuana."

Spencer cuts through a side street and turns down an alley. He slows behind a row of buildings and parks beside a Dumpster.

I check for business signs as we get out of the car, but the buildings around us are unmarked and only faintly lit by the streetlights from the roadway.

He presses on a door handle. It doesn't budge.

"Breaking in?" I cross my arms and sink my shoulder into the brick building. "Am I finally seeing a glimpse of that bad boy inside you?"

He jiggles around in his pocket and produces a key. "No, but I am working on being spontaneous."

"Spontaneity isn't something you can work on, Spencer Sway."

We step inside, and spotlights shoot from the ceiling to illuminate sculptures and paintings.

"My dad's gallery," he says. "It's closed today. And it's the most amazing place in Cedar Falls."

"Your dad is an artist?"

"The owner. An art aficionado, I guess. The gallery barely breaks even, but Mom supports his habit. Some of these are by local artists, friends of my parents. Most are from artists up north. Take a look around. I'll be right back. I have a surprise."

I make a slow circle around the room, taking in these creations, all unusual.

He returns carrying two clear plastic cups full of something dark red. In the crook of his arm, a cork sticks from a bottle.

"Fancy."

"Nope." He passes me a cup. "It's the cheap stuff my dad doesn't like to serve. He won't even notice it's gone."

We trip through the corridors, drinking our wine and staring at paintings splattered with colors that stretch so far I can't take them in without moving my neck right and left, up and down. They're strange and lovely and untamed.

"You don't look bored," says Spencer. "I wasn't so sure you'd find it as amazing as me." He stubs the toe of his shoe on the wooden floor. "I mean, as amazing as I find it."

"It is amazing"—I down the last of my wine—"and so are you, somewhere under all that unrealized potential."

We stop to refill our glasses, and the wine dwindles down to nothing. In the lobby, I lounge across a black velvet couch that's more of an oversized ottoman. Half a dozen people could sleep there and never so much as brush their toes together.

Spencer's cheeks are red from wine as he stretches beside me.

I trace my index finger down the bridge of his nose. "I do believe you're drunk on two glasses of wine, Spencer Sway."

His purple-stained lips curve upward. "Why do you always have to say my full name?"

"I like the sound of it. *Spencer Sway.* What do you call it when all the words start off repeating the same sound?" I love that point when I'm drunk enough to talk nonsense. Drunk enough to forget all the sensical things I don't want to remember.

"Onomatopoeia?"

"No, it's . . ." I think about the vocabulary Wen's always tossing around. ". . . alliteration. Shame on you, Spencer. You're going to fail that SAT and never make it into that college."

Close to my ear, he whispers, "Please don't talk about college." He touches his mouth to my collarbone and kisses the column of my throat. "Is this okay?"

The logical part of me says this isn't okay. The illogical part of me wants this closeness, and tonight, illogical's winning out. I like the feel of him.

With my eyes closed, I breathe a dangerous word. "Yes."

Maybe it's Felix, a few miles away in camp, waiting to cart me away, waiting for me to tell him I'm his. Being here with Spencer makes it better somehow, reminding myself my body is my own, that I get to choose who touches me.

"Tell me something," I say with our mouths inches apart. "Why're you here with me, instead of anybody else in Cedar Falls? You're far too pretty to be a loner."

He rolls onto his back and stares at the rafters. "So, I read this Vonnegut book for class once, and it said something about getting close to the edge. That when you're on the edge, you can see things you don't see from the center."

My heart aches at those words. I collect my focus the best I can. "Well, still waters do run deep."

"Everybody in this town is standing dead center." His smile turns serious, and he meets my eyes. "I hate this town, everything about it. How my mom's always worried about what people think about her, what people'll think if I don't get accepted to SJU." He skims his thumb over my knuckles. "Hey, I told you how I did that exchange program last year? How I spent the year in Spain? When I came back to Cedar Falls, everything was the same. All my friends cared about was basketball games, girls they were trying to nail, who was running for mayor. Of course, my friends were Craig and Jeremy, so go figure."

"The guys at Whitney's?" *The gorillas.*

"Those would be the ones. I got wasted at a party, and I don't know, I started talking, telling them what I thought about them. This town. Jeremy and Craig were the ones to throw the first punches. Someone should have ended it before it went that far, but we were all pretty drunk. They wanted everything to be the same when I got back, but nothing was. And I wished—I wish—I'd never come back here at all."

What he's saying scares me, and it's not easy to do that. What he's told me means something big in his world.

"If you could go anywhere," I say, "where would you most want to go?"

"Sailing from Sydney to Cape Town would be a dream." His voice takes on that quality Wen's gets when he's starry-eyed over a book. "Someday, I want to sail around the world."

"I've never even been in a boat."

Thinking about things I haven't done always makes me think about Mom. I wonder if she's adrift somewhere, having some great adventure. I don't really care where she is, but I wonder if she's wandering or staying still.

Either way, she's left Wen and me to wander all alone.

"You'd love it," Spencer says as he skims his lips along my jawline. "Drifting over the water, heading off to places behind the horizon."

I want it. I do. And the wanting hurts because it's something I'll never have in my Wanderer life.

The weight of Spencer sinks over me. I gasp—I don't believe anything has ever surprised me so much before—and he pulls back. But I grab his wrists, anchoring his hands to both sides of my head and his knees at the sides of my hips.

It's an alluring, messy distraction, but this room feels safe, holding the two of us and our dreams of other worlds.

I hope Spencer's fine with it staying this way, though, clothes still on.

I make a soft sound against his mouth before I pull away. "When are you going to tell your family you're not going to that college?"

His eyes twinkle with amusement. "What do you mean? Of course I'm going to SJU."

It hits me like a slap across the face.

He dips his mouth toward mine, but I press against his chest and dodge his lips.

The gallery lights swirl from the wine as I sit up. Over my shoulder, I say, "But I thought—I thought you weren't going to do that."

"Go to college? I don't *want* to. But there's a difference—a big one. What else am I going to do? Assuming I have what it takes to get in, I'm going to SJU next year. Nothing's changing that." He yawns into his hand and shrugs. "Maybe I'll finally be able to do more traveling someday. After SJU, after I work a bunch of years in some windowless office."

Just like that, he's giving up. All talk and no action— Spencer Sway to a T.

The realization hits me—Spencer Sway is no different from everyone else in Cedar Falls. He almost had me fooled.

"You lied to me."

If this was the slightest bit funny, I'd laugh at the irony—a markie lying to me for a change.

"It wasn't a lie." He sits up and rubs at his eyes. "I was—oh come on, do we have to take this so seriously?"

I feel so impossibly stupid, for coming here tonight, for allowing myself to be the mark in a con I never saw coming. For putting myself in jeopardy—Wen and our whole camp, too—because of some stupid, selfish urges. For being a little less myself and a little more my mother.

We wait for the early morning hours to leave the gallery, until our limbs aren't heavy and we're all sobered up, but it's still dark enough to slip back into each of our lives unnoticed.

Spencer drives me to camp without talking, easing his car around curves and over potholes. In the vanity mirror, I find the reflection of my eyes. They looked dangerous before I left, lined with streaks of black eyeliner. Now, with everything he said ringing in my ears, there's a little uncertainty the makeup can't hide.

It's windy, and the lanterns of camp dance through the trees. When I was a kid, if we came back to camp late at night, I'd press my face to the window of the truck, watching the lights beckon us home.

Spencer guides us off the main road and underneath the trees that keep camp hidden.

"Stop right here," I say.

Before I know it, he's around the car, opening my door. "I'll walk with you."

It's a bad idea for him to come this close to us. Someone could see. And I shouldn't blur the lines between our two worlds. I don't tell him *no*, though, and let him walk beside me until the smoke from our campfires tickles my throat.

My sandals slow in the pine needles. "We're here."

"If you say so."

"Everything you said last night—that's why you like

me, isn't it? I'm the sweet promise of somewhere else."

"Is that so bad?"

He's playing with me because I'm a piece of somewhere else. But I won't be his toy.

As the shape of his back moves away from me, I realize something horrible's happened—I let the momentum of Spencer and me build to a dangerous speed.

And we just crashed.

CHAPTER 20

"Let's start it up." Wen lets go of the Chevy's bumper and grabs on to his knees to catch his breath. "We're far enough away."

I bear my shoulder into the tailgate of the Chevy, my boots sinking into the mud as I heave the truck a few more inches by myself.

Camp is off in the distance. I rest my hip on the bumper. Everyone's tucked away in their trailers except for someone softly strumming a guitar.

Wen and I are both dripping with sweat, even though the October air is cool, and he's probably right—we're far enough away that Rona won't hear the engine starting.

Anyone else wouldn't care too much about us sneaking off into the night, but if Rona heard us, she'd march down the road and order us back to our beds.

I wouldn't go, of course, but Wen would hang his head and trail her back to camp, his tail between his legs.

That can't happen tonight. I need my brother.

This is a two-man con.

"Shouldn't be this hard to get away," I say.

I use a bottle of hand sanitizer to clean the dirt and sweat from my bare arms as Wen drives. By the time we've reached town, I've applied mascara and lip gloss, brushed my tangles into submission, and swapped out my boots for a pair of sandals.

"You feeling good about this?" he says.

"Fortune favors the bold."

Wen takes off into the Cedar Falls Inn a few minutes before I do. For this con, my brother is a stranger to me, waiting in the shadows in the event I need some muscle. A sad excuse for muscle, but he's all I've got if everything goes south.

I park myself on a bench right outside the hotel bar, a freshly printed newspaper folded in my lap. I've got an ID in my pocket that would get me inside the bar, let me order whatever I wanted, as much of it as I wanted. Tonight, though, I'm me—in one sense. I'm sixteen.

Wen snags a seat within earshot, right inside the bar. The waitress rolls by, and he orders a strawberry daiquiri, the most under-twenty-one drink in the history of alcohol. I cringe. She cards him, of course, but our handiwork with the laminator seems to pass the test.

Hotels are the best places to set this con into action. Travelers usually keep a lot of cash on them, and lonely businessmen are as good as putty in my hands.

For nearly thirty minutes, I work the newspaper between my fingers, bite my lip, look down the corridors, waiting. Waiting for a figment of my imagination.

I'm alone with my thoughts, and my thoughts are a dangerous place to be, with Felix sneaking into my nightmares, with Spencer swaggering through my daydreams.

Spencer—I can shake him, but not his memory.

I may never travel anywhere the Chevy can't take me, but what I have is better than sitting still. Spencer has dreams of seeing the world, dreams that'll never come true.

A man pauses by the hotel lobby's elevators. He runs his gaze up the length of my brown legs, pausing at the hem of my skirt, high on my thighs. He takes care to flash the gold Rolex hanging from his arm. A fake Rolex, upon closer inspection. This is a man who wants to be someone he's not. Sonia read enough high-end magazines to learn the difference, and she taught me everything she knew.

Hello, three hundred dollars. What a pleasure to make your acquaintance.

I rise from the cushion, toss my hair back, and give him a small smile. "Excuse me, sir." I rest my hand in the crook of his elbow. "You wouldn't be Mr. Garcia, would you?"

"Sorry, miss. It's Dwayne Jenkins."

I slump back on the bench and give him my I'm-about-to-cry pout. "Sorry to trouble you."

"What seems to be the problem, young lady?" He sidles in beside me, his arm wrapping around my shoulders, his hand stroking my arm.

I fight off shivers and squeeze out a few fake tears. "You see, I bought this lottery ticket last week, using my older sister's ID. And I won. It's quite a chunk of change, and I've really been hurting for money lately."

"Well, that sounds like tremendous news to me. No offense, but I'm having a helluva time seeing the problem."

I sink my teeth into my painted lower lip and whisper, "I'm underage and can't cash the ticket in."

He removes his hand from my arm and scoots away. "How underage are you?"

Figures Dwayne would ask about that first. "Three lousy weeks short of eighteen."

"Can't you give the ticket to your sister and let her claim it for you?"

"April's got a bit of a drug problem, you see? I can't trust her, and it'd be as good as killing her to give her the five thousand dollars—"

"Five thousand dollars? That is one chunk of change."

"It's a fortune to me. I drove here, all the way from Macon, because this man I met online—Mr. Garcia—

said he'd cash the ticket for me. He said he'd do it if I split the winnings with him. He hasn't showed up, though, and I don't think he's going to." I press my hand over my mouth. "There I go, spilling my guts."

"What if someone else cashed it for you?"

"Who would do a thing like that?"

"Well, I would. For half, I mean. You have the ticket on you?"

I show him the newspaper, with the clear winning numbers, and the ticket—the altered date unrecognizable to the average Joe. This con is so easy it's stupid. The only legwork is changing the date on the ticket so the markie thinks he's got a ticket from last week instead of this one. Wen's handiwork is nothing short of amazing.

"Okay." He whistles. "I'll take the ticket, cash it, and give you half the winnings after they come in."

"You'd do that?"

"'Course I would."

"There's another problem, and I'm just sick over saying it, but how do I know I can trust you? I mean, you seem like such a smart and worldly man. You could be a con artist, for all I know."

He squints like he's thinking that one over. "You know anything about good faith money? How about I give you a couple of hundred in exchange for the ticket? I can call you up after I've claimed the prize money, and we can split it—maybe after your birthday. We could have ourselves a little celebration."

I smile. "That sounds like fun."

His wallet is a sea of green, spreading open before me. He counts two lousy hundreds and slips them into my hand. Wen likes to say I can look at money and make it grow legs and walk on over to me. I wish half the stuff Wen says were true.

"It kills me to ask this, Dwayne, but you suppose we could make it five hundred?"

My breaths are coming fast, my pulse pounding in my ears. We wind around the turnabout outside the hotel and barrel down the road. It's almost like being high, getting away with it, the five hundred dollars tucked safely inside my bra. It's better than high.

"Aren't you excited?" I say, slapping at the dash-board.

Wen presses his lips together, a sad excuse for a smile. "'Course I am. Five hundred's a record for you. . . ."

I sigh. "I know, Wen. It's not even close to enough."

"I'll do what I can, too, Tal. I will."

CHAPTER 21

WEN ANGLES HIMSELF ACROSS THE DINER TABLE, watching my pen scratch numbers onto a paper napkin. It's midmorning, and we're using twelve of our hard-conned dollars to treat ourselves to breakfast.

The numbers I've scribbled on the napkin aren't high enough. Wen's checked my math three times with the same result. We're still more than eleven thousand dollars short. Any way we total it, we have to up our game if we're going to bring in the twenty thousand.

"Have you thought about talking to Boss?" he says.

"I think Lando's calling the shots now."

Wen downs the last of his milk and wipes the white mustache left behind. "Maybe Lando would let you give him some now and some later. I mean, you've proven you can bring money in."

Lando would sooner park his wheels in front of some tract home and become a markie than let me out of the deal without every cent paid to Felix.

"I don't think that would work."

Wen rests his forehead against the window, which has been recently painted with pumpkins for Halloween. "We could run away for a while, me and you. We'd come back with our pockets weighed down with the money. You'd have done it then; you'd be free."

I want to say yes—I do. But I can't pretend the road isn't an uncertain place for only the two of us.

"This isn't right," Wen mutters at the figures on the napkin.

"I know."

"No, really. It doesn't add up. We should have exactly four hundred more than this. You must have lost some of it."

"That's impossible. Have you ever known me to lose money? I'd sooner lose you."

"Or someone's stealing it. Who knows about our stash?"

There aren't many people at camp I absolutely trust. It could be anyone.

"Does Sonia know?" he asks.

I snatch a piece of bacon from his plate. "Sonia wouldn't steal from us." As soon as the words leave my mouth, I wonder if I'm wrong.

"Either way," he says. "Our stash isn't safe in the trailer anymore."

Through the windows, a bouffant-haired woman waves at us from across the street. It takes a moment before I recognize her—Blanche Fairchild, the bookstore owner. She's wearing a sheer, lime-green tunic with purple pants that remind me of encyclopedia pictures of India.

Wen waves back, plastering on a great big grin.

I lift my hand. "She's a little off, I think."

He frowns. "Don't say that."

I pull the keys to the Chevy from my pocket and throw some cash on the tabletop. We've been in town most of the morning, and it's time to cut our adventure short. Out on the sidewalk, he says, "Hey, can we go back to the bookstore for, like, an hour?"

"No."

"Why not? I let you do what you want with that markie."

"Seriously?"

"Come on, Tal. I have, like, ninety pages of a book to finish."

"You can't read ninety pages in an hour and—" I lose track of my thoughts as we step around the corner, where a patrol car is all lit up with someone in the backseat.

My eyes must be playing a trick on me. That long mane of black hair streaked with white has got to be some unknown markie's. The woman's shoulders shift so her profile's framed by the window. In the backseat sits Rona.

Wen lunges off the curb, not even looking for traffic. I grab his shoulder, yanking him behind a bench with me and ducking down low.

"We have to do something, Tal."

"We can't." It's not me; it's our code. If one of our own takes a pinch—gets arrested—we scatter.

The police car bolts down Main Street, lights flashing and sirens blaring as it carries Rona away.

We get to our feet, and Wen's glaring. "Listen," he says. "Rona and you may have your problems, but you've got to put all that aside. She's the closest thing to a mother we've got."

I don't speak.

"What? You think I don't know Mom's gone forever? I may say shit about her coming back, but I know the truth. Maybe Mom doesn't really give a damn about us, but Rona does."

Wen's never said anything like that before. Half of me is glad he knows our mother really isn't our mother anymore. But the other half hurts for him.

He kicks the ground and stomps to the truck, the bookstore abandoned.

Everyone's in a frenzy at camp. Murmurs of Rona's name are mingled with legal jargon like *fraud* and *fel-*

177

ony. They're saying she can't fight the charges. All she's got on her side is some stuttering public defender. They say she's definitely going away for a long time.

Rona got busted for running a rental scam. Some Wanderers broke into a vacant cabin and rented it out for Thanksgiving week to a bunch of different toureys. The markies shouldn't have realized they were duped until moving-in day. Realized that there was no way into the house, that none of them had a right to it, that their money was gone forever—along with us.

This time, the cops caught on, and Rona took the pinch because her pay-by-the-minute cell number was used for the ad in the paper.

Sonia knocks on our door a little before dinnertime. "Thought you might want to know what's going on."

We sit on the trailer step together, both of us tucking our feet under ourselves.

"I heard Lando talking," she says. "There's a hearing at the end of the month. They can't get Rona out of there unless we post bail. Lando says we don't have the money."

"How much?"

She whistles. "Thirty grand."

"How much does the bondsman need to post bail?"

"Twenty percent. Six grand."

Guilt bites at me. I'm sitting on a pile of money that could have Rona back in camp by nightfall. But my money isn't for buying Rona's freedom. It's meant to buy my own.

"Don't you worry, Tal. I know Rona's going to be okay." Sonia tips her face up to the sun with her eyes closed. "The Spirit of the Falconer, he'll make sure of it."

Even if I believed, even if I shared in Sonia's uncanny ability for simplifying the biggest of problems, her words wouldn't bring me comfort.

Because the Falconer didn't keep our mother out of prison. No matter what Rona or Wen thinks happened in those weeks before Mom's arrest.

The week before the law found our mother, we pulled over at a rest stop outside Texarkana. Wen and I—five and six at the time—went tearing toward the drinking fountains like banshees as Mom and Rona rolled down the Buick's convertible top and shared a cigar.

Wen and I watched from the shade of the building as an owl perched itself on the Buick's hood ornament.

Mom yelled some profanities at the thing, while Rona flapped an old towel and made the bird fly away.

Later that week, when I sent Wen's beach ball sailing into the forest, Mom took Wen's hand and they went in search of it. Not two minutes passed before Wen screamed. He was wailing his lungs out when Mom carried him out of the brush, high on her hip. They'd found an owl, dead and torn to shreds.

Rona and Mom had exchanged a look I didn't quite understand.

Wen's sobs turned to sniffles, and Rona said, "You see now, Greta? The Spirit of the Falconer, he's trying to show you something you're too blind to see."

"What I see," said Mom, "is nothing at all."

Later, after Wen and I fell into Rona's care, he woke me up one night and told me he'd heard Rona talking. Rona swore Mom had ignored the Falconer's warnings that the arrest was coming.

I told him it wasn't true, but I think Wen's gone on believing the Spirit of the Falconer was trying to save our mother.

Wen comes trudging down the road and pushes past Sonia and me. He walks straight through the trailer door, without a word. I tell Sonia I'll catch her later and go in after him.

"You all right?" I hop on my bed and pat the spot to my right. "Talk to me."

"I was just closing up the windows of Rona's trailer." He sinks in beside me, his breath shuddering out of him as he tries not to cry. "Don't tell me you don't care, Tal, because somewhere inside, I know you've got to—"

"I care, Wen. I do." I wrap an arm around him in a sideways hug and rest my head on his shoulder.

"Money, again," says Wen. "Always money. That's her ticket out."

I'm so afraid he'll ask to use our savings. More afraid I'll tell him yes. I can't tell him yes.

His voice quiet, he says, "I'm not asking that. Don't worry." Nobody reads my mind as well as Wen does. "But have you thought *what if we could make more money?*"

My palm starts humming with the expectation of cash. I could convince him to do anything right now. It will never be enough for both of us—me and Rona, too—but it would certainly be more for me.

I don't even mean to manipulate him, but it comes so naturally. Even with the person I love most in the world, I'm an opportunist.

"We'd make enough for both of you," he says.

As words bubble from my throat, I can't bring myself to do it. "It would never be enough, not for me and Rona."

"We have to try, Tal."

I shake my head until he says what I can't deny— my own words thrown back at me: "Fortune favors the bold."

CHAPTER 22

AT DARK, WEN AND I CASE THE STREETS ON THE hunt for a scheme. It's a little colder downtown. Seasons are changing, and with the shift comes the packing of camp and the turning of wheels. Before we hit the road, I popped inside the trailer for my brown-leather bomber jacket, a favorite thrift-store find. We're dressed to kill. To kill a con, that is. To knock some scam out of the park. Which one, we're unsure.

Something about town doesn't seem right.

I'm not one for omens, but I do believe in hunches. The mood is different, chaotic. The anger, the whispers, I can feel them in the air. Ladies clutch their purses. Men walk with heavy steps and furrowed brows. All of them are carrying orange fliers.

Downtown has a slope to it, with the government buildings up high and the shops and restaurants down below. At the top of that hill, brake lights congregate. Something's going on up there. Something serious.

"Tal." Wen sounds uncertain behind me. "You have

to see this." He's plucking one of the orange fliers off the sidewalk as I turn. A big, gray shoe print is stamped on the front, but the type is clear: GYPSIES IN CEDAR FALLS! BEWARE OF CRIME! TOWN HALL MEETING AT THE COURTHOUSE AT 6!

"It must be because of Rona," says Wen.

But that's not entirely true.

Spencer warned me the town isn't too friendly toward Wanderers. I don't know how or why, but this town's prejudice starts with me. Everything goes back to that parade.

We don't pull a con that night, not with all the heat from the still-in-swing anti-gypsy rally. I'm less of a con artist for letting it scare me off. And I'm less of myself for being so vulnerable, opening myself up so I let this town hurt me.

Wen's snoring as I sneak out of the trailer.

This time, I don't worry about starting the Chevy at the edge of camp. With Rona locked away, there's no fear of someone stopping me.

Downtown Cedar Falls is abandoned except for a crowd of people spilling from a bar onto the spotless sidewalks. After cutting down Main Street, I travel to the edge of the city limits, all the way to the jail.

Despite all Rona's talks about jails, there are no bars—there are just Plexiglas windows up high. Some are lit, but there's no movement inside.

I picture Rona looking out one of those windows, even though this probably isn't where they keep the prisoners. I wonder if she sees the moon framed by that little opening and she's pretending she's with the camp. She has to be thinking about all of us. Definitely Wen. And maybe me.

She might even be thinking about when she created the rift between us.

I look to those jail windows again. What I said to her that night wasn't quite fair. From stories and a handful of memories, I should have known Mom well enough to realize she would do what she wanted, no matter the damage. Rona didn't run Mom off. She only tried to smooth over the damage Mom left in her wake.

No one knows why I hold Rona at such a distance. Maybe I don't even know for sure. What I do know is letting Rona inside means letting Mom in, too, and I've built that wall out of brick and mortar.

No matter what Wen thinks, I do feel bad about Rona. For putting a barrier between us like I did that night and for being out here while she's locked away.

I've got enough money to set Rona free. If I believed in signs, I'd call that one. At least Felix is bringing only imaginary bars into my world. Still, I want that money to save me.

I sit inside the truck until the last lights go out inside the jail, but my guilt never dims.

CHAPTER 23

WHEN THE RAIN STARTS, IT PLUMMETS FROM THE SKY in heavy drops that smack against the roof of the tent trailer and drip through the old patches that aren't holding—which is every last one of them.

Not a drizzle for months and then an outright downpour.

Weather's the one obstacle we can't con our way around. Sure, that compass inside me leads camp southwest during the snowiest of months, and I'm not afraid to take us north when the heat gets unbearable. Nobody dares argue with Boss about the convenience of my talent.

Rona hates the rain, how we all pack ourselves inside our tent trailers, RVs, and campers, and catch the leaks with pans, and duct tape the holes the best we can. She hates the way we stake everything to the ground, keeping our world from blowing away in the wind.

Maybe she's watching rain fall from the window of her cell. If her cell has a window at all.

By early afternoon, the clouds overhead are dark and thick with hours' more water.

"That's it." Wen closes up his book and sets it beside his pillow. "I'm going to scream if we don't get out of this tin can."

We decide to take the Chevy into town to hide from the water for a while.

Wen dumps the Cool Whip container onto the floor. There's definitely something going on with our money, so we can't leave it behind in the trailer anymore. The truck's not a good spot, either, with its doors that won't lock right and the probability of getting towed. I split the money into two thick stacks that we stow on our own bodies. It isn't safe, but it's the safest option we've got.

Wen buttons his shirt over his half of our cash. "Are we going to keep this up forever?"

"No." I run my fingers around my waistband, making sure my bills are disguised. "We're going to set ourselves a trap."

When we walk outside, Sonia and Emil are standing there, looking like drowned rats, and Wen invites them along. I suppose I can't blame him; it's miserable here, and Emil is his friend, and Sonia is very pregnant. I get inside the truck without uttering a complaint, at least verbally.

Downtown is packed with cars, so we take a parking space at the end of the block and walk under the eaves of the stores. The wind blows the rain sideways until my jeans are dark with water halfway up my knees. Every step swings the ice-cold fabric against my skin and weights the money closer to my hips.

A car creeps closer, idling in the road beside us. I look over and my breath catches.

Spencer's on the other side of the rain-streaked passenger window. His chin dips, and our gazes connect. He gives me a weak smile, but I look away. His tires roll down the road, keeping a car length ahead of us.

Wen shakes his head at Spencer and then me. Emil and Sonia stare into the stores along the sidewalk. They don't seem to notice.

Spencer never said he really would skip college in favor of traveling the world. But a lie by omission is a lie just the same.

Emil cups his hands against the fogged-up windows of the first coffee shop we pass and peers inside. "It's warm in here. Look at the windows." Bells jingle on the door as he holds it open for Sonia. "Let's go in here, babe."

"Ooh," she says. "They have flavored marshmallows."

Raindrops streak with Spencer's red brake lights as he double-parks in front of the next storefront. I stand perfectly still for what feels like an eternity, watching the warm white air billowing from his car's tailpipe. I can feel his urgency, him waiting for me to find a way to join him.

It doesn't make sense, but all I want to do is get inside that car.

Just then Sonia and Emil disappear into the coffee shop, handing me the kind of freedom that tastes much better than any designer marshmallows.

"Make an excuse for me, will you?" I pat Wen on the cheek and run toward Spencer's car.

"Tal, no," whines Wen. "Oh come on, Tal."

The heat hits me as soon as I open the door, warming through my wet clothes and drawing me inside. We both stare for one infinite, wordless moment across the console.

I want to find the angle, to be the maestro of some great scam. But I also want to give in to temptation.

Spencer pulls away from the curb, joining the stream of traffic. "I'm so damn sorry about the other night. I—"

"Just drive," I gasp.

I look back and see Sonia through the foggy coffee shop window, her chin cradled in her hand, and her smoky, kohl-lined eyes staring right at me.

We're a safe distance from the coffee shop before Spencer speaks. "I've got to pick up Mags at Ice-Skating for Tots. I hope that's okay."

"Sure."

His fingers inch close to mine and stop short. He leaves them frozen, but when I don't meet him halfway, he returns both hands to the wheel.

The storm becomes a drizzle, and he slows the windshield wipers. "I thought I might never see you again. After the other night."

"I thought the same thing."

He pulls the sedan into a parking space in front of an indoor ice rink and leaves the engine running. "I've got some explaining to do, I guess."

"I'm all ears."

"All my parents have ever talked about is college— all my life that's the way it's been. And they didn't say it like it was a choice. College has always been a cer- tainity." He plays with the vents, flipping them up and down. When he catches me staring, he stops. "I've been on this prescribed path for as long as I can remember. You probably don't understand—and that's not a slam. I'm glad you don't know what it's like to be tied to someone else's plans for your future."

But I do. I know about being wild and free until the day traditions show up at your door and rob you of your dreams.

The anger I've been feeling for him ebbs away. "I'm sorry, Spencer."

Not only for that other night. For the life he wants and won't have.

"No, I'm sorry—" He focuses on the entrance to the ice rink. "Shit. She's already done."

Margaret's rubbing the fog from the windows and peering into the parking lot.

"I've got to go inside to get her." He opens his door but hesitates. "Just so you know, I was never trying to lie to you about my plans. I think I was lying to myself."

He jogs toward the entrance before I can say a word.

Margaret skips ahead of Spencer down the concrete steps, in a sky-blue leotard with a turtle-shaped backpack and a pair of red ice skates slung over her shoulder. As Spencer buckles her into a booster seat, he says, "Mags, you remember Tal?"

"Her brother does magic."

I fold my hands over the headrest and smile. She's determined not to forget Wen's little sleight of hand. "That's kind of a secret. Do you think it could be a secret only the three of us shared?"

"Why?"

"Because we're friends. Friends keep each other's secrets." This feels dirty.

Spencer slides into the driver seat and flicks his eyes to the rearview mirror. "Hey, how about ice cream? I bet that would make you forget the magic trick."

Margaret finishes her mint chocolate chip, and Spencer sets her up at the pinball machine with a handful of quarters.

He settles in the booth across from me. "Food's always the best motivator when it comes to Mags."

His little manipulations remind me of the way I sometimes work my brother.

I pluck a maraschino cherry from the top of Spencer's melting banana split. "So, why JSU?"

"SJU." He grins. "Stonewall Jackson University, named after the Confederate general. Let's see. Lots of reasons. It's competitive as hell. It's in Charleston—so not too far away. My parents went there."

"When?"

"For college. Mom was poli-sci, and Dad was art history. Had the time of their lives, met each other, got married, moved up to Massachusetts while my mom went to law school, and then they moved back here."

"What do you mean, *back here*?"

"Cedar Falls is my mom's hometown. She had an offer from a Philadelphia firm. My parents actually chose to come back, if you can believe it. I mean, she's ambitious and so is my dad, but they could have done so much more. It's like they don't think they missed out, though. At least, as far as I can tell." That piece of hair falls into his eyes as he looks up at me. "Your parents must let you do whatever you want, huh? You're so lucky."

"I don't have parents."

He covers his mouth and says through his fingers, "I am such an asshole."

"You're really not, Spencer." I sigh and watch the traffic outside. "I have a guardian. Rona. The woman who got arrested—small town like this, I'm sure you've heard about it."

He nods. "I've heard. It's not on my mom's docket. But I've heard. So, what about your dad?"

"He's dead," I say. Spencer cringes and opens his mouth, but I put up my hand. "It's okay. I never knew him. He died when I was two. And my mom—" I try to smile. "Don't I wish I knew where she was. She cared more about her own freedom than me or my brother. She abandoned us, and Rona let her." I realize I've told him something I couldn't even tell Wen. "Nobody else knows that about my mom. Not even my brother."

All the secrets I've been stowing away in the shadows inside me for years, they're out there—and somehow Spencer's still looking at me the same.

There's a safety in knowing I can tell him anything without consequences.

Except Felix. That future is the one thing I can't admit, not to Spencer, not to myself. He can't know my camp thinks of me as something to be bought and sold. A *commodity*, as Wen would call it.

"So your future," I say, "it has to be that school?"

"I guess it doesn't have to be SJU, but if I'm going to college, it might as well be there. It would be selfish to go anywhere else when SJU would make them proud. They're not trying to be jerks about it. It made them happy, and they think it'll be the same for me."

I stare at the black-and-white tiled floor. He's not selfish like me. He'd give up the whole world to go to that school and make his parents proud.

"What about your own happiness? Do you ever think about that?"

His banana split has become a milk shake, and he pushes it to the side of the table. "Lately, I keep looking back at all the moments that told me I didn't fit in here. Rewinding to that fight with Jeremy and Craig, that year in Spain, even that kid on the parade float."

That float, it's been sitting at the edge of my mind ever since Spencer made me remember that day and this town.

The plastic seats creak as he slides forward. "Does that sound crazy? I mean, am I a crazy person for thinking like this?"

I drum my fingers on the tabletop. "What if I told you the kid was me?"

He slowly lifts his chin. His crooked smile becomes a laugh. "You must think I'm pretty gullible."

"If I wanted to tell you a lie, I'd make it worth my while. I got bored and snuck up on the float."

"All right, then." He reaches across the table, and his knees bump mine as he takes my chin in his hand. "If it's true, look me in the eye and say it."

For one of the first times ever, I'm not lying to a markie, but I'm too stunned to speak or dodge away. "I can prove it," I finally say. "The float was a cloud. I wanted to know what it felt like to fly through downtown on a cloud."

We step into the parking lot after Margaret's quarters run out. There's a weightlessness that's come from letting go of that secret, and my feet move lighter across the pavement.

Spencer pats down his jeans. "I think I left my wallet on the table."

As he jogs inside, I briefly wonder if I stole it when he wasn't looking. A habit I couldn't kick.

I open the back door for Margaret, and her turtle

backpack falls onto the rain-dampened asphalt.

She shrieks and tugs at her black curls. "My turtle!"

"It's okay. Turtles are supposed to get dirty." She looks unconvinced, so I dust off the turtle's shell. "See, no harm done."

I take a knee and shovel the scattered items inside—a pack of gum, a yo-yo. As soon as my hand closes around a picture book, the wind picks up, and the pages flip open.

Staring back at me is an illustration of an owl.

I stay low to the ground, the gravel biting at the ripped knees of my jeans, as I blink at the page, as if the thing will flap its wings and lift itself out of the book.

"Tal?"

I squint up at Spencer.

"We should go," he says.

"Yeah." I shut the book and shove it into Margaret's bag. "We should."

As we coast around the winding roads toward camp, my mind is bursting with all the stories from my childhood—of the Falconer, owls, and compasses. I know better than anyone that at least one of those myths isn't real.

The tires slow their roll until we're right outside the boundary line between Spencer's world and mine, closer than he's driven before. He leaves Margaret buckled in and walks around the car to where I stand.

"You don't have to walk me in," I say.

There's only so far he can travel before he's crossing into our camp, and that's an imaginary line we've both drawn in the sand.

"I know." He moves his feet through the damp fall leaves. "Can I tell you something about that day? The parade?"

"Sure." What I really mean is *please*.

"Sometimes I think about you, on that float, how I wanted to do something like that, too—hijack a parade float just because I wanted to fly. Even back then."

What he's said is a gift-wrapped box I'm not allowed to open.

"Come find me, Tal, if you get bored."

"I will."

He steps away, but as I turn my back to him, his hands catch my waist, spinning me around. Spencer's kiss is gentle and quick enough to make me want more of the things I never knew I wanted: markie things like books and borders and his hands in forbidden places.

CHAPTER 24

THROUGH THE SCREEN AROUND MY BED, I WATCH the Chevy barrel between the trees. Wen doesn't ever tell me where he's headed anymore, and I don't bother to ask.

Town is off limits for cons after Gypsy-gate, and camp holds Felix and Sonia, my future and my fear. I'm going stir-crazy.

"Talia," I hear through my door. "Are you in there?"

Felix. I could duck low and pretend to be out, but with my luck, he'd sit outside and wait for me to come home.

I open the screen and cross my arms. "Morning, Felix."

He smiles wide, flashing teeth that make him look wolfish and that make me feel like lunch. "Can I come in and talk to you?"

"Sure. Not that I see the point."

I climb on my bed, dangling my legs off the side and tapping my heels against the wood.

Felix glances at the booth by the dining table but climbs up beside me, the weight of his hips jarring the mattress. I dig my fingers into the underside of the bed to keep from rocking against him.

"You got lots of books."

I lift my chin to the piles stacked around Wen's bed. "Those are Wen's."

But Felix stares at the one on my bed, right beside his hip. He opens it across his lap, and the pages fall open along the creased spine. To Africa. At first, I think he's checking out the pictures, but he stares too long.

"This is really something."

"Yep," I say.

"Beautiful place."

I can't help myself from saying, "Doesn't it bother you you'll never see it?"

"There are lots of things I'll never do." He closes the encyclopedia and sets it beside him. "I try not to think about them. 'Course it bothers me."

It can't bother him as much as it bothers me.

"We haven't spoken much since I've been with your camp, Talia. I wish we'd gotten off to a better start." I concentrate on the crickets outside, the wind through the trees, anything but what he's saying. Something catches my ears. "When we leave here . . . I can't wait to take you with me, back to my camp."

His hopeful smile chips away at my anger and

my fear. He wants me, and he can't have me. I'm no stranger to wanting, and I'm no stranger to wanting what's out of reach.

He wants other things, too—the same things I do—and he's decided to push those foolish desires aside. That's where we differ and where we always will.

That earns him a little bit of something I've never given him before: honesty.

"Look." I set my hand on top of his. "I'm really sorry, but this isn't going to work. I can't go anywhere with you. And I'm sure you're perfectly nice and all, but I'll never be yours."

He squeezes his eyes shut. "I wish it didn't have to be like this."

"I know. When I said I was sorry—"

"I can't go back to my parents without you," he blurts.

I take my hand back.

"The shame—I couldn't bear it. And I'm ready to take my place as a man in my camp. With you by my side, I can. I was only asking if you'd come with me to be polite. I'm a nice guy—I swear I am, so I wanted to tell you I'm going to have a chat with Lando."

I take shallow breaths until I'm able to speak instead of scream. "Are you threatening me?"

"No, ma'am. I don't mean it like that. Shit, no." He hangs his head toward our shredded linoleum floor. "If you hated me—well, I couldn't stand that."

My fingers curl into fists, and I dig them into my hips to stop myself from doing something that will make everything worse. "You need to go."

"Hear me out. If you say you'll go along with the marriage—nicely, I mean, without causing anyone any trouble—I'll talk to Lando. I'll make sure your little brother always has a place with us, even if we decide to move along to another camp or go roving. I'll pay Lando good money, even."

The air around me spins, then stills.

Saying yes would be the selfless thing to do. I would die for Wen, but marrying Felix for him is another thing entirely.

Felix leaps off the mattress and thunks onto the floor. "Would you think about it? Pretty please? You don't have to tell me now. Just think it over." He takes a look around, at our faded curtains, the rubber bands holding our cabinets shut, our battered floor. "You deserve better than this hovel, you know?"

The screen door screeches closed without another word.

I grab my jacket and tug my feet into boots, then stuff our money into the waistband of my jeans. I'm out the door in sixty seconds. Wen has the Chevy, but I have to get away from camp.

Locked up, Rona has no need for her truck, a little beige Mazda with primer shining gray through the paint. She keeps her keys stowed in the trailer beside a music box my mother gave her. She wouldn't mind me taking the truck for a spin or two.

I pounce up the two metal steps to her trailer door, and the screen swings open. There stands Lando.

"What are you doing in here?"

"How is that any of your business?" He pushes past me, and I catch a flash of green sticking from his pocket.

I wouldn't think Boss's son would bother stealing from people in his own camp, but the money we've had go missing makes me wonder.

I won't dare accuse him. Not until I'm sure.

A crowd of about twenty people is lined up in front of city hall as I idle at a stoplight. All of them hold signs that say things like CRACK DOWN ON CRIME and SAVE OUR TOWN FROM GYPSY TRASH.

With the Mazda seat humming against my thighs, I think about Rona, handcuffed and locked in a cell, with those townspeople outside, sharpening their pitchforks and lighting their torches.

Most of all, I think about me. After the deal Felix offered, I shouldn't be trying to scheme my way into the bride-price. My selfish urges shouldn't be stronger than my love for my brother.

I find the Cedar Falls High School easy enough. All the townie kids forgot about the party and the fake ecstasy—that's what Spencer told me—so maybe it's okay to show up here.

But I know better. They didn't forget, not really. Wen and I became one blur in their drunken night, a little cash that's now missing from their wallets.

In the parking lot, I spot the familiar shape of a girl in a navy blue skirt and cardigan: Whitney. Her legs are wrapped in mustard-colored tights that make me think of the old magazines Rona and my mother stole from a beauty shop when the conning business was slow.

I duck, but Whitney waves. It seems rude to keep on driving. Like manners have ever been a great concern of mine.

She props her arms on the edge of the open window and smiles.

"Hey there, Whitney."

"Well, hello . . ." She trails off, like she's unsure of my name.

"I think you know it's Tal." There's no sense in keeping the ruse going now. "So how does winning feel?"

"Oh, please." She laughs and taps her fingertip against her lips. "We had a mutually beneficial relationship. You just didn't know it. I helped you to make some quick cash off my friends, and you made my party legendary."

"You weren't the one who nearly got arrested."

"Listen, I'm sorry about the cops. You're not angry, are you?"

"A little." More like impressed.

A bell rings behind us, and she throws a glance over her shoulder. "I'll catch you later, Tal."

I drive down the aisles of the parking lot. Finally, I see Spencer's silver sedan. I riffle through my bag for something to write on. All I find is the orange flier. I scribble a note, slip it under his windshield wipers, and drive off.

Behind the gym, and mostly out of sight, I park Rona's Mazda. In the woods near the back of the high school, I prop myself against a tree and try to dream up my next con.

Bells ring, and a flurry of activity begins. Across the way-off parking lot, Whitney disappears into her convertible with two other girls, leaving one seat empty. I imagine myself sitting there, not because I want to be with them, but because I wish I knew what it felt like to be one of them.

I close my eyes, and, before long, the orange flier drops into my lap. I read what's penciled on the other side. My message: MEET ME IN THE WOODS BEHIND THE GYM.

Cupping my hand over my eyes to cut the glare of the sun, I scan Spencer's body from his feet all the way to his lopsided grin.

"You got my note. Guess I forgot to sign it."

"Only you." He looks around like there are answers dangling from the tree branches. "I've got to drop Margaret off at ice-skating. But, uh, afterward, we could go back to my place. If you want."

CHAPTER 25

"LET ME SEE YOUR ROOM, SPENCER SWAY."

Halfway up the staircase, I lean over the banister. In the foyer, Spencer swings the front door shut, sealing the mid-October air outside.

He drops his backpack on the hardwood floor. "You really care about seeing my room?"

The house is empty, other than the two of us, and while I have no business being here, it's the only place I want to be. After Felix's proposition, I need a good, strong distraction.

I sprint up the rest of the stairs before he actually says yes.

All the doors are closed at the top of the landing. "Which one?"

He strides up the stairs behind me and folds his arms over his chest. "Guess."

I start opening doors, the first a bathroom. "Cold," I say. The next one has pink-painted walls and shelves full of stuffed animals. "Brrr. Definitely not this one."

Plaid wallpaper lines the walls of the next room. Bookcases are brimming with yearbooks and textbooks, and on the wall hangs a map of the world.

I hug the door frame and smile up at him. "Warm?"

"You're on fire." The way he says it isn't all sexy-like—it's kind of self-conscious.

The room has a smell, not bad or good, but something indescribable that's so definitely Spencer. New clothes, laundry detergent, book paper, and a little cologne his parents probably gave him for his birthday. There must be a scent to all of us that we'll never be able to smell. Mine must be pine needles and lake water and rain and dirt and summer.

He keeps one foot in his room and one in the hall while I stop in front of the world map.

Little blue-tipped pins stick into almost every continent, but there's not one in Africa. All the places he's been. My own map, the one that exists in my mind, has a cluster of pins stuck in only the US. For sixteen years of solid traveling, I've seen almost nothing.

Spencer sits on the bed, watching me go through all of his stuff. "We could watch a movie downstairs."

"Maybe." A movie downstairs might bore a markie girl, but I wouldn't mind it, doing what he probably does every day, walking around in Spencer's shoes all afternoon. I'd even like to dive into his closet, wrap myself in one of his plaid shirts, and blend into those wallpapered walls.

"I might be able to score something out of my parents' liquor cabinet."

"Booze and drugs and hijacking parade floats aren't the only ways I chase my boredom away, Spencer Sway."

"Hey, I'm sorry."

"Don't be."

A few weeks ago, getting drunk was another way of traveling. I would have chosen oblivion over anything else.

On his desk is a folded navy sweatshirt with burgundy letters—s, j, and u. The tags are still attached.

"A gift?" I say.

"You bet."

I saunter over to him, move his knees apart with mine, and step between them. "Spencer Sway, you are going to spend the first half of your life making plans and the second half regretting them."

"Then I'll make better plans."

"Like what?"

He smiles. "Like Africa. With you."

This is a lie I wish I could believe.

His right hand spins his watch around and around his left wrist. He unhooks it and drops it on his nightstand.

"You don't believe in time anymore?"

"I don't know." His fingers circle the wrist where his watch had been. "There's a lot I don't believe in. Nine-to-five jobs and small-town bullshit. We've all got something we're supposed to believe in that we just don't. What do you not believe in?"

Images of owls and lanterns blaze right through me. My lips part, but everything truthful is trapped behind my tonsils.

"I believe in me," I say. "That's it, and nothing else."

"Oh, I assumed Wanderers had a whole different belief system. A religion or something."

"Wanderers do. I don't." I've never told anyone else I don't believe. Not even Wen. "They believe the Spirit of the Falconer—a Wanderer from the past— watches over us. They believe in omens, in owls, in a lot of things." I circle the room so fast that I make myself dizzy. I face him and rest my hands on the desk behind me. "That's not it, though. My camp believes in me, too. . . ."

I tell him everything. The powerful dogma of our camp, their believing I'm their compass, that a divine force guides us to the places we're meant to be. How I let everyone go on believing in me, and I carry their faith on my shoulders.

He doesn't say anything, not for a few moments, but then he walks to me and whispers, "I'd make a good Wanderer. I believe in you, too."

He leans close, like he's about to touch his tongue to an electrical socket. It's always like this with Spencer. Tentative at first, maybe a little shy the way he holds back, but once he's touching me, every bit of his uncertainty vanishes.

I like the feel of his hands on my hips, the steadiness of them. I close my eyes and tilt my head to the ceiling as they roam and sink into the dip of my lower back.

"Why do you have all this money?"

My eyes fly open. My cash shifts under his touch. I bolt away and tuck the money back into place. "What's it to you?"

"Well, it's . . . crazy. You can't carry that much cash safely. Why do you need that much on you anyway?"

He's right. It is crazy. Everything about our plans, exposing a thief and earning the bride-price, too. "Please don't act like you know my life, Spencer."

"Tell me more then. Make me understand."

"What do you want to know?"

"What are you doing next, you and your brother? You're going to leave Cedar Falls and head somewhere else after your guardian's out?"

Uncertainty is no friend of mine, and I've never been so uncertain about my future. Even if I break free from Felix, what good is freedom to the kind of girl who chooses herself over the woman who raised her? A girl who threatens her own brother's well-being?

A door slams downstairs. Voices trickle up from the hallway, and Spencer straightens. "So, that would be my parents. I guess they're home early."

I crane my neck toward the window where tree branches aren't too many feet away. I could make it out the window.

"Relax." He collects my hands in his. "I'll tell them I'm having a friend over for dinner."

"You need a better cover than that. A whole backstory. How we met, what I'm doing here. Ordinarily, I'd wing it, but you're such a rookie. . . . You'd ruin this for sure."

We settle on a variation of the story Wen told in Chicken and Billiards in Pike. My parents are involved in a real estate transaction, a transferring of property—one of their old summer homes they're sick and tired of—one that requires they oversee some repairs. My brother and I are only here until the job is complete. If his parents ask too many questions, I'll be vague about our fictional loft in Chicago and the private school my brother and I attend.

We decide to use my real name and my brother's, too. That bit of truth might make it harder for me. It's easier to become someone else when everything's a lie.

He bounds down the stairs, with me tiptoeing behind him.

Spencer's mother—Judge Sway—sits at a bar stool sipping wine, with her blonde hair swept off her face, while his father stirs a pot on the stove.

"It's too peppery for my taste," says Spencer's father. He swirls wine around in his glass and whistles. "But look at the legs on that."

The kitchen has high ceilings, dark mahogany cabinets, and stainless steel appliances. I tagged along with Rona once, when she ran the rental scam, into a home with a kitchen a lot like this one. She called it a million-dollar home. Sonia would swoon over this place, the same way she loved that sparkly new trailer Emil provided.

"What are you guys doing home so early?" says Spencer. "I thought you had a full calendar, Mom."

She answers without spinning around, her voice moneyed and honeyed. "The defense asked for a continuance on the Williams case, which pushes everything to my already full, 9 AM traffic calendar. Your dad closed up the gallery early because Margaret's coach called and said she wasn't feeling well." She whirls around, pausing as she looks past Spencer to where I stand.

Judge Sway makes her living measuring truthfulness; I'm terrified she'll look right through me and see me for what I am.

"This is Tal." Spencer steps free from me, leaving me feeling exposed. "She's staying for dinner."

Spencer's mom rises from her bar stool, her warm smile spreading. "Lovely to meet you, Tal."

"Nice to meet you, too, Mrs. Sway. Judge. Your Honor."

I'm usually so much smoother than this. It's dinner, not a con, not a scam.

This would be different if I was a normal girl—sweet sixteen and having dinner at a boy's house.

"Ella. Call me Ella. I insist." The phone sitting beside her buzzes, and she types away on it, muttering about a "sequestered jury from hell" as Spencer's father lurches forward.

"Glad to know my son has good taste. Marcus. Nice to meet you, Tal."

Marcus Sway looks so much like his son, with a strong nose and a square jaw. The hair, though; it's different. All I love about Spencer's hair is absent from his father's. That unruly piece that's a little too long and dusts Spencer's eyebrow is gone. It must need years of combing to stay put, and Marcus has finally mastered it. I hope Spencer never tames his.

Spencer repeats my cover story almost flawlessly. Ordinarily, I would take the lead but not here with the Sways.

Margaret teeters into the kitchen, still wearing her spandex ice-skating costume.

"What's wrong with you, Mags?" Spencer touches the back of his hand to her forehead. "You're sick?"

"She says she has a sore throat," Ella says.

Marcus slams the refrigerator shut and spins toward the island. "She's probably faking. I think she's just tired of ice-skating. She keeps going on about magic lessons instead."

"Mags, say hi to Tal," says Spencer.

Ella flicks her eyes up from her phone. "Margaret knows Tal?"

Margaret's wide, serious eyes catch mine. "Spencer kisses her in the forest."

Marcus throws a dish towel onto the counter and gives Spencer a look. "Way to be a good influence, Spence."

I choke back lies they'd never believe. It wouldn't take much for them to realize exactly what I am.

A smile touches Marcus's eyes, and I relax.

Around their dining-room table, we eat a meal Marcus prepared: pasta, salad, and garlic bread. Ella says she works long hours, and Marcus's schedule is more flexible, so it's never made much sense for her to cook. She drinks the last drop of red wine from her glass, and Marcus is quick to refill it.

She presses a hand to her temple. "I feel like I should be drinking it out of the bottle after my day. Those protesters are camped right by the window of my chambers. Can you imagine a judge having this problem in Philadelphia?"

"Which protesters?" asks Marcus.

Ella huffs. "You haven't seen those half-wits and their anti-gypsy propaganda?"

The word *gypsy* makes my back go ramrod straight. They wouldn't be saying this if they knew who I was.

Marcus tops off his own glass. "Honey, you need to open up your window and tell those people to get a life."

"Hear, hear." She clinks her glass with his.

Marcus taps a finger to his cheek. "Do you remember that parade years ago?"

Across the table, Spencer's eyes meet mine.

Ella groans. "Do I ever." She passes the bread basket to me. "Tal, I'm sorry. We're being horribly rude, talking around you." She angles herself toward me. "So, years ago, a group of Wanderers passed through town, and this little girl from their camp climbed up on the float for Swanson's Washers and Dryers."

It takes a few seconds to realize Ella isn't playing a game with me, only being friendly. Me, I always see the worst in people, and I especially expected it from her, the mother.

"Swanson's Washers and Dryers float?" asks Spencer. "I thought that thing was some kind of cloud."

Marcus points his fork toward Spencer. "Those were bubbles, son. You remember Mr. Swanson's daughter, Becky?"

"Uh, the artist who begged you to display her paintings?"

"That's the one." Marcus rolls his eyes. "She designed the float. What a nightmare. It's one thing if you've got talent, but that poor woman doesn't have an ounce."

All this time, I thought it was a cloud, but I was floating on soapsuds.

Ella slaps at Marcus's arm. "Don't be rude. The poor thing is trying, at least." She tilts toward me again. "Anyway, Mr. Swanson found the girl's mother"—I bite back the word *guardian*; it was Rona—"and he started screaming that the kid was trampling his daughter's artwork. At the same time, some Wanderers were picking the pockets of people standing at the sidelines, and a full-blown riot broke out on Main Street."

The beautiful story of that day—the one Spencer and I crafted in our minds—is something dirty and sordid.

Embarrassment washes over me, and I stare at the napkin folded in my lap. "That's quite a tale."

"Marcus had Spencer there," says Ella, "and it was an absolute clusterfuck." She glances at Margaret and covers her mouth.

Marcus laughs and scoots the wine bottle a few inches from Ella's placemat. "All right, honey, that's enough."

This isn't how I imagined his mother, his father, their roots, and this house. This glimpse leaves me with a longing I can't tame.

We finish eating, and Marcus collects our plates and silverware and carries them to the sink.

Ella shuffles through the mail. "Hey, Spence." She tosses an envelope at him and winks. "I bet I know what that is."

Spencer stares at it unopened. I peek around him, at the tremor in his hands that nobody's mentioning. The top left corner reads *Stonewall Jackson University*.

Marcus turns off the water and rests his elbows on the kitchen island. "Well, open it."

The envelope rips, and Spencer pulls out a thin white sheet. He swallows. "My interview's November fifteenth."

Marcus wraps an arm around Ella's waist, pulling her into a sideways hug, before turning back to Spencer. "We're proud of you."

Ella untangles herself from Marcus. "That's the week before Thanksgiving break." She uncaps a Sharpie and writes on the calendar beside the fridge. "You'll have to miss school. Do you think you'll have tests that close to the holiday?"

"Nope," says Spencer. "Everything's going according to plan." He tosses the paper onto the counter and takes my hand. Leading me toward the stairs, he calls back, "I'm giving Tal a tour of the house."

From the kitchen, Ella yells, "Door open in your room, okay?"

In the shadows of the upstairs hallway, his hands are still shaking. I press my weight against Spencer, bringing my mouth to his ear. "She seriously underestimates what I could do to you with the door wide open."

We pass through, and he leaves it cracked, six inches of space between the door and the jamb, buying us some privacy.

He falls back into the downy-soft mattress, pressing the backs of his hands over his eyes.

The bed lurches as I sink in beside him.

"Are you okay?"

"I—I'm not sure I thought I'd actually get an interview."

"Tell them you're not going."

We're not so different—Spencer Sway and me—expectations have become our prisons. His has a built-in escape hatch. All he has to do is say the word.

He lifts up on his elbows. "To the interview or to SJU?"

"Both. Your parents are nice people—they're good people. They'll listen."

"That only makes it harder. If they were assholes about it, I could tell them to go to hell and be done with it. To them, there's nothing in this world that could make me any happier than security. A solid, dependable future." He blows out a breath. "Besides, going to SJU is one thing. Having no plan at all, that's scary as hell."

We lie there on top of his plaid comforter, the sounds of the house whirring beneath us, and I close my eyes and slip into that place between dreaming and awake. There, I imagine ending up here in Cedar Falls, and I wonder if Spencer's wrong about small-town life.

His voice is husky, cutting through my thoughts. "You ever been in love before, Tal?"

The room whirls, and I sit straight up, blood rushing to my head as what I've started comes into focus. This little charade has gotten out of control.

"Don't throw around words you don't understand."

"I understand it fine." One of his hands squeezes the tense muscles in my shoulders. "The question is: do you?"

"You remember that list of things I told you I don't believe in?" I look over my shoulder and wait for his nod. "You can go ahead and add love."

CHAPTER 26

Rona's Mazda gives off a high-pitched whine as I guide it into its spot beneath the drooping branches of a sycamore tree. Sounds from camp—hollers and cheers—trickle through the rolled-down window.

Camp is usually completely dark by now, every lantern long ago dimmed, but tonight—I now remember—is Boss's birthday, so the games are still in full swing.

I shouldn't have missed tonight.

As I kill the engine, the words Spencer said in his bedroom come rushing back to me. My breath gets away from me, and my cheeks burn with regret, with desire, with the embarrassment of forgetting who I was for a whole night.

I lock the truck, wishing away the word Spencer threw around so carelessly.

Someone's set up a basketball hoop in the dirt road between trailers. With his dress shirt untucked and his sleeves rolled to his elbows, Lando dribbles a ball at Emil's feet. Emil's skinny hips are set wide, and his face is gleaming with sweat as he plays defense.

Most of our games came from a southwest-roving caravan known for putting up twenty-four-hour carnivals in parking lots. Hoops bent into ovals make it a lot harder to sink a shot, and bouncy plywood backboards will send that basketball right back to you. It takes more than a killer slam-dunk to win—it takes a con man.

Lando shoots, and the basketball floats through the net with a perfect swish, missing the backboard entirely. From the looks of Lando's grin and Emil's scowl, Lando's winning the game.

Since Boss's health worsened and it looked like Lando might be heading up camp soon, nobody's seen him horsing around with the rest of us lately, only exercising his power.

This glimpse of Lando reminds me of a time when camp was a civilized place to live. He catches me staring and tips his chin at me. I look away and turn down the road toward my trailer.

No lights are glowing through our tarp walls, so I take a spin around the outside and peek through the netting. Wen isn't stretched out in his bed.

Laughter slips between the trees. Laughter unmistakably belonging to Wen.

Deeper into the forest, my breath fogging the air in front of me, I follow the glow of lantern light and the strangest flickering shadows. A little closer, and I find a great big paper target swinging from a low-hanging branch.

Sitting on a blanket spread across the mossy ground, Wen's grinning at someone beside him. I round a tree trunk and see Sonia.

She pours half a sleeve of peanuts into a bottle of Coke and gives it to Wen before emptying the rest into her own bottle. He laughs at something she said. As he's drinking his peanuts and Coke, he turns his eyes to the clearing.

He spots me and hangs his head in shame.

My brother shouldn't feel guilty for being with Sonia. We were all inseparable not too long ago, and Wen's never been good at holding grudges. On the other hand, if I'm not feeling charitable, I can hold a grudge so long the thing will grow legs and live independent of me.

My feet crunch through the pine needles. Felix cranes his neck around a tree that had been blocking him from my view—Sonia isn't the reason Wen looks so damn guilty.

My name forms on Felix's lips like he's figuring out if it's really me. As I move under the lanterns, he beams and lowers a BB rifle to his side. "Well, it must be my lucky night. Are we finally going to spend some time together?"

He lurches forward, but I meet his eyes and he rocks right on back. He's the one who's armed, but my stone-cold stare's intimidated him.

Wen's eyes tell me he's sorry as I crawl down beside him. I hug his fleece-covered arm between my hands and rest my cheek on his shoulder.

"Tal, you're just in time." Sonia's got a game in her voice. She gives me a wink Felix can't see. It almost cuts through the tension. "We're waging a little bet. Wen agreed to be our moneyman. Keeping things fair and square, aren't you, Wen?"

Three paper targets hang like ghosts in the forest. It's another carnival game. The winner shoots the shape of a star out of the paper before all the ammo runs out of the gun. It sounds simple enough, but nothing's simple about these contests.

"You can join us, Tal, if you want to," says Felix. "I'll even load for you."

"Not really in the mood. If I was, I'd load for myself."

"Well, have you ever shot a BB gun?" he asks. "It's not that hard."

"Oh, I think I can hold my own."

Wen outright hiccups with laughter.

"Who's winning?" I say.

Sonia's grin is a white flash in the forest. "You don't have more faith in me than that? Pity." She passes Wen her peanuts and Coke and plucks the gun from Felix. Shots whistle through the air as she shoots a clean ring around the star. She isn't even out of BBs as the star flutters to the ground.

"Wen? Ten me, good sir." Sonia collects a ten-dollar bill.

"You know, Sonia," he says, "I don't believe I've ever seen anything as backwoods as a pregnant girl with a BB rifle."

She rubs a hand through his short hair. "Oh, I am backwoods, baby. All the way."

For one fleeting moment, there's a glimpse of the old Sonia, the girl who would clasp her hands over my eyes when I was doing sixty-five on the freeway and whisper in my ear, "Trust me?"

"Care to go again, or are you running out of money?" she asks Felix.

He yanks a billfold out of his pocket. It's not that Sonia's taking advantage of him. He's one of us; he should know better. He whips out two fives and hands them to Wen.

As Wen pockets the money, he says to Felix, "You run many cons for your camp?"

"I'm not too familiar with it. No. My uncle is our Boss, you see? So I'm more in charge of managing stuff."

As Felix looks through his sights, Wen rolls his eyes. That explains so much: Felix's fancy RV, his naïveté, and his desire to take me home like a prize and make his folks proud.

He fires at the target haphazardly, peppering the paper with tiny holes and not doing a bit of damage to the star.

A small laugh passes between my lips. He looks my way but keeps on firing. This time, he shoots the clip clear off the paper and sends the sheet flapping against the trees.

"Son of a—" he mutters.

I'm laughing hard now and not even trying to hide it.

"If you think you can do better, Talia, be my guest." He holds the rifle out flat like an offering.

"Ten dollars doesn't entice me. You can't afford to play me."

He fumbles with his money and produces a fifty-dollar bill.

"Tal," says Wen. "We don't have that much to spare—"

"No," says Felix. "She wins, and the money's hers." He meets my eyes. "You don't win, then you don't owe me anything."

"Other than a marriage?"

He sighs. "Other than that."

"Pass it over, then."

Sonia gets me all geared up with a fresh target and a newly loaded gun. Nothing's ever felt more right than taking Felix's money. Handing him his balls might be my ticket to proving that marrying me won't make him more of a man.

I look through the sights. My finger is light on the trigger, careful to not release too many BBs at once. I fire a single shot into the middle of the star.

"Harder than it looks, huh?" says Felix.

Over the top of the sights, I see I nicked the target a few inches too high and a little to the right.

"Here's a free lesson for you, Felix: the barrels are bent. You take a couple of shots to figure out how off your sights are, and only then do you start firing." I raise the gun, adjust my aim for the bent barrels, and shoot an almost-perfect ring of BBs around the star until it flutters to the ground. "Simple as that."

"Simple as that," Felix repeats as he watches me collect his fifty from Wen.

Once my laughter starts, it's contagious. Traveling from me, to Wen, to Sonia. Even Felix joins in.

The moment isn't even strange when it's happening. Only minutes later, when we've all moved on, and Sonia has challenged Felix to a real fair-and-square game.

We feed a bonfire, empty an ice chest of beers, and, after a few hours, Sonia and Felix are nearly tied. My small, calloused hands even move over Felix's smooth ones once, showing him how to keep his trigger finger from getting away from itself. As the night wears on, I can't hate him. I don't love him or even like him—not really. But he isn't terrible like I thought.

Night breezes whistle through the trees by the time we run out of ammo. Sonia and Felix yank down all the targets before the wind can take off with them.

I shiver and run my hands over my arms.

Wen's got a blanket wrapped over his shoulders like a cape. I sidle in beside him, and he drapes a corner over me. The blanket smells exactly like expired sunscreen.

We used it last spring when we slept on the beach in Florida. Before Lando got control, it was our ritual to spend one night each season sleeping under the stars. Now we're forbidden to sleep too far from camp. *Safety,* says Lando. But what he really means is control.

Wen asks quietly, "What'd you do today?"

If he knew how I'd spent that evening at Spencer's, he'd ache to hear it described in graphic detail. Telling him would mean dangling a carrot he's never going to eat.

It's wrong not telling him about Felix's proposition. We're too far from the money to even think about paying the bride-price back. With Cedar Falls on alert, we can't hustle another cent. I'm as good as married to Felix but selfish enough to keep hold of my freedom a little longer.

I'm torn between having a million things to tell Wen and an equal number of secrets to guard. Either decision I make is equally cruel.

"Same old, same old," I say. "How about you?"

Under the blanket, Wen slips me two crinkled-up bills. I take a peek, and the lantern highlights a pair of hundreds.

"Holy shit," I whisper. "You must have pissed off someone good."

"Nah . . ." He tugs at a loose thread on his shirt. "Wasn't like that."

Emil comes tromping up and puts an end to our conversation. Everyone but Wen and me heads between the trees, in the direction of camp together.

Over her shoulder, Sonia smiles at me. I almost smile back until she gestures toward Felix and bounces her eyebrows three times.

I mouth, *No way in hell.*

Even if I spent tonight free-falling into the life I used to adore, the life of a Wanderer, nothing's changed things with Felix. He might not be awful, and he did treat me more like a girl and less like an object, but a few hours of him being an all right guy didn't stir anything magical within me.

As the fire dies out, Wen and I collapse onto our backs and stare up through the branches.

Stars pop out of the sky, a million pinpricks of light that barely shine from the middle of Cedar Falls. Spencer can give me dreams of Africa that may never come true, but he can't give me the stars.

What I can have is all this, a place where Wen and I can be kings of the world any night we choose. Sitting still is never going to be the life for me. Even if, for one night, sitting still in Spencer's house was something I feasted on.

Wen yawns into his hand. "We should head back."

"Let's sleep out here. Like we used to. Lando's having too much fun to send a search party after us."

The mid-October air is almost too cold, but we curl into the blankets, my arms around Wen's waist and his around my shoulders. He reaches out and dims the last lantern.

This night was everything I love about our Wanderer lives. The freedom, the fearlessness, the invincibility. The rush of uncharted wilds. The luscious promise of somewhere else always on the horizon.

His face pressed into the blanket, Wen murmurs, "Good night, you thief, you vagabond."

"Good night, Wen."

CHAPTER 27

AS SPENCER DRIVES TO A RESTAURANT DOWNTOWN, his hand moves from the place where my knee peeks through the tear in my jeans all the way to my thigh. It's confusing and delicious.

I've been expecting this since early October—a whole month—his hands to wander, one to creep up my shirt, or elsewhere. Maybe he thinks I'm easy. Not that I could blame him. Easy is exactly what I'm putting out there and not with only Spencer. Mid-con, there's no limit to what I'll say to markie boys. The way I look at them, lick my lips, and move my hips—that's maybe the biggest lie of all.

"Spencer. Do you want *more*?"

He steals a glance at me but looks away fast and takes his hand back. "No. I mean—I mean, of course I *want* more. But I don't expect it—I don't want you to do anything you don't want."

I don't even know what I want.

I'm not sure what kind of girl I am. Maybe the kind who says sexy things but stays all-look-and-no-touch.

Wanderers aren't supposed to give ourselves to anyone but our spouses—and not until marriage. That's a doctrine I'm not sure I agree with, though I haven't defied tradition yet.

He clears his throat. "So you know, I haven't before. There weren't any girls I cared about before I left for Spain last year, and there haven't been since."

I should tell him I haven't, but I don't say anything. That's never going to be part of my relationship with Spencer, and I don't want to talk about commitment, not at all.

"That wasn't some line." He dials down the music and faces me at a red light. "I told you so you'd know I'm not the kind of guy who . . . who'd try to pressure anyone."

"I've never doubted the kind of guy you are."

"Good. I don't want you to think that's why I'm here with you."

"Why are you? Here with me?"

We're quiet for a long time.

"Because when I'm with you, I see colors that don't exist." It isn't suave or debonair, how he says it. Only a little shy and a lot too honest.

As he's parallel parking, the reflection in the side mirror makes me do a double take. Lando's walking down the sidewalk, headed right toward us. The lettering on the mirror catches my eye: OBJECTS IN MIRROR

MAY BE CLOSER THAN THEY APPEAR. I slide down the leather of the seat until my knees touch my forehead.

I hold my breath, as if not breathing will make me smaller, an invisible thing Lando won't see through the transparency of glass. "That guy outside, he can't see you with me."

"That guy up there?"

"Yeah."

"Why?"

"It doesn't matter."

Spencer punches the accelerator and joins the stream of traffic. "Tell you what. Let's forget dinner out. My parents aren't home. We can hang out there."

Gravel pings against the doors until Spencer breaks the silence. "Tal, why are you still doing this? If that guy we saw on Main Street scares you so much, then why?"

"What else would we do? Get all socially secured, with cards to prove it?"

"You could get a job. Go to school for a while or get your GED. Then you could go anywhere. See all the things you want to see. Travel the world."

"Wen's fifteen. I'm sixteen. Some social worker would have us both in foster care in no time if we got caught."

He works the watch around his wrist. "Look, I don't have all the answers. You'd have to find a way of keeping yourselves from social services until you both turned eighteen."

"You make it sound easy."

"It wouldn't be easy. I'm not saying it would. But, Tal . . ." He swallows so hard I see his throat bounce. "I don't want you to leave Cedar Falls."

I'm a force when I want something, moving time and space to get the money in my pocket, shiny things into my hands. But Spencer's stolen all the swagger from my step, the seduction from my eyes—the con man inside me—leaving me this nervous, uncalculated girl before him. He's the first thing I've wanted that I can't find a way to own.

Words bubble up from deep inside me. They're sitting in my mouth: *I don't want to leave, either.* Swallowing them down is going to hurt us both.

He peels his eyes away from the road and looks at me like he can see right through me. "Tal—"

Sound explodes around us. The car swerves left, then right, throwing us against the windows as we cling to our seats. It feels like thunder and an earthquake and a hurricane—every natural disaster at once.

The brakes bring us to a screeching halt. I follow his unwavering stare to the windshield. It's shattered into a million pieces. Around a bloody center.

We've killed something. I've done some terrible things before. Nothing's ever felt so sickening.

Wordlessly, Spencer opens the driver door, and I slide out behind him.

In the road, he takes a knee. A few steps closer, I notice the gray, dead mass in the road.

"Spencer," I breathe, "is it . . . ?"

He whispers the unthinkable: "It's an owl."

If for only a second, I might believe.

Several houses up the street, another gray and bloody thing lies unmoving on the asphalt.

"Just fell from the sky," he mutters. "All of them."

All of them.

I skim the road slowly, starting with an owl by a light pole, then by a brick mailbox, then by a parked motorcycle. And up a ways, there's another. And another. And another. They're everywhere, bloody, feathered corpses. All fallen from the sky.

CHAPTER 28

Spencer drives to a repair shop and calls Ella to tell her about the accident and ask if he can put a new windshield on her credit card. Ordinarily, I'd marvel at someone coming by money so easily.

Scratchy news reports come through the radio inside the waiting area of the repair shop. Talk of hail at high altitudes, sonic booms, lightning strikes, noxious fumes, and the apocalypse.

Owls are still tumbling from the clouds and smacking onto the courthouse steps. They're crashing into driveways, clogging up roadways, diving into swimming pools. Two traffic accidents have been reported, shutting downtown for at least another hour.

But none of the markies' explanations can be right.

Once, we were on a long journey, before Mom's arrest, when my brother and I were kids. We stopped for the day in this town that might have been in Kentucky, or maybe it was Tennessee. State lines sometimes run together in the same way as memories.

It was raining tiny drops of water that floated down so slowly four-year-old Wen kept trying to catch them on his tongue. We walked through this gas-lamp district full of curious little shops with windows lined with handmade dolls and confections.

Mom sat us on a park bench and bent to the ground, big gold hoops skimming her shoulders and the beginnings of a scam glowing in her eyes. "Stay right here, and don't you move a muscle," she said. "Mommy is going to come back with some money for lunch."

Stiff as the toy soldiers standing at attention in the shop windows, Wen did what Mom asked. But I was never good at sitting still.

As soon as Mom's coat swished around the corner, I pressed my nose against the glass of one of those windows, mesmerized by a giant snow globe. Inside the globe was a tiny town, with tinier cars and even tinier people, and a thin road winding around the perimeter, a perpetual loop. I wondered if those people wandered around that loop, always ending up in the exact place they'd started.

A woman came to the window. I almost ran, but she smiled at me and picked up the snow globe, inverting it and spinning it around in three slow circles before she tipped it upright and let snow float down over the houses. I imagined the people inside stepping outside their tiny houses, watching the snow coat their world in a white blanket.

The woman smiled, but when she did, her hip bumped the table. The snow globe teetered against the edge before crashing to the floor. Breaking their world.

I ran.

Now, in Cedar Falls, the world is broken just the same. Instead of artificial snow falling gently, it's dead owls.

I can't ignore the very real possibility I've been wrong all along, that everything is real. And maybe by storing the secrets of these omens inside me—by not believing in them or fearing them—I was the one who broke the world.

After the windshield is replaced, I make excuses to Spencer and ask him to drive me home.

We idle at a stoplight, and he turns to me. "Did I do something, Tal?"

It's always him, that's what he thinks.

But it's never him. It's always me and my Wanderer ways or my restless feet or my bad omens dropping from the sky.

My voice is grit and anger. "It's not you."

That kills all conversation, so there's nothing to do but close my eyes and listen to his wheels on the road. The sound is both a breath of fresh air and a dunk in the lake's freezing, murky waters. Not at all like it was before I came to Cedar Falls. I want to hate Spencer for ruining my turning wheels, my one great love.

And I want to hate him for being someone I could never hate.

We're almost there when he says, "You're upset about the owls. That's okay. I'm sure lots of people are having a heart attack right now, too."

He parks at the edge of camp as usual and turns to me. "The thing you told me about the owls, how they're omens, you said you don't believe. You don't, right? You heard that guy on the radio. There's got to be an explanation."

Rona read us a children's book when camp was stopped near the mountains a long time ago. *The sky is falling. The sky is falling.* That's what it said. And now it is.

Spencer would find a way to reach to the clouds and hold them in place for me if I asked him to try.

"Don't you worry, Spencer Sway. Of course I don't believe." My voice doesn't sound convincing.

"I'll see you soon."

I nod, but as I walk away, I'm not sure he'll see me soon, or ever again.

Spencer pulls the car beside me and rolls down the passenger window. He arches himself across the seat. "I don't know much about falling for someone, Tal, but I think I might be."

Dropping low, I tilt inside his car. And I say the truest thing I've said in my life. "If this isn't falling, then the rest of the world is doing it wrong."

Dead owls are gathered around the outermost edge of camp, not thrown away like trash but laid together lovingly. The epidemic has reached camp, but we won't have the same reaction as the markies, looking to science to subdue their fears. We'll turn ourselves upside down.

Sonia and Emil sit in lawn chairs a few doors down from my trailer. Sonia's eyes are closed, and a paperback romance dangles from her fingers while Emil smokes a cigar.

"What's happening?" I ask.

Emil glances up but doesn't say a word, and Sonia opens one eye.

"Do you guys know about the owls?" They still don't speak, so I fold my arms. "Is someone going to answer me? Sonia?"

She scoots to the edge of her chair. "You're embarrassing yourself, Tal, and you don't even know it."

I step back. This isn't the Sonia who I went shooting with in the woods, or the one who's been wanting to patch things up, or the girl I spent my childhood tromping through the forest beside.

She grabs the arms of the chair and arches from her seat. Leaving her novel behind, she meets me in the middle of the road, out of earshot of Emil. "Felix told me what he offered you—he'd make sure Wen always had a home with the two of you."

"That's not any of your business."

"It's camp business, which makes it everyone's business. Why the fuck haven't you taken him up on it? How could you do that to Wen? Take the offer while it's still on the table. You might as well. You're marrying Felix, no matter what."

"Not *no matter what*."

She snatches my wrist and hisses into my ear, "I saw you getting in the car with that boy last month. Tell me you're not being stupid. Grow up already."

Calling me stupid is one thing. Telling me to grow up is another. I won't grow up if it means selling out the way Sonia did. I won't trade my dreams for Sonia's reality.

I shake her off. "Go to hell, Sonia."

Inside my trailer, I press my back against the screen door until the cold metal seeps through my sweater and chills my skin.

Wen tosses his encyclopedia aside and leaps off his

bed. "You're finally back." Behind him, encyclopedia *A* is open to *apocalypse*. "Do you know what's happening? Dead owls are falling out of the sky. Well, we don't know if they're dead before they fall or when they smack down on the pavement—"

"I know. I saw them. One of them crashed into Spencer's windshield."

"You don't think this is 'cause of us, do you?" He moves closer. "Because we buried that owl?"

I work my hands through my hair, collecting it in one big heap and tying it back with a rubber band. "Don't be silly."

As long as I'm breathing, I can keep up lying to Wen. I don't know how much longer I can lie to myself.

Camp is abuzz as we wind down the main road. Wen heard there's a meeting in a few minutes. Some of the children are crying. A group of old men are sitting under Boss's awning, sharing stories of owls that warned us of famine and flood.

At the center of camp, Felix's eyes sink into me. Wen and I move to the back of the crowd.

Lando walks to the middle of the half circle the camp's formed. "Everyone, gather 'round."

People push inward until I feel like I'm being crushed.

Someone yells from the back, "Where's Boss?"

Lando lifts his chin and projects his voice. "My father's real under the weather today, so you're stuck with me."

Murmurs rise and then fade away.

"How's my trap coming?" I whisper to Wen.

His hand goes to his pocket like he's remembering the money he's carrying and verifying it's still there. "Nothing yet. I checked this morning."

Lando clears his throat. "Today's events are something none of us have seen before. Something evil is upon us. Even the markies are concerned. Our most sacred animal is dying around us, falling out of the sky. The Spirit of the Falconer is warning us against something, and I don't know about the rest of you, but I'd rather not stick around and find out what he's trying to tell us about this place. Way I see it, we don't have any choice but to pack up our camp and get the hell out of here." People stumble to their feet, but Lando holds out his hands. "No, no, no. Let's hold our horses. We'll load up tonight, and leave in the morning. Five o'clock. Before the town wakes up."

Someone in the front asks about Rona, and Lando claims he'll come back for her with bail money. Wen and I trade looks. We know we can't put our faith in him.

The meeting ends, and people head to pack their

trailers, find their kids, prepare for travel. I stay still, letting the others dip their shoulders and dodge me.

Leaving early means I'll never see Spencer again—I'll never say good-bye. The film of our relationship pans wide and comes into focus, startling me with sudden clarity of what was tucked away inside me. Spencer made me feel safe—the way nothing had before—without obligation.

Wen wraps his arm around my shoulders and nudges me onward.

As the day fades to twilight, a funeral pyre is set up. Wanderers lay the owls atop the straw one by one. Marius says a few solemn words before lighting them on fire.

Wanderers don't bury their dead. Being buried is the worst fate of all: trapped underground and doomed to one place for all of eternity. Only if someone is hated is he buried. Instead, we burn the bodies and scatter the ashes over the nearest river so they'll wander for all eternity.

Outside our trailer, Wen stops and looks to the sky. "I wonder if Rona knows about the owls. She was always talking about omens."

"You feel bad about her, don't you?"

"I feel—" Tears stream down his cheeks. He swallows and turns his face from me. "It's not that I don't want to help you with the bride-price, Tal. But we've got all this money. It feels like betraying Rona to not help her."

The sight of my brother crying has always been my weakness. Wen may be sensitive, but he's not a crier—Rona's arrest is ripping him to shreds.

I take his hands in mine and tug him into the shadows before someone sees his tears. "I'll help her, too, Wen. I promise."

"You can't promise that. It's too much money."

"No, I promise it. I don't know how, but even if I have to come back for her myself, I'll get her out."

Wen fills one plastic tub with his books and another with his nice shirts. On my knees in my bed, I secure the latches on the cabinets with rubber bands.

"What are people saying in town?" he asks.

"Lightning, hail, a sonic boom, some kind of fumes, the apocalypse."

"You know what a sonic boom is? It's when an object moves through the air faster than the speed of sound—"

"It doesn't matter, Wen."

He stops packing and moves to my end of the trailer, then rests his chin on his hands on the edge of my mattress. "You're upset because of the markie. How are you gonna walk away from him?"

I plaster on a dark smile to keep from crying. "The same way we always leave."

CHAPTER 29

Towns are just towns to us. No town is better or worse. They're all the same. Jumping-off points in the journeys that make up our lives.

That's a lie, actually. We try real hard to believe it now, but Wen and I weren't as good of liars when we were kids.

Back then, we couldn't help but make a judgment about each location we tumbled into. We loved and hated places for the silliest of reasons. We'd love a town for having cool arcades or a carnival, even if it was the kind without a real Ferris wheel, like the ones that go up in the Kmart parking lot. And we'd hate a town for a stupid reason, too—because it smelled like sulfur or because the McDonald's didn't have a PlayPlace.

Wen and I would bawl our eyes out when we had to leave the good places and jump and shout over leaving the bad ones. Now we live by the rule Rona imposed right after Mom got put away. "What's the rule?" she'd ask, her eyes dreamy flashes in the rearview mirror.

Wen and I would lift in our seats, craning our necks like little birds, as we said, "We never look back."

I've never been much for rules, but that's one I've always followed. I wish I could follow it now.

Wen snores softly as I dress in the dark.

My hands pause as I lace my boots because hanging from the doorknob of one of the high-up cabinets is my equinox crown. The one Rona made me. She'd stop me if she knew I was going to betray our traditions.

But she's locked up, and I'm free as a bird, and my decisions are all my own. At least for tonight.

Sheets snap behind me, and Wen sits up in his bed. "Are you running away?"

"No." I stuff the keys to the Chevy into my pocket. "I'll be back in the morning."

He yawns and rubs his eyes. "But we're leaving at daybreak—"

"Before sunup, I'll be back. Nobody will ever know."

He blinks the rest of the way awake. "Are you going to spend the night with him?" Louder this time, he says, "Wait! You're going to spend the night with him?"

My silence answers the first question he's ever been uncomfortable straight-out asking me.

He swings a leg over his bed and then falls all the way to the floor. His feet make a sound so loud it's a wonder he doesn't bust through to the ground. "Tal, wait, please! You can't do this. Not without a blessing. It's just not done."

"Wen, stop it," I whisper. "I need to do this."

"And you don't care what that makes you?"

Tears stream down my cheeks.

"Oh shit. I'm so sorry. I meant because you're engaged. I didn't . . ."

I wipe my eyes on my sleeve and try to push past him.

He lodges his shoulders in the doorway, blocking my path. He'd only have to yell out, and every trailer, camper, and tent would be aglow. Everyone would come running, and there would be no leaving, no night between me and Spencer, and no good-bye. All I'd leave behind me would be a trail of dust and maybe even Spencer's broken heart.

Wen would say he did it for my own good, and he might be right.

I try to move past Wen, but he stands his ground.

"Why would you do this?"

"Because Felix made me an offer. I should have told you. Sonia knows, so she's bound to tell you soon enough. Felix said if I'd marry him without causing trouble, he'd talk to Lando—he'd pay Lando, even— so you'd always be with me and Felix if we went to another camp. You and me'd always be together."

Wen stares at me in a way that would make my throat ache if I didn't look away. "Oh, Tal. Not for me. You can't—"

"I might." Emotion thrums over my vocal cords. "The point is, I don't know. Everything's uncertain. Tomorrow, we're going to be somewhere else, somewhere far away from Cedar Falls. I'm never going to see Spencer again, but I want tonight. I'm not sure how many choices I've got left that'll be my own, but I want to make this choice. I want this choice to be mine."

Wen's bare feet shift away from the door. As I step past him and into the night, he says to my back, "I trust you."

I only wish I trusted myself.

 **CHAPTER 30**

THE HOUSE IS DARK WHEN I STEP INTO THE FOYER. As I replace the key under the Sway family doormat, screeching comes from the tree in the yard behind me.

I take three deep breaths. I've heard this in the forest before. An owl.

Without turning around, I push the front door shut and block out the sound.

The stairs creak under my shoes. I imagine Marcus and Ella flipping on the lights, tumbling from their room in their bathrobes to find me standing in their house all alone after midnight. All the lies I've ever told will run together, leaving nothing but the truth sitting on my tongue. That's how I'll vanish from Spencer's life, not with a bang or a whisper, but a midnight confrontation. But the hallway stays dark all the way to his room.

A ribbon of light glows from under the door.

As I turn the knob, my hands shake, because doing this means the distance between the outside world and me is about to crumble.

Spencer's sitting at his desk, scrolling through a website. In his Google search box are the words *typical college interview questions*. He whirls around in his chair. He's still dressed in jeans and a plaid shirt, all the buttons undone and a T-shirt underneath.

His lips part, but I say, "Shh," and cross the bedroom.

He meets me at the end of his bed, the very center of his hunter green rug. "You're breaking into my house now?"

I inch forward until our bodies almost touch and work my hands into the space between his plaid shirt and his T-shirt. His warmth radiates outward so that I don't know where his body heat ends and mine begins. "Come down to the basement with me."

"You don't have to whisper, Tal. My parents are at a fundraiser, and they won't be home until after three, and Margaret's at a sleepover." He hooks his thumbs into the belt loops of my jeans, tugging our hips closer but still a respectable distance apart. "I don't really care where they are. All I want to know is what I did to deserve this surprise. And how I can do it again."

I shift my gaze to the bed. "I guess we can stay right here."

He raises his eyebrows. "What do you mean? For what?"

I press my fingers to his lips, then replace my finger-tips with my mouth. Crushing my whole body against him, I answer his question without speaking. He doesn't sink into me, not at first, but when he does, I'm oh-so-aware his body wants this, too.

He gasps into my mouth and tilts his chin toward the ceiling, breaking away. "Um, Tal. What are you—" His jeans scrape the comforter as he backs away from me.

I could tell him everything—that the next few hours are the only thing standing between the road and me—but there aren't words that don't sound like good-bye. I want tonight. This one memory. Perfect or terrible, I want this to be ours, unmarred by him knowing this is truly the end.

No matter what happens, wherever I go, we'll both carry these parts of each other forever. I want to share this with him more than I've ever wanted anything. It's not going to be perfect, not this night, not with the doomed-from-the-start history of us, but it's the only shot we have of giving each other something to hold on to long after my wheels hit the road.

I crawl over him, and as I grab his belt buckle, his breath catches. "I don't know about this."

"It's okay, Spencer. I'll respect you in the morning." But my fingers tremble and don't cooperate. The control I'm trying to keep is slipping through my hands.

Spencer wraps his fists around mine, steadying me. "Are you all right?"

I stare at his hands, still holding mine tight. "In the car, I should have told you, but I've never done this before, either."

Our gazes connect, and his eyes are oceans I'll never cross. "If you want to stop, Tal, we can stop."

Rona would kill me. Sonia could never understand me taking off my clothes for a markie.

I realize what I'm really afraid of—he's the only thing I've ever wanted that hasn't made any sense.

"I don't want to stop." I dip into the depths of myself and say, "There are few things I've ever wanted more than this."

From an orange shoebox in his closet, Spencer locates a little foil packet that manages to make my always-steady pulse race like hell. As he kicks his jeans to the carpet, I prop myself up on my elbows to get a better look at him. He's wearing navy boxers with a plaid waistband and little yellow airplanes that won't take either of us anywhere.

My stare makes him blush down at the carpet.

Seconds pass without him touching me, leaving me fully dressed while he's damn near naked. I find his hands and guide them to my body, making him aware I'm not look-don't-touch. Not anymore.

"Spencer." My voice runs away from me as I whisper, "Please."

His fingertips find the edge of my T-shirt, carefully exposing a small slice of my stomach. His mouth meets my skin, and warm bubbles fizzle under my surface.

We undress each other the rest of the way until there's only the slip of the sheets against our skin. He slides into the bed beside me, and my heart nearly pounds out of my chest. As I stare up at the plaster ceiling, his traveling hands take me to places that don't exist in anyone's atlas, all the way over that edge he's always talking about.

Our bodies frozen inches apart, he says, "There's something I have to tell you."

"Will it make me want to do this more or less?"

"Knowing you?" He cringes. "Less."

"There's tomorrow," I say, even though tomorrow for Spencer and me won't come. There's my tomorrow and there's his, but never a tomorrow the two of us will share. "Tell me then."

All apprehension vanishes, and he looks at me, really looks at me, so even though we're naked beside each other, his gaze connected with mine makes me feel the most exposed.

He says my name, breathes it into my neck. Here, in Spencer's house, in his bedroom, with the weight of him over me, there's no markie world and no Wanderer world.

There's only Spencer Sway and me.

CHAPTER 31

WITH MY EYES HALF OPEN, I BREATHE THE SCENT OF laundry detergent and new clothes. The smell of Spencer. The world around me comes into focus, and I'm in my own bed, in our tent trailer. Alone.

I peel back my quilt, and I'm still wearing Spencer's plaid shirt.

The screen door swings open, and Wen glances at me and then looks away. His face turns the most horrible shade of red. Maybe Wen and I should be spared those private details of each other's lives. I'm not ashamed. It's just that I never imagined this would drive a wedge between us, when nothing had before.

I pull my quilt under my chin and tame my bedhead with my hands. "Hey."

Wen doesn't look at me. "I guess you want to know why we didn't leave?"

Everything spins as I sit up too quickly. The sun is bright through the screened-over window beside my bed. The day is wasting away, and we're all sitting still in Cedar Falls. "I didn't even think about it."

He hops on his own bed. "Some people got up real early this morning—way before sun-up—so they could start loading their RVs, and Lando wakes up Boss, and—get this—Boss said we have to stay."

"Said?" *Said* is for those who speak. "What are you talking about? He spoke?"

"Yep, he crooked his finger to Lando. Whispered one word: *Rona*. Lando brought him his chalkboard, and Boss scratched, *Not without Rona*. But Lando said the camp still doesn't have enough money to bail her out."

"You're kidding."

"No. So, um, now that we're not leaving, will you still get her out?"

"A promise is a promise."

The gift of time doesn't leave me the relief I might have expected. Not after the way I left last night.

The buzzing of Spencer's garage door opening was what woke me. The clock on his nightstand said it was 2:23 AM. Spencer didn't budge. Beside me, he lay asleep on his stomach with his fingertips grazing my rib cage and his other arm slung over the bed. The front door slammed shut, and Ella's and Marcus's voices trickled up the staircase. They were home from their benefit and oblivious to the fact I was naked in their son's bed.

I listened as his parents shut themselves inside their room, and when the house went quiet again, I slipped free from Spencer's touch, crept from his bed, and threw on my clothes.

In the dark of his bedroom, I stood still for one moment that stretched to infinity, eyeing the place where the sheets moved low on his back as he breathed. I couldn't wake him and tell him I was leaving for good. For someone who only ever said good-bye to places, it wasn't a word that easily dripped from my lips when it came to people. Every time we packed, there were farewells to be said. I was afraid there were only so many good-byes inside me, afraid of what would happen when they were all used up.

I couldn't, wouldn't say good-bye, so I wrote my farewell on an oversized Post-it from his desk and stuck it to the bed, inches from his splayed fingers.

I wanted nothing more than to climb between his soft sheets and arrange myself beside him. Or wake up in the Sway house and know all the Wanderers were gone from town and that I wasn't one of them anymore.

A sliver of light from the hallway lit up the rug as I cracked open his bedroom door. Spencer's plaid shirt was balled up on the floor, taunting me. I was never any good at resisting temptation.

I slipped my arms inside the sleeves, tiptoed down

the stairs, and took off out the front door, taking with me two pieces of Spencer Sway, neither of which he's ever getting back.

Wen hops from his bed and walks down the trailer to the spot beside me. He digs into his pocket and flicks a few bills between his fingers. "Oh, I almost forgot. Seventy-three extra bucks."

"Where'd you get this?"

For each day he's taken off into town, he's come in with forty or fifty dollars to add to our pile. Whatever he's doing is working well.

"You forget I'm capable of making money without you, Tal."

Making money—a phrase that has become synonymous with stealing, scamming, conning, and even risking our lives.

"But how?"

"Chess," he says. "Hustled some old guys in the park."

"You keep it." I hold it out to him. "My pockets are bulging as it is."

Chess is a game I understand all right, but I'm no chess hustler. My mind doesn't work the same way as Wen's, mathematical and always five moves into the future. It's a shame, because the hustling money is good.

"We have more time here," says Wen. "I thought you'd be glad."

I must be frowning. "Sure."

"You're not going to see him again."

He knows me too well. I've closed the door on Spencer and me, and I won't open it again.

Last night was supposed to make everything better. I don't regret what I did, not at all, but now I don't know how I'll marry Felix. I can't possibly stand the feeling of his hands moving down my body or the weight of him crawling over me.

"Spencer's my past. I'm scared as hell Felix is my future."

Wen squeezes his knees until his knuckles turn white. "You're not doing it for me. You're not. I can't live with that."

He's got tears in his eyes. It's hit him, how serious the threat of Felix is, and it's an ugly thing seeing it rip him apart.

I lay my head on his shoulder. "The only way out of this is to come up with the money or leave. And if we leave, they'll find us, and we'll be right back where we started."

"But how are we going to get the money? We can't run any cons now. Not with those yayhoos and their fliers."

Usually the cons silently call to me, like the crackle

of electricity down telephone lines, but today there's no wishing a plan into action.

Cedar Falls is off limits, like Wen said, but maybe that's the answer.

"That's it," I say. "We've got to head to another town."

CHAPTER 32

THERE'S A WIDELY KNOWN MAXIM IN THE WORLD OF grift: *You can't cheat an honest man.*

So as I watch Wen screech into a parking space in front of the Denny's in Pike, I hope it's not an honest man he finds.

Down the street from the restaurant, I sit lengthwise on a park bench, kicking up my heels. Wen disappears inside, wearing a starched shirt and slacks. I close my eyes and imagine the exchange inside.

He'll strut through the doors, order some food at the lunch counter, and make small talk with the waitresses and the other diners. On his right hand, he's wearing this great big emerald ring—fake emerald, that is—and he's talking with his hands, flashing it as he talks, drawing every bit of attention to it he can.

When he goes to pay, he'll shake an amount of cash most people have never laid their eyes on, every bit of our savings from the Cool Whip container. He'll say good-bye to everyone inside, and right as he's about to step onto the sidewalk, he'll declare, "My ring! It's missing!"

They'll scramble to the diner floor, everyone who's inside, combing the tile, over dropped forks, dried-up french fries, and not-so-lucky pennies. But no one, not no one, will find that ring.

"A reward!" Wen'll yell. "Four grand for anyone who finds it. I'm staying in room forty-five at the Holiday Inn. Room forty-five at the Holiday Inn!"

My brother knows this con as well as the back roads of the South. He'll come through, I'm certain.

Imagining my brother working the room like a pro brings a smile to my mouth, the first smile since I left Spencer's bedroom. For a few moments, I had let him slip my mind.

I don't know if it's the part of me I left in Spencer's bedroom or the part of him I'll always carry with me, but I'm either less of a Wanderer or more of a markie.

There's this image I have of future Spencer with gray hair around his temples and a closet full of business suits, a wife who wears pearls, and 2.3 children. And me, I'm a flicker of a memory to him. I wonder where I'll live inside Spencer's mind. A faceless girl with a long-forgotten name. Some easy girl he laid.

Where I'll fit him into my memory, I don't know, and that hurts most of all. By creating that night with Spencer, I thought I'd have something to carry with me forever, and that it would be enough. Now I don't want to live in the shadow of that one night forever.

I look up, and the Chevy's already coming toward me. Wen cranks down the window, wearing a cocky grin that a good scam brings.

He drops the ring into my palm. "Do your thing. It's looking good in there."

"That's what I like to hear."

"Try the suit by the lunch counter. Meet you two streets over at the park. Be safe."

The Chevy roars down the road as I saunter toward the Denny's with the ring, a small lump in the pocket of my bomber jacket. That's not the only thing I've got on me. Over five thousand dollars is pressed around the waistband of my jeans. That makes my heart rate pick up. It's one thing to walk around with that much money and another to con with it. One wrong move, and my money could be gone in a flash.

The bells on the door jangle as I step inside. I stand beside the gumball machine, the earpiece of my sunglasses resting against my painted lips and my hand on the hip I'm popping. There's a feeling in the air, a rhythm I can feel pulsing through the room. Maybe it's the knowledge I've got at least five hundred dollars coming my way.

The patrons look me up and down. I take them all in. I notice the leer of a fortyish man wearing shirtsleeves and dress pants, his suit jacket slung over the back of his chair.

I pull up a seat, leaving one bar stool between us. There's no reason to appear too eager, and it's more natural if I let the mark come to me. I order a Coke with cherries and wait for him to strike up a conversation, let me pull him into my trap

Not ten seconds later, he shoots me a grin. "Just how is your day going, miss?"

"Not half bad." I dip my fingers around in my drink, fishing out a cherry. "How about you?"

"Couldn't ask for more."

He swings his jacket over his shoulder and takes the bar stool beside me. "Where you from?"

"Savannah."

"Pretty little place."

"Sure is." I lift my Coke from the counter, making sure condensation has glued my napkin beneath it. As I drink, I let it flutter to the floor. I laugh and push back from the counter, collecting the napkin and slipping the ring into my palm.

"What's this?" I pop up in my chair, flashing the fake emerald in the light.

The man's jaw drops. "That's, um, mine," he says, reaching for it. Sheepishly he adds, "Must've dropped it off my finger."

"Looks like it's worth a lot of money." I whisper as I

examine it, "If it's really yours, then you wouldn't mind putting up a little bit of a reward, would you?"

He scoots his bar stool closer. "Fifty dollars should do it, right?"

"Fifty dollars. You must think I was born yesterday. This ring must be worth five grand."

"How 'bout three hundred?"

"I don't even believe it's your ring."

Sweat beads on his brow and rolls down the sides of his face. He uses a napkin to mop it up. "So it's not my ring, but I do know where to find the owner, and you don't. What's it going to take?"

"A grand."

"Would eight hundred dollars do the trick, then?"

Eight hundred dollars. Much more than I expected. "We've got a deal."

"Hey, hey, hey!" says someone in the background.

"Excuse me, sir," says a boy from behind us. "I have a feeling this young lady is shaking you down. I've seen this happen before." He turns to me, tipping his trucker cap higher and eyeing me. "You're gypsy trash, aren't you? You and that fella, who was in here, flashing his cash."

I can't breathe, but I step from my chair, keeping my pulse level. "What in the world are you talking about? I found this ring, and he's paying me a little reward. Nothing but an honest exchange here."

The man I was trying to scam grabs a cell phone from his pocket and dials. "Maybe you can explain it to the cops."

I set the ring on the bar counter and hold up my hands. "Hey, relax."

The boy grabs me by the back of my neck as I move toward the exit. He digs his thumb deep into my skin, then deeper. I can't help but cry out. "You're not going anywhere," he says.

"I wasn't doing anything wrong."

"There's one way to find out." The man plucks the ring off the counter and lifts a fork. Using a prong, he scratches at the stone. Green dust scrapes off.

The boy spits on the floor of the diner. "We know all about your kind."

I yank free and back up to the bar counter, with both of them closing in on me. But the bells on the door jangle, and all our eyes shift to the entrance.

It's Wen. I suck in a sharp breath. *No. No. No.* If one of us gets caught, the other one is supposed to make a run for it. These aren't our rules.

Go, I mouth.

"Okay, the jig is up," Wen says, ignoring my warning. "There's a perfectly good explanation for all this." He's grinning like a fool, but his words shake a little. I hope I'm the only one who notices. He points to a smoke detector on the ceiling at the other end of the restaurant. "Do y'all see that camera? Well, you're on *To Catch a Con Artist.*"

This is about to get really good or really bad.

"*To Catch a Con Artist?*" asks the man I was trying to scam.

"Haven't you heard of it?" I say, fake-smiling so hard my jaw aches. "The television show." I turn to the room, clapping my hands. The whole restaurant joins in.

Wen sets one hand on the shoulder of the man and the other on the boy's, guiding them away from me and farther into the diner. "Okay, here's what you need to do. All of you look at the camera." He points to the smoke detector. "Now say, all together now, 'I caught a con artist!'"

They exchange looks before staring up at the "camera" and mumbling the words.

"You'll have to get a little closer," Wen says, backing away. "Right beneath it. That's good. A little closer." He inches toward my side and whispers one word: "Run."

We hit the door, and Wen knocks a table over behind us to block the doorway.

We take off like jackrabbits, pulses in our ears as the men chase us down the sidewalk. But we're younger and faster, our bodies accustomed to running from markies.

We jump in the Chevy and hit the locks. Wen's mouth is gaping open as we fly down the street, past the man and the boy.

We make it onto the highway, and I collect my hair in one hand, sweeping it away from my neck. The skin is tender and hot to the touch, but I could have been hurt much worse. So could Wen.

"How did you know?" I gasp.

"I don't—I don't know. A bad feeling, I guess."

"You always know."

CHAPTER **33**

I SIT CROSS-LEGGED ON THE FLOOR OF OUR TRAILER while Wen stretches a new shirt over the dining room table, our makeshift ironing board. He starches and irons the fabric until the collar's stiff and the wrinkles steamed away.

"Why are you going this time?"

"Same reason as always," he says. "Money."

I can't argue with that. We do need the money.

He goes into town every day while I stay at camp avoiding anyone and everyone. At first, I'd begged him to stay close to camp, not to go into town for fear Spencer might see him and know I hadn't gone anywhere. Wen got crabby by the second day, sighing at the stack of books he'd already read, so I told him to go on and leave as long as he promised to make himself as anonymous as possible.

"What's the scam?"

He yanks the shirt off the table and shakes it out before slipping his arms into the sleeves. "Whatever it needs to be. Depending on the mark."

"I should be going with you."

"Don't worry yourself, Tal."

I stay on the floor after Wen swings the door shut, after the Chevy starts up, and long after the hum of the engine disappears up the road. I wanted to go along, but catching a glimpse of Spencer behind the glass of the diner on Main Street would be unbearable.

I clean everything in the trailer that isn't bright and shiny, all the windows first, and then I spray tire cleaner on the tent trailer's tires. I do all the things I did before, trying to wedge myself back into my routine. It feels like a dress that's a size too small now. I can only get into it if I don't let myself breathe.

In the tent trailer's lowest cabinets, I gag on long-forgotten jugs of sun tea I'd made when we were camped near Biloxi, two towns before Cedar Falls. They're near solid in spots and growing mold around the edges of the waterline. I carry them past the edge of camp to dump them.

A voice at my back deflates everything logical that had risen up inside me and made me think I might be able to slip back into Wanderer life unchanged.

"You're still here."

I whip around and face Spencer Sway.

His hair is sticking up all over his head, and his sweatshirt is wrinkled. He looks like hell. I didn't want this. I wanted my last memory to be the two of us swimming in blankets and his dark lashes brushing against my cheeks as he asked me if I was okay.

I want to touch him, but I cross my arms, erasing the possibility of them circling him. "You shouldn't be out here."

"That's all you've got to say to me, after that night in my room, after you never even fucking said good-bye?"

He's never spoken to me like this.

I dump the last bit of tea, watching it spread and darken the ground because I'd rather look at anything over the anger flashing in his eyes. "My note was my good-bye. I didn't want to say it again."

"*We're leaving town tomorrow. Have a good life, Spencer.* That's not good-bye."

Hearing what I said repeated back sounds like wet gravel under bald tires. I was so afraid I'd say too much that I didn't say enough.

"I wanted to see this place after you guys were gone," he says. "I made it halfway up the road when I thought I saw lights. You said you were gone, and then way up that road, I saw lights. Lights. Do you realize I thought I was losing my fucking mind? So I drove closer, and here you are." He holds his arms out wide.

"Here you all are!"

The rumble of voices isn't far, and there's nothing that's going to make Spencer go away fast. I have to deal with him, talk about this.

Without asking him to follow me, I stalk off toward the clearing where he's always dropped me off and park myself on the hood of his car. "We . . . we got delayed. We're still leaving."

The sedan jars as he sits beside me. "Why?"

Coming clean is always such a disaster. But he has to know leaving isn't optional. Skulking away from him in the night was necessary.

"It was because of the owls. Everyone thinks we're headed for an apocalypse, or something, and that we gotta get out of here before it hits."

"That doesn't make sense."

"Neither do owls falling from the sky. But now we're not leaving after all. It's, uh, because Rona's still locked up. As soon as we get her out, we're gone."

"So you'll be leaving soon?"

"Sooner. Later. It could be tomorrow or a month from now."

He works the zipper on his sweatshirt, the metal teeth wheezing in the quiet forest. "You act like it doesn't matter."

It matters. I've never wanted to stay put so bad, but those desires are tragedies I shouldn't form into words.

Above, between the low-hanging branches, the sky is darkening, a not-so-perfect way to end this. "You should get out of here, Spencer, before someone sees you."

We get to our feet, and he puts his back to me. He opens his car door and stands staring inside as the keys in the ignition make the sedan ding. He slams the door shut.

"That night," he says, "I told you I had something to tell you. It feels stupid saying it now, but I want you to know." He moves closer, until the tips of his shoes brush against my toes. "I want to tell you."

He goes in to kiss me, just missing my mouth but making heat pool where his lips touch. I close my eyes, tipping my mouth to his, in time to hear him whisper something I don't want to hear: "I was going to say . . . I think I might love you."

The world whirls around me, and I realize I've rushed away from him like he's burned me.

This wasn't what I wanted. I'm not the kind of girl who runs because she wants to be chased.

Tears drip from my eyes, roll down my cheeks, and leave dark spots on the cuffs of my sleeves. *Love.* The sound of it rings in my head and hurts like hell, a migraine of a word. Using that one word—*love*—he's made us into something so sugary sweet we have to be phony. Like cotton candy and Pixy Stix and promises.

"You're a coward," I say.

"A coward?"

"You're all talk and no action. All you do is talk about seeing the world when you're really just going to SJU. What do you think you're doing with me? You can't have me, Spencer—no one can—and I can't have you. And that's why you said that to me—because you'll never have to act on it."

His Adam's apple bounces. The light that was once in his eyes, I've destroyed it. I've gone too far.

His blank look goes hard. "No, Tal," he says. "You're the coward. You couldn't even give me a real good-bye. I've been standing here for an hour, trying to decide if I should walk into your camp and confront you. I should have realized how pointless all of this is— my fake idea of you."

It stings. I've been someone else with every outsider I've ever known except for him. With Spencer, I was always the real me.

I take a step back and whisper, "You know me."

"Not really." He stares at the ground and runs a hand through his hair. "When the Wanderers are near, I don't know who you are. You're not the same girl you are when the lights are low and we're alone in my room."

I take a step closer, and he moves away, keeping our distance a constant.

274

"In case you were wondering, your note wasn't a good-bye. This is."

He gets inside his car and slams the door. No matter what happens, I think he'll always remain in my mind, like some scam I planned that failed.

Without ever meeting my eyes, he starts up the engine and takes off down the road. As the shadows swallow up his sedan, I realize that even if I never see him again, Spencer Sway and I will never be through.

CHAPTER 34

WEN SHAKES ME HALFWAY AWAKE, BUT I WANT TO stay lost in oblivion for longer. I tug my blanket over my head.

"The trap," he whispers. "I checked just now."

I sit up too fast, and our trailer spins. The late morning sun is bleeding through our screens, and Wen's holding his finger to his lips and our Cool Whip container against his chest.

"Some of it's gone?"

"A fifty."

A fifty—one-eighth of the four hundred dollars we left as bait.

I last checked the Cool Whip container the afternoon before. Someone snatched the money while we were eating dinner in the heart of camp.

"When do we do it?"

I throw back the covers. "No time like the present."

He hugs the container against his chest and stares at me.

"Don't look at me like that." I finger-comb my wild tangles and slip my jeans up my legs. "We need to do this before Lando has a chance to hide it."

A few people are buzzing at the heart of camp. Boss is parked beneath the shade of his RV, a thin tube from his oxygen mask running from his ears to his nostrils. Today's one of his bad days. I hope he'll listen.

I scan the crowd for Lando. He isn't around.

"I think he's in Boss's RV," whispers Wen.

"Hey!" I cup my hands around my mouth. "Everyone needs to gather 'round. We need an emergency camp meeting right now."

People exchange looks and move in closer as murmurs shift through a building crowd. Sonia's staring at me in a way I don't know how to interpret. I used to know every type of smile she'd try on, every freckle on her face.

I scan for Felix and am relieved not to find him. I still haven't said another word to him about his proposition.

Boss holds his chalkboard up to me. It says, *Not supposed to call meetings.*

I bend down to Boss's level out of respect. "If this wasn't truly important, Boss, I wouldn't do this. But you gotta hear what we're going to say."

The door clangs shut, and heavy feet tromp down the steps—Lando.

His hand closes around my upper arm, and he hauls

me upward. My bicep burns as we come face-to-face. "What the hell do you think you're doing? If Father says there will be no meeting, then there is no meeting."

Loud enough for everyone to hear, Wen says, "We wouldn't be here if it wasn't for you."

Lando releases me and kicks up a dust cloud heading toward Wen, but Boss holds up his hand and motions for him to let Wen speak. Lando lowers his fists.

"We've, uh, noticed some money going missing." Wen's voice quivers as everyone turns to him. "We've got some savings, you see. Like, uh, like most of you do." I glare—we can't let them know the amount of cash we were hoarding—and he adds, "Meager savings, that is. But it's a lot to us, so we marked some of the bills."

Tiny, almost-invisible pen marks you'd have to be looking for to see.

The scratch of the chalkboard sends us all spinning to Boss. He beckons me closer. In tiny letters, he writes, *Who is the thief?*

"I—" My throat closes up on me. "I think it's Lando."

Boss shakes his head as someone in the crowd yells back, "You think it's Lando?"

"We don't think it," says Wen. "We know it."

Lando chuckles to himself. He removes his wallet

from his back pocket and tosses it to me. "Go ahead and find your marked bill, if you're so sure it's me."

I skim through Lando's wallet, over fives and tens and twenties and hundreds. There isn't a single fifty.

Horatio steps from the crowd with his hands buried in his pockets. "Well, we could always search his trailer. If Boss would let us."

I bend down beside Boss, sitting on my heels and resting my fingers on the wheelchair. "Boss." His eyes slowly trail my way. "You up to hearing me out for a minute or two? I know he's your son, and it's hard for you to see the ugliness inside him. But I'm so sure I can find that money in his trailer."

His hands don't move toward the chalkboard.

"Boss, please, I'm begging you."

Carefully, Boss scratches along the chalkboard, his hands slow and shaky. He holds the chalkboard up for the crowd to see.

Not the thief.

Boss wraps his cool fingers around mine and squeezes. His lips barely moving, he whispers, "Need more proof."

I back away from Boss as the crowd disperses, and I head for my trailer. Wen comes to my side, and I whisper what Boss said.

"How are we going to prove it?" he asks.

"We'll find a way."

Camp's as good as lost to me if Boss requires solid evidence. That's another truth I can't tell Wen.

Spencer's car pulls into the ice-rink parking lot right on time. I wait for Margaret to swing the car door open and to skip up the steps before I make my way to him.

Right now I need to not feel so alone, and there's only one person who can fill that void.

I drop beside the open passenger window and rest my hands on the window ledge. "Hi."

Spencer's eyes glow for the briefest second before he squeezes them shut and stares straight ahead. "What are you doing, Tal?"

"I've got something important to say. I—I told you I didn't believe in love—"

He knocks the car into reverse.

"Wait!" My fingers curl around the window ledge, as if my sheer will can keep him parked long enough to hear me out. "You're not letting me finish."

"Should I?"

"Yes, because out of all the people in the world, you've gotta know more than most that some things are true, even if you can't say them. And I—" *Love*—I want to say it back to him, I do. But that word rushes to my head and makes me dizzy and vulnerable. "All I'm asking for is a second chance. I don't know if I'll ever find the right words to tell you what's deep down inside me, but . . ."

When I can't say more, I think I've lost him forever. Until he shifts into park and looks at me. "Why? Tell me—just give me this."

I meet his eyes and exhale. "Because there are depths of me I didn't even explore before you."

My teeth chatter in the cold air as I wait for some sign I've said enough—given him enough—so he knows how I feel, even if I'm too broken to say the words aloud.

He leans over and opens the door for me. "Where to?"

I'm a little out of breath as I slide into the seat. "Anywhere but here."

We end up naked in Spencer's basement. There's a deadline on the horizon, even though we don't have a precise date or time. Now that Spencer knows me pulling out of town is inevitable, it's a ticking clock that never goes silent.

I run my fingertip down the bridge of his nose. "Your interview's a couple of weeks away, huh? What's it going to be like?"

"Why do you want to know?"

"Well, interviewing so you can pay them to teach

you things just doesn't make sense. Shouldn't it be the other way around?"

Spencer's eyes narrow up at the ceiling before he cracks up. "Your logic might be my favorite thing about you." He gets to his feet, wearing nothing but his boxers. "Okay, you want to know what it's going to be like. Here goes." He runs his hands through his hair and straightens the imaginary tie attached to his imaginary shirt.

He turns to his right and says with a deep voice, "Mr. Sway, welcome. How did the drive down to Charleston treat you?" He flips back to his left. "Not bad at all. I drove a steady fifty-five miles per hour for the three-hour drive, observing all traffic laws and paying careful attention to all road signs."

I tuck the blanket under my armpits and sit up. "Oh, please don't stop there."

He jumps to his right and deepens his voice. "Mr. Sway, tell me about yourself. Why are you interested in Stonewall Jackson University? What will you contribute to our campus community? Does your high school record accurately reflect your abilities? What do you see yourself doing ten years from now?" He goes back to his left and adjusts his fake tie again. "And wearing a great big grin, I'll be trying to say, without really saying, 'Well, sir, I'll be majoring in political science with a focus on rhetoric, all the while being an active participant in campus politics. I'll go to law school, marry my college sweetheart, and move back to my hometown of Cedar Falls. There, I'll take a sweet job as a county prosecutor, and by the time my mother, Judge Ella Sway, retires, I'll be a seasoned attorney ready to fill her place. I'll retire, take a few vacations—nothing too taxing because I'll be too geriatric for anything strenuous, maybe a cruise—and then one day I'll up and die.'"

I'm not laughing anymore, and neither is he.

"I'm sorry." He runs his hands over his face and drops beside me. He gives me a weak smile. "That got real dark."

The basement grows colder as sweat dries on my skin. I sit up to feel around the floor for my sweater. He stretches across the futon to turn the lamps on. I hear him take a deep breath.

"Tal, what is that?"

The brush of his fingertips trace my spine. Spencer pushes the hair off my bare shoulder and presses into the sore skin at the nape of my neck.

I flinch, and my memory flashes to the markie's hand there in that diner. "It's nothing."

"So are you gonna tell me what happened or should I ask again?"

"I said it was nothing."

"You're black and blue. It's not nothing."

What he's thinking is clear.

"Spencer Sway." I force a laugh and tug my sweater over my head, pulling my hair from beneath the collar. "If anyone ever laid a hand on me, you better believe I'd kill him."

"I wouldn't think less of you if someone hurt you, Tal."

I can't tell Spencer I got hurt trying to con my way into a life of my own choosing. It's the one thing I'd be embarrassed for him to know—that I'm for sale.

"What if there was something I couldn't tell you? How would you feel about that?"

"You can tell me anything."

I cut my eyes back at him, then at the walls of the basement, and rest on my elbow beside him. "What if I really couldn't?"

"If you can't tell me, then why are you saying anything at all?"

"Because we've only got a week or two here, and I may not be around much. There's something I've got to do."

"What?"

Raise several thousand dollars to win back my soul.

His warm hand moves from my shoulder to skim his fingertips over the bruise. "Some kind of a scam, right? Because you need money." I really hate it when the truth seeps through. "Is it dangerous?"

"Don't know. I don't know what scam it's going to be yet."

He slides his jeans up his legs, stands, and zips them. "I'll be right back. Don't run out on me again."

With my clothes back on, I sit on the edge of the futon, my forehead in my hands.

He returns with a stack of bills folded in half. I lunge for them and count the money fast. Five hundred and forty dollars in twenties.

"That's all I can get now, but I've got more in the bank. There's not much I can get easily, not without my parents finding out. Whatever I can manage, it's yours."

The cash is heavy. I've never held so much without trying to figure out a way to make it mine. Here it is—a gift. I'm holding the balance of my future in my hands.

I pass it back to him. "I don't need you to save me, Spencer Sway."

He frowns. "I'm not saving you, Tal. You're saving me."

I shake my head. Accepting his money proves I'm nothing more than someone who takes advantage of people, someone who searches for the angle. I thought I could be more than that. I want to be more.

"Really, Tal, I'd like you to have it. This is what I want to do with it—give it to you."

Maybe nobody will ever know the story of Spencer and me and these months we've spent together. But just in case, this shouldn't be the moral.

I can't say that to him, though, so I lie. "It's never ending. If they know I got the money from you, they'll ask for more. I have to hustle or con the money—that's all there is to it."

"Then we'll find another way to get it. Whatever it is, I'll help."

"What, you're gonna hustle people at pool for me? Thousands of dollars worth of hustles? Besides, we get caught, and your parents'll never forgive either of us."

He collapses against the futon, folding his arms behind his head. "I don't care what they think."

"I don't believe that for one second. If that was true, you'd cancel your interview now. Or is that what you really want?"

"'Course it is. It's not that easy. I guess I am a coward."

"You shouldn't listen to me," I say.

I was the one who planted that seed in his mind. I want him to be happy—and maybe I'm crazy for thinking I know anything about Spencer's future happiness—but I don't believe he'll find it in Cedar Falls.

"Let me help you, Tal."

"I don't think you have any idea what you're getting yourself into."

"You don't know what you'd be getting *yourself* into. I already have the scam in mind." He laughs up at the ceiling. "You're a dangerous girl, you know that?"

"And why am I so dangerous?"

"You take away my sense of self-preservation."

 **CHAPTER 35**

I GO LOOKING FOR WEN AT THE BOOKSTORE FIRST.
It's empty—only towers and towers of books, all organized in neat rows. My brother's fantasy.

I scan the aisles. No Wen.

A door cracks open as I'm about to take off. Wen steps
out, looking alarmed. The sign on the door says STOCK-
ROOM. He shuts it behind him. "What are you doing here?"

"Looking for a book. It's called *Where the Hell Is
My Brother?* Have you heard of it?"

He blushes and puts on a dopey smile, like he does
when I catch him lusting over markie things. He sits in
a cushy red chair in the back corner of the store, where
a book is perched on the armrest, *The Fellowship of the
Ring.* A bookmark sticks out from the middle.

I point to the stockroom door. "What were you
doing back there?"

"Bathroom. Blanche said I could use it when I come
here to read."

"Blanche? You're on a first-name basis with the

crazy book lady?"

Arching himself over the armrest, he whispers, "Please don't say that in here, will you? I like coming in here to read about as much as you like hanging out with markie boy."

"You're still refusing to call him by his name, huh?" I curl into the red chair adjacent to him, and kick my feet up on the table. "Well, you should try to learn his name, because Spencer Sway has offered to help us plan one last con. The greatest con of all."

It's barely dark as I watch the forest boundary from inside our trailer, blurs of green through the screen windows.

"What if someone sees?" asks Wen.

"Let them see."

The shape of a paperback book—a new one, no doubt—presses through his back pocket. "You're sure spending a lot of time at that bookstore."

"You're sure spending a lot of time with markie, Talia."

"Touché."

The trees light up in three quick flashes. I take off, and this time Wen follows.

The man on the radio is still talking about the owls as we seal ourselves inside the car. Spencer's eyes flick to me before he reaches for the volume dial. I push his hand away. I want to hear.

The radio host is talking to some big ornithologist—a bird expert named Dr. Houseman—who's come to Cedar Falls because of the owls. He says there are around eighteen species of owls in North America, and some counts are higher. Between all the corpses he's collected, they've found fifteen different species. He doesn't have any explanation for that.

The host asks him if he knows what killed the birds. He gives the same answers as those first reports: a sonic boom, fireworks, power lines, lightning.

"Or the apocalypse?" says the host.

Dr. Houseman laughs, and so does the host.

I turn off the radio myself.

In the dark of the car, Spencer's focus shifts to me. "If that's true," he says, "then I figure we're all going up in the flames of a meteorite, no matter where we are. We might as well be smoldering together."

We take the highway northbound, headed away from Cedar Falls and all the way toward Pike, me in the passenger seat and Wen in the back. I close my eyes and imagine we're all running away from everything, searching for that place in the world where we could all stay together—the three of us orbiting around each other and nothing else.

I wonder how it might be to keep on driving with

Spencer and my brother, to head straight for some ship and sail all the way to Cape Town.

I open my eyes and watch the black road passing between our wheels. There's no sense having such dysfunctional fantasies.

"Okay," I say. Even though everyone is clearly aware of how they fall into the con, I like feeling in charge, doling out responsibilities as if I'm the criminal mastermind here, not Spencer. "I'll be keeping an eye on the crowd. Wen will collect bets from the other team. Spencer, you'll make sure the Cedar Falls team loses big time—and, of course, you're driving the getaway car."

The home team, the Mighty Fightin' Lumberjacks, are all dressed in their best and brightest reds and whites, filling the bleachers to full capacity while the away side—the Cedar Falls Mud Dogs side—is barely a quarter full, even though this is the first game of the preseason.

The scarce Cedar Falls attendance means there's less chance of being seen by someone who knows us from Whitney's party. Still, we don't take chances.

The three of us scatter in the parking lot. For this scheme, we're all strangers.

Wen rushes to the other side of the court and moves through the home side. He stole a Cedar Falls sweatshirt from an unlocked car in the parking lot, so he blends right in.

With the brim of one of Spencer's hats pulled low over my face, I'm hanging by the exit, in the event the game gets too hot—our game, not basketball.

Basketball, itself, is a sort of con, each side taking turns trying to break through the defense to slip the ball past the other team. Cons are like that, trying to break through the mark's unwillingness to trust, and then sneaking something past him while he's standing in front of you.

Spencer says the Mighty Fightin' Lumberjacks haven't won a single game this season, and school spirit be damned, those Lumberjacks are going to bet good money Cedar Falls is ahead by halftime tonight. Cedar Falls is the district champion, three years running.

Spencer, our inside man, is working behind the scenes. He already jogged off around the outside of the gymnasium after he parked. I almost feel guilty he's crossing over to the dark side for me. Our worlds are bleeding together more and more with every day, not because he's here with us, but because I actually care about him dirtying his hands and his conscience.

He's threatening every goal his parents have set before him. Even if those dreams aren't his own, my guilt doesn't feel good.

Cheerleaders line up near the concession stand to

form two tunnels for the players, one of red-and-white pom-poms and one of navy and yellow—or blue and gold—like the Cedar Falls side is chanting.

Blue. And. Gold. Blue and gold.

From under each arch of pom-poms, a stream of hulking boys jog onto the court. And there they are: number fifty-four, Jeremy Hale, and number twenty-three, Craig Castle. They both grin at the meager Cedar Falls audience as they run to the court. It has yet to kick in.

"Hey." Spencer faces the action and leans against the other side of the exit door, a good seven feet from me.

Keeping my eyes on the players, I say, "Everything okay?"

"Better than okay. Perfect."

The game starts. I hold my breath.

Jeremy's basketball shoes shift and shimmy ever so slightly across the gym floor. Sweat drips down Craig's arms and forehead, and he mops at his face with his jersey. I smile. Things are heating up—in a good way, for a change.

"Tal."

"No names," I whisper as Spencer comes to my side.

"I'm not going to my interview next week."

I face him before I remember myself and the con in action. I settle against the wall and stare straight ahead. "What do you mean?"

"I'm going to talk to my parents. Tell them SJU was

their dream and never mine."

It's hard to keep my game face on when my happiness for Spencer is threatening to burst out of me.

As the quarter drags on, Craig gnashes his teeth together. Jeremy's face darkens a shade of red with every second of the clock. If I had more of a soul, I might feel bad for them.

The game's almost tied as the clock counts down to halftime—no thanks to Craig or Jeremy. The ref blows his whistle because one of the Lumberjacks fouled on the Cedar Falls team.

Craig steps to the free-throw line. If he makes it, Wen and I are screwed.

He aims—I don't breathe—and the ball bounces off the rim. Craig frowns at the hoop and bounces on the soles of his sneakers. They play the last few seconds, the buzzer goes off, and that's it: Cedar Falls is two points behind the Lumberjacks.

We made the bet for halftime, so once Wen collects, we can bail.

The rest of the team jogs over to the sidelines, but Jeremy keeps on running. He heads all the way down the length of the gymnasium and out the doors, holding the crotch of his basketball shorts. Craig isn't far behind.

Jeremy and Craig don't know why their game is blown tonight. They don't know why there's a fire down below. They don't know Spencer put Bengay in their cups.

"Did you see that?" Spencer's laughing so hard he's swerving the car all over the road. "I mean, did you see him grabbing his nuts in front of the whole crowd?"

"Priceless," I say. In the backseat, Wen's busying himself with a paperback copy of *The Winter of Our Discontent* he found beneath the seat. "Hey, Wen, you saw, right?"

"Yeah, um, great."

Spencer came up with the idea to rig the game like that. Somehow, screwing over guys like Jeremy and Craig fits into Spencer's moral code. I guess we're all that way, making up our own rules so we can feel good about the choices we make.

Mom must have her way of rationalizing taking off without us. Wherever she is, she's probably telling herself she did the right thing. Even if she's wrong.

"Either of you hungry?" Wen presses his face between the front seats. "My stomach is sticking together."

We stop at a roadside diner between Pike and Cedar Falls. Only some of the lamps above the tables are on. It looks closed until we notice one waiter moving around inside.

Bells chime as we step across the threshold. The waiter flips on the rest of the lights, avocado-colored ones that make our skin look green.

For the briefest of moments, I wonder what would happen if the whole world ended and nobody but me, Wen, Spencer, and the waiter are left. If it happened like that, nobody would care if the three of us—four with the waiter—wandered or stayed put.

Now that the owls have fallen out of the sky, the world ending wouldn't come as much of a surprise. That thought unsettles me.

Between bites of egg the light has dyed green, Spencer counts the cash on the Formica tabletop.

"What's the total?" I ask.

Spencer adds the last twenty to the stack. "Twenty-eight hundred and twenty dollars."

Wen thumbs through Spencer's book. "Best haul we've ever had in one night."

It's not enough, but it's so much closer. "Not bad. Not bad at all."

I take Spencer's hand under the table and, before I know it, we're all talking about the game.

"Man," says Spencer. "I don't know how you do this all the time."

"Did you almost lose your nerve?" I ask.

"Sort of. They all put their stuff down and went outside for their team prayer before suiting up. I was going

296

through Jeremy's bag when Coach walked back in. I swear, I almost threw up."

"What'd you do?" says Wen.

"Hit the ground. I hid beneath the bench—pressed on the disgusting locker room floor—until Coach left. I thought I was done."

Under the table, I squeeze Spencer's thigh. "Didn't it feel good to see them lose?"

"No," says Spencer. "It felt incredible."

We drive back to Cedar Falls with everything we want to leave behind forgotten. There are no Wanderers or markies, no owls or Falconers, and no Felix. Tonight there's only us and this laughter that fills all the empty places inside me.

CHAPTER 36

I PEER OUT THROUGH THE METAL SCREEN OF THE door. It's getting late, and Wen hasn't made it back to our trailer. He said he was going to check on Rona's place over an hour ago.

Firelight slips between the RVs across the road. People are still gathered after dinner. My face is half frozen in the November air. I almost wish I'd gone to sit near the campfire, but it's getting harder to sit there and pretend I'm still one of them.

I get into bed and read from one of Wen's encyclopedias. I wish we had *O*, so I could read about owls and omens. There's a burning inside me for more information, like if I could get my hands on that book, I'd have all the answers.

Instead, I pick up *L* and read about lions and Libya and liars.

A raw scream travels through the windows.

The book drops off the bed and thuds against the floor. I'm out the door and running. Gravel stings my bare feet. Even torn to shreds by the scream, I know it was Wen's voice doing the yelling.

Bodies buzz around something at the center of camp. They're riled up.

I shoulder through. There, with everyone looking on, Horatio pins Wen's arms behind his back.

Lando throws a punch into Wen's face while Horatio holds him still. Wen wails again. This isn't a bare-knuckle fight. It's not a fight at all—it's a beating.

I dart closer. "Stop! No!"

Blood pours from Wen's nose down the front of his shirt. I lunge forward and get several jabs into Lando's back, but an arm snakes around my waist and drags me backward.

"Let me go!"

Emil squeezes his fists into my abdomen. Emil is Wen's friend, and yet he's allowing this.

"Stop fighting me," he whispers into my ear. "We have to let this happen. He has to learn his lesson."

I go still. "His lesson?"

There's nothing Wen could have done that would make him deserve this punishment. The last time I saw this happen, a boy had stolen from the family bank. Later in the week, that boy disappeared. I thought he'd run away, but all his stuff was still at camp.

"You know that bookstore he's been hanging out in?" says Emil. "He's been working there. A real markie job. Felix saw him in there today and told Lando."

Tears trickle down my cheeks. With my arms pinned to my sides, I can't even wipe them away before someone sees.

This is my fault. All mine. Wen's watched me walk along the ledge between markies and Wanderers, teetering and about to fall off into the markie world for months now. I was supposed to set the example.

Lando fishes around in his pocket. His hand comes out sporting a pair of brass knuckles.

I claw at Emil's arms with each punch Lando throws, screaming until my throat is sore and my ears are on fire.

Wen holds an ice pack over an eye that's black as night and dangerously swollen as I dab at his cuts. It's the two of us inside our trailer now, me and this battered boy who barely resembles my brother.

On the counter is a bottle of Vicodin Emil left when he carried Wen inside. I shake them out in my palm and pass Wen a handful.

"So, how'd all this job business start?"

He throws back the pills and swallows them. "Blanche offered me a job that first day I went in there without you. A few hours a week, under the table."

All those times Wen barely spoke, snuck away without me, those had nothing to do with his awkwardness over me and Spencer, and everything to do with the bookstore, his own little markie fantasy.

"What all does she know?" My bowl of water swirls with red as I dunk the rag and touch it again to his cuts.

He cringes at my touch. "She knows about us. Says she's a sympathizer."

"What does that even mean?"

"I don't know, Tal. It was weird, so I didn't ask." He moans as my fingers put pressure on his swollen jaw. "I couldn't not take the job. Not with you owing the bride-price back to Lando."

I should have taken Felix up on his offer. If we weren't trying to scrape together the bride-price, Wen wouldn't have taken a job at the bookstore, and he wouldn't have been beaten bloody.

"You shouldn't have done it for me. Got yourself tied down to a markie job."

"It wasn't you. It was . . . I don't know. I wasn't tied down. We think we're so free, going where we want, when we want. But earning my own money, knowing it was coming in day after day, it made me feel freer than I've ever felt before."

"That's not real freedom." I slump down to the floor of our trailer, leaning my cheek against the edge of Wen's mattress. "And neither is this."

"What is it, then?"

"I wish I could tell you."

"Right before Lando hit me, he leaned in and said I'd have to quit the bookstore because I couldn't go to work looking like this."

"You didn't know Felix saw you?"

"No."

Wen was never the illusionist in our two-man show—I was. I don't know how much longer I'll be able to go on running around with Spencer without camp discovering. How long until my magic will run dry.

Wen sinks down beside me and wraps an arm around my shoulders. "You're not mad at me, are you?"

"Of course not."

"Maybe we were both just playing around with this markie stuff after all."

"Please don't say that."

"All things have to end, I guess. I had a good time. You had a good time. Let's try to forget."

"What if we ran? I know I've always said we couldn't stay on the run from them, but what if we settled down somewhere, hid out for a few months until Lando forgot about us?"

His lips turn up but he moans, and his almost-smile becomes a grimace. "A little town like Cedar Falls?"

Warmth rises in my cheeks.

"Oh, Tal, don't tell me you were starting to think

things might work here. You're supposed to be the logical one. I'm the dreamer. All of this—it's gotta end." He
focuses on the stack of encyclopedias beside his pillow,
then digs an envelope out from under his mattress and
hands it to me. "Oh, this is for you."

I flip it open, and it's stuffed with cash. A quick
count of the hundred-dollar bills, and I realize it's the
last of the money I need. Every bit of the bride-price.

"You stole it from the book lady? 'Cause if bookselling
pays this well, then we've got to stop our thieving ways."

He doesn't smile. "Blanche had a real heart for our
problem."

"Damn it, Wen, thank you." My fingertips skim his
swollen cheek. "This wasn't worth it, though."

"It was."

He snuffs out the lamp, and I lie in my bed, listening
to the crickets, waiting for him to begin our ritual. After
too much silence, I say, "Good night, Wen."

There's an impenetrable quiet as I wait for him. He
clears his throat. "Good night."

All the broken parts of me ache for all that's lost in
the moment.

"Wen?" I say softly. "Good night, you thief, you vagabond."

All he gives me back is nothing at all.

The smell wakes me up, sharp and smoky like good barbecue.

What really coaxes the sleep from my limbs are the brightness and the searing heat. I lift up on my elbows and stare out my window. Filtered by the screens, a fire crackles in the space between our trailer and the forest. Wen stands beside the flames, shirtless, even though the weather is cold and biting.

It's not unheard of to do our burning in the middle of the night, when the black sky can swallow up the smoke and keep our secrets hidden away from the outside world, but there's nothing Wen has that needs burning.

I work my feet into a pair of shoes and yank the quilt off my bed, wrapping it around my shoulders like a cape and heading out the door.

My feet crunch through the frozen grass as I step closer to him. Stacked in the dirt are all his encyclopedias.

Wen barely turns. "Go back to bed."

"Wen, you can't."

He grabs an encyclopedia off the stack and tosses it onto the flames. They lick at the book, spreading the pages open, and turning them orange, highlighting the words my brother stayed up late devouring.

Pain twists in my rib cage. Fighting with the tears trapped behind my eyes, I whisper, "You're gonna be so sorry tomorrow."

He takes another book into his arms and hugs it against his chest before sending it spiraling into the flames. "I'm sure I will, but it's got to be done."

Sparks fly at our toes, and I take a step backward.

"You really should go back to bed, Talia."

Too long, I wanted him to fit in with camp, and now he does. With the firelight flickering across his bruised ribs, Wen's crossed the line he always danced around. He's a Wanderer for good. That hurts most of all.

A soft gust makes me wrap the quilt tighter. I step away from the fire, beside the stack of encyclopedias. The letter embossed on the spine of the top book, the one next in line to be burned, is *A*.

A for *adventure*, *academia*, *Algeria*, and *agony*. *A* for *Africa*.

Wen's facing the fire, his back shuddering as the book burns. I can't bear to watch *A* go up in flames, so I tiptoe to the pile and slip it beneath my blanket. Squeezing the four corners into my skin, I carry the encyclopedia against my heart and never turn back.

CHAPTER 37

Spencer and I settle into the couch and click on the TV while Margaret flips through a book of magic tricks.

News coverage in a place like Cedar Falls should involve prize-winning African violets and high-school sports coverage. Tonight, it's all about the owls and the hordes of media filling up the one hotel in town.

"Is this bothering you?" asks Spencer.

"It's fine."

The truth is that not being okay has nothing to do with owls and everything to do with the wall Wen's built around himself that I haven't been able to break through.

Spencer turns off the TV and stands by the edge of the couch. "Let me take you somewhere now."

"Where?"

His fingers circle my wrists and slide until our palms join. He pulls me to my feet. "Coffee, ice cream, pancakes, Africa. I want to go somewhere with you. Right now."

I go limp, leaning the weight of me away from him

and deep into the couch cushions. He grins and tugs harder, hauling me to my feet and against him. My whole body hums with the feeling of us pressed together. I'm suddenly conscious of the tiny places where our unclothed skin touches: my index fingers against the fine hairs at the back of his neck; his rough thumbs grazing the space where my jeans and sweater don't quite meet; my bare toes brushing over his bare toes.

"Stay with me," he whispers. "Don't leave with the Wanderers. Ever."

"I'd have to change to stay here. To fit into your world."

"You wouldn't."

"I would."

He says into my hair, "The rest of the world doesn't matter."

I've never felt this, my heart leaping away from my body, every inch of me aching. I should fight the feeling. I should pull away. Instead, I push harder against him, and it makes me want more. More of what, I don't know, but whatever it is will be my destruction.

A glass shatters in the kitchen, and the room rushes back to me. We let each other go as Margaret's shrieks drown out all the wanting.

We break apart, and Spencer runs into the kitchen.

"It's broken! It's broken!" Margaret's standing barefoot on the taupe-tiled floor, and she's surrounded by shattered hunks of cobalt-colored ceramic.

Spencer grabs her around the waist and sets her onto the counter. "You didn't cut yourself, did you?" He lifts one of her feet and then the other.

"Nope."

"Stay right there. Don't get down." He jogs to the walk-in pantry and comes back with a broom. He scans the tiny pieces scattered over the floor. "Mags, what *was* this?"

She lifts her hand to her mouth and bites at her nails. "The cookie jar."

"Are you serious, Mags? That was Nana's. It was an antique. Mom's going to be so upset."

Tears roll down Margaret's cheeks. I sidestep the broken pieces and wipe her tears away. "Hey, it's okay. We can buy another, can't we? What did it look like?"

He doesn't answer, focusing on sweeping broken bits into a dustpan.

"Spencer?"

"Don't read too much into this." He sighs. "It was an owl."

The smoke from the burned encyclopedias is inside my throat, even though it's been days, and Wen's ragged breathing is in my ears as I lie awake. He hasn't breathed right since Lando took a fist to his ribs.

Two hours before sunrise and I haven't slept. Any courage I could have built up would have made its appearance already if it was going to show up at all.

I dress quietly, so I don't wake Wen.

As I'm carefully guiding the screen door back into the frame, I look down at the mini-flashlight in my hand. It's no good for protection. I go back for my heavy-duty Maglite.

Lando's asleep in his bed. He never even stirs as I close his door behind me.

I turn my flashlight beam on him and say, "Here's how this is going to go down."

He throws back the covers and comes at me. Backing me into the wall, he says, "Talia, what the damn hell are you doing in here?"

I lift my chin and harden my eyes. "I know you're the thief."

I watch his hand hanging loose at his side, how his fingers curl inward and make a fist. If he were to hit me, I don't know if the rest of camp would say I had it coming or if Boss would give a damn about me.

Lando raises his arm, and my own hand tenses around the flashlight, ready to swing. He slams his palm into the cabinet behind me, inches from my ear.

"Whatever you think you know," he says, "you're

wrong."

"I'm not wrong. But it doesn't matter if you are the thief or you aren't. All that matters is that everyone's about to think you are."

He laughs as he rubs his chin. "What are you getting at?"

"Three hundred marked bills are in this trailer. I know because I put them here today while you were out."

Lando leaps away from me. He dumps the fruit bowl on the counter, sending oranges and pears bouncing to the floor. He goes for the first cabinet on his left.

"You'll never find them," I say. And that's the truth because I've never set foot inside Lando's trailer until right now. "They're hidden too well. Nope—no one's gonna find them until I convince Boss to let us search this place. Then I'll be the one to find them."

"You're bluffing."

"Am I?"

He glances in the direction of Boss's RV. "My father would never let you search my trailer."

"What if I told you he asked me to prove you're the thief? You really think he trusts you?"

"You wouldn't part with three hundred dollars just to frame me."

"You don't know what I'd do."

"What's your angle?"

It's time to play. "A little old-fashioned blackmail."

"You think I've got enough to pay Felix back? Because I don't have near that kind of money."

"This isn't about Felix. It's about Rona." I don't know for sure if he has enough for Rona—but he has to think I do. "You've got it. I know you do."

This won't make up for Lando beating Wen, but at least I'll fulfill my promise to my brother.

Lando cocks his head to the side, as if he's considering that. "Bailing her out might take time."

"I wouldn't let it take too long, if I were you."

CHAPTER 38

WEN BRINGS THE CHEVY TO A STOP AT THE CORNER of Main Street and Ivy. I squeeze the door handle but don't press down.

"I could go with you, you know?" I say. It's the first day of Spencer's Thanksgiving break, and we're supposed to celebrate, but he'll understand if I'm late.

"Nah."

Wen's face is swollen and purple and ghastly in the sunlight. He's on his way to tell Blanche he won't be coming to work today and not ever again.

"Wen, you can tell me if you don't want to go alone."

"I'll be all right. I promise."

On Main Street, I jaywalk against the DON'T WALK. The bell tower chimes noon, and I quicken my pace.

Up the street a ways, Sonia's standing by herself. She's arching her upper body inside the passenger side of a car, her belly brushing against the door.

I take slow steps—I don't want to interrupt any

scam she might be running—and follow the sidewalk to the diner where Spencer's supposed to meet me.

As the space between us vanishes, I notice the silver color of the car, the familiar shape of the bumper, a sedan.

Spencer's car.

The engine turns over, and Sonia stands. She backs onto the sidewalk, pressing her hand into the middle of her back as Spencer pulls into the street. I break into a run, but he guns it down the road. His taillights are faint dots at the end of Main Street by the time I reach the diner.

He left me. Knowing I was on my way to meet him, Spencer left me behind.

Sonia's dark, smudgy eyes catch me, and damn it, she looks ashamed. She saw us through the coffee shop window that day, Spencer and me racing down Main Street together. I was stupid to believe a glimmer of our friendship still shone for her.

"What did you say to him?" I demand.

She lifts her chin and crosses her arms. "You're awfully self-righteous, considering what you've been doing with that markie."

I'm right up in her face now. "Tell me what you said to him."

The whites of her eyes redden and fill with water. "That there's one of him in every town. That you're engaged to be married to someone else, and now you're ready to move on."

She reaches for me, and I dodge her grasp.

"You don't understand, Tal. It's better this way."

"Better for who? Because I can't think of a single person any of this is better for."

"For you." Her chest rises and falls like she's trying to hold something deep inside. It all comes tumbling out in sobs that wrack her shoulders. "And for me. Everything can go back to the way it was before now. You'll be with Felix and I'll be with Emil, and they can run the scams for us, and we can have babies together and travel around, and we'll be just like we used to be."

I should tell her to never speak to me again, rip her hair out, wrap my hands around her throat and squeeze. But I'm empty inside.

There's something so damn sad about realizing our friendship is something from the past that's never going to be our present.

It doesn't even matter. Spencer learned the truth about Felix, and he left me.

Our Chevy flies to a stop beside us in the street, the wheels smoking from peeling rubber onto the road.

Wen's grinning as he rolls down the window. "Hey, I ran into Horatio. Good news!" He looks to me first, and then Sonia's teary face, and his smile falls away. "Um, uh, Rona's back."

Lando came through. My plan worked. Winning should feel good, but I can't think about anything besides Spencer Sway.

I glance down Main Street, where his car disappeared seconds before, and I get inside the Chevy.

Wen leans across me and out the passenger window. "You getting in, Sonia?"

She wipes the mascara streaks from her cheeks and nods. I scoot to the middle seat.

Sonia presses a hand to her chest as she hiccups. "Guess this means we're leaving. Rona coming back, I mean."

"Yeah," says Wen.

"Nothing holding us back now," she says.

With my eyes closed and the Chevy swaying me from side to side, I should be thinking up places for that compass inside me to lead us next.

There's no lying to myself anymore—I don't want the road beneath my wheels. I want to chase Spencer all the way to his front door and tell him everything Sonia said was a bald-faced lie.

But I couldn't lie to him now, not even if I tried.

"You didn't tell the book lady yet, did you?"

Wen stretches across his mattress while I'm sitting

on the edge of mine. We wait inside our trailer for Rona, who's at the heart of camp now, giving Lando and Boss a rundown of her time on the inside. "I'll do it tomorrow."

"You really don't have to. When you stop showing up, she'll get the idea."

"No. It's only right I say good-bye. You should say good-bye to Spencer, too."

I could drive away from Cedar Falls without ever seeing Spencer again. Maybe that's how it ought to be.

"Did you see him today?" he asks.

"Our plans changed."

I couldn't bring myself to tell Wen about Sonia betraying me. The opportunity was there—a dozen times over, I could have confessed—but I can't stomach the thought of him thinking badly of her. Maybe that means I've forgiven Sonia for marrying Emil, for saying what she did to Spencer, for falling out of best-friend love with me.

Wen holds his hands to his sore rib cage as he exhales. "You got Lando to get Rona out, didn't you?"

He's on to me, but I keep my voice level so I don't give anything away. "Why do you think that?"

"Because your poker face isn't that good."

"Really?"

"Okay," says Wen. "I saw you sneaking back in before sun-up. You were wearing your post-con smile."

Our door creaks open, and the beam of a flashlight blinds me. My eyes adjust, and Rona's black-and-white hair comes into focus.

Wen goes to her first and falls into a hug.

She pulls back and strokes Wen's bruises. "Your poor, sweet face."

"What's going to happen with your case now?" he says.

"It'll be fine." A grin spreads her red-ringed mouth. "Lando put up the bail, but there aren't any bounty hunters out there who'd have the smarts to find us. As soon as we leave here, we'll never look back."

A sad sound escapes me.

Rona's eyes dart my way. "Wen," she says, "would you mind running down to my trailer and taking a look at the back window? It's like the damn thing sealed shut on me."

The screen door slams behind Wen, and Rona whispers, "Tal."

I hop down from my bed. So much has changed since she was last at camp. Maybe she can tell I'm different, missing things: my illusions, my adoration of this life, my virginity.

Her arms encircle me first, and I melt into her. She squeezes me so hard I can't tell if it's her shaking or me. We stand there, vibrating together until she pulls away.

"Jail got me thinking, Tal. All that time—and I . . . I'm so sorry I ever kept anything from you. Greta hurt me, too, when she took off, and I didn't want you and Wen to know that pain."

I swallow. I should say I'm sorry, too, but I am thought and action. Putting words to my emotions has never been my strong suit.

I turn my back to her and stare out the screens and into the black forest. She doesn't know the means to my freedom is in my possession. It aches through me, knowing I had the money to set her free all this time, and I chose my own freedom over hers. I am my mother's daughter through and through.

"These owls have had me thinking about Greta a lot," she says.

"What do you mean?"

Rona and I have never discussed the last time the owls showed up. Everything I know comes from my own memories and what five-year-old Wen told me.

"Oh, I'm sure you remember the rest stop, when that owl parked itself on our hood ornament, or the one Wen saw out in the forest when he lost his beach ball. It was before Greta left."

"Before she left," I whisper. Not before *her arrest*. But before *she left*.

Realization washes over me.

If I believed the Spirit of the Falconer was real,

maybe I could believe he wasn't warning my mother about her arrest? Maybe he was warning us she was about to leave the wandering world behind?

But I don't believe. I can't and I won't.

Rona cocks her head to the side and looks me up and down. "Tal, what's going on with you? Whatever it is, I'm ready to hear it."

I face her and square my shoulders. "We've made the money to pay the bride-price back. Me and Wen did. I'm buying myself back from Felix."

"And what will you do, then?" she says. "It doesn't have nothing to do with that markie boy, does it?"

The trailer fills with silence. I can't admit aloud—not to Rona and not to myself—Spencer and I are over.

Her face is wistful. "No matter what, you can't stay here."

Even though she's right, I still have to say it. "Why not?"

"You'll be trading one kind of captivity for another."

It's time to say good-bye to Cedar Falls, to Spencer, to markie life. I was never cut out for anything but the road beneath my wheels. I mask the truth and say, "At least freedom is mine to trade."

Rona takes a deep, shuddering breath. "I guess you've got decisions to make." The door creaks as she sinks her weight into it.

Just as she's about to walk away, I blurt, "Wait."

We stand there, staring at each other for an instant that stretches on too long.

"I never was fair to you. To me, you always lived in Mom's shadow, and there was nothing you could do— and you tried all sorts of things—to get yourself into the light."

Tears slide into her smile lines. "You had your reasons."

"I'm not saying it was all my fault, but it wasn't all yours, either. And I appreciate you, for all you did for me and Wen."

Her hands move from my chin to my shoulders, and she takes a step away, the weight of her palms steady as she studies my face. "You look just like Greta now. But you're not Greta. I should have seen it long ago."

CHAPTER 39

TWO HOUSES DOWN FROM THE SWAYS', I PULL TO the curb and shift the Chevy into park.

My brother and I are on a different kind of mission this morning, the kind that doesn't involve aliases or five-finger discounts—just finding two people who deserve our good-byes and our apologies. I'm up first.

Wen stares at his reflection in the vanity mirror. He runs his fingers over his yellowing bruises but flips the mirror shut when he notices me watching. "What will you say to him?"

My jeans catch on the duct-taped seats as I slide out of the truck. "I haven't thought that far ahead."

This whole time, I've been conning Spencer into thinking my future belonged to me.

I would tell him about the arranged marriage and how Felix's family bought me the same way they'd buy a used RV, if I knew for certain revealing my secrets would make a difference. That's a leap of faith I can't take.

"Give me a few minutes," I say, "and we'll head

downtown."

My fingertips scrape against the brick retaining wall around the Sway's property line. I knock on the door, and when no one answers, I ring the bell.

The bolts click, and I almost lose my courage.

"Hey, Tal." Marcus Sway's hair is in his eyes, and he's running a dish towel over his hands. "What can I help you with?"

I peer around his shoulder into the foyer and up the staircase. "Is Spencer home?"

"No, Spencer's probably halfway to Charleston by now."

"His interview." I step back, a few feet from the Sway family doormat. "It's today?"

Marcus's brow wrinkles, etching the lines of his forehead deeper—he doesn't understand—but he quickly smiles. "I thought Spence would have told you."

"Oh, he did. He did. I must have forgot." I back down the porch and stumble on the last step. "I'll see you later."

He told me about his interview, all right, the exact date. But then he told me he wasn't going. Everything he's learned about me—I just hope it wasn't me who changed his mind.

"Hey, Tal!" yells Marcus. "You should come by for dinner tonight. I closed up the gallery to do the prep work. I'm making Spencer's favorite—paella, and flan for dessert."

"Thanks for asking, but . . ." My skills, they're failing me. "I've got things to do."

"That's a shame. I know Spencer'd love to have you here."

I stop halfway down the driveway. "You don't know how much I want to be here."

Wen shakes the loose change in his pockets as we walk through downtown. We're headed to grab one last slice of thin-crust pizza before he says good-bye to Blanche and we leave Cedar Falls in our rearview mirror.

A flash of plaid drags my focus across the street. It's a gray-haired man in a flannel shirt, not Spencer. How stupid—Spencer's probably sitting across from an admissions officer right now.

We freeze as Lando fills up the sidewalk in front of us. "What are you kids drifting around town for?"

"Hello, Talia," says Felix, from behind Lando.

Wen covers his bruised, swollen cheek. "We're going to get a pizza."

"Not today, you're not," Lando says. A burst of orange paper crinkles in his fist—one of the anti-gypsy fliers from that rally over a month ago. "These are tacked up all over town."

Down the street, they're everywhere, orange fliers cautioning the town against Wanderers. Taped inside windows and stapled to telephone poles, they're bright beacons of warning. I don't know how I hadn't noticed.

Lando thrusts the flier at me. I pretend to study the words I know all too well.

"We're leaving day after tomorrow," says Lando. "Till then, no more town privileges. Head on back to camp, you two."

If they crack down on all our comings and goings, I'll never see Spencer again. I can't let his last memory of me be the image painted by Sonia.

Time must have sped on by, because, beside me, Wen's making excuses for my silence.

Lando looks at Felix and says, "She doesn't look well. You drive them back in their truck. I've got some business to attend to."

We fall away from Lando. I look across the street and blow the hair clear from my eyes.

Every bit of the momentum moving my body disappears.

Spencer stands under a street lamp in a navy blue suit, his hands in the pockets of his trousers, and his eyes steadying all the chaos around me. I don't dare break his stare. If I look away from him for a second,

I'll lose all my nerve, my free will, my fire.

He didn't go to his interview.

I imagine traffic clearing and walking across the street and never looking back. I've never needed anyone else, and I don't—need him, that is—but I want him.

They wrench me down the sidewalk, past the pizza parlor, my brother on one side, gently, and Felix on the other, more forcefully.

Spencer took a huge step in his world. It's time for me to do the same in mine. I will the words into my throat, and cement my feet into the sidewalk.

"I'm not going back to camp."

Lando freezes several storefronts away and doubles back. "What did you say, Talia?"

Wen's voice in my ear is more of a whimper. "Please, you have to come with us."

I repeat, louder this time, "I'm not going back to camp."

Lando backs me against the brick space between the drugstore windows and the pizza parlor, forcing my gaze away from Spencer. He says low, "I know you get off on being defiant. Now's not the time. Get on back to camp. Now."

"You mind taking your hands off her?"

I cringe at Spencer's voice, not from across the street anymore, but feet away.

Squinting at the bright winter sky, Lando turns to

Spencer. "Who the hell are you?"

It gives Spencer enough time to wedge himself in front of me. I have this momentary fantasy where this works, and Lando holds up his palms like a white flag and draws away from Spencer, my brother, and me.

But around Spencer's shoulder, Lando's expression is impenetrable. Until he laughs. "Is he why you've been difficult? Really, Talia?" He rakes his eyes from Spencer's clean patent leather shoes to his burgundy tie. He claps Felix on the shoulder and shoves him forward. "You don't know what you're doing, kid. This is Talia's fiancé. She's bought and paid for."

"Bought and paid for," Spencer repeats. He looks at me, and as the last pieces of the puzzle slide into place, his confusion fades to a look I only see as pity. To himself, he whispers, "The money."

All I can do is nod.

Felix says to Lando, "Do, um, you want me to fight him?"

Lando scans the street, papered with orange fliers. He won't want trouble out in the open.

Spencer works the knot of his tie loose and pops the first two buttons of his collar. "That could be arranged."

His shoulders lift, and I plant one hand on his chest, pushing him back.

I look to Lando. "You need to get out of here."

"You need to get your ass in the truck before I put

you there."

"You're forgetting our midnight meeting," I say.

"You think I've got twenty grand for the bride-price now?" Lando asks. "No matter what you think you know, there's no squeezing blood out of a turnip."

"No," I say. "We've got the money. Every last dollar. My freedom's mine."

"Talia," whispers Felix. He has this look on his face like he's about to either cry or vomit.

"I'm so sorry. Marrying me won't make you more of a man. You're just doing what you're told to do. You've got to see that."

He swallows hard. The small sadness I feel surprises me.

Spencer holds out his hand, but my fingers are just out of his reach. "Come with me, Tal. We'll figure out everything together."

He waits, his hand solid, unmoving, stretched out for me and only me.

I put my hand inside his and squeeze.

Lando and Felix both slink away, until it's only me and Spencer and Wen, standing on the corner on Main Street in downtown Cedar Falls.

Sometimes, the expectation of something is better than the real thing, but Spencer wraps his arms around me, and there's nothing as good as this. We stand there in this moment of staggering perfection. Nothing can steal my bliss, except knowing what's to come—decisions and longing and maybe even regrets.

One breath later, the moment has passed, and I'm so impossibly sad.

I extend my other hand to Wen, letting him know this is it, the time for us all to leave. Joining the markie world is all he's ever wanted. What we'll do now, I don't know. But we've got choices now that the bride-price is squared away.

But Wen slides his palms down his face and screams at the sky, "What the hell are you thinking, Talia?"

"Hey, relax, man," says Spencer, moving toward Wen.

I touch Spencer's elbow and pass him by.

I take Wen by the upper arms, making this just him and me, with the futures we both desire close enough to touch. "It's like you said that day in the lake. I'm street-smart and you're book-smart, and we can make it. Come with me. Just for now. We'll go back to camp later and pay off Lando and get our stuff. There'll be no one coming after us. Not ever."

"No." He backs away like I've struck him. "I'm through chasing markie dreams."

My chest burns with those words. He's the one who always wanted this. "What about you and the book-store? It can be yours now."

"That was a fantasy," Wen whispers. "Come on, Tal. If you want to go back later—and you will—you won't be able to. Not after the ruckus you're causing. Lando will make sure of it. I'm not going anywhere, and neither are you."

"Can't you see, for me there's no going back?"

"But you're not just my sister," he says. "You're my best friend."

"That's why you have to come with me. We find each other, always."

Wen's panting now, looking around him or inside himself for something that might make me change my mind.

He grabs a fistful of my jacket and hangs on tight. "I won't let you go."

This person threatening me is not my brother anymore. This is not Wen.

I shove at his chest and move out of his reach. Over my shoulder, I say, "Make sure Felix gets the money."

"Don't do this," he yells after me. "I'll hate you, Tal! I'll hate you if you keep walking!"

As much as I want to turn around, not once do I look back.

In that selfish moment, as I leave my brother alone on the sidewalk, I've become exactly who I never wanted to be—my mother.

Spencer's voice is soft behind me. "My car's this way."

I hook my hand into his and let him lead me between the buildings. He rips off his tie and tosses it into the backseat.

I fall into the car seat and rest my forehead against the window, squeezing my eyes shut hard enough to hold all my tears inside me.

As Spencer fires the engine, I open my eyes. Painted on a building's brick façade, in the most haunting green and yellow paint, is a mural of an owl.

CHAPTER 40

I THOUGHT THE DAY I LEFT THE WANDERING WORLD, if that day ever came, I'd stand by the side of the road and watch the caravan move on without me. I never dreamed of running away with an outsider, a markie boy named Spencer Sway.

He walks me to the front door after dinner, and even though his whole family is walls away, he kisses me hard, his lips moving mine apart. Pulling back, he looks at me like he expects something, maybe some words to bubble out of me, words even now I can't say.

He lets me get deeper into his house before he swings the front door open and throws his voice. "Good night, Tal."

The door slams shut, and I wink at Spencer before I close myself inside the basement.

With my ear pressed against the door, I hear Marcus ask, "You didn't walk her to her truck?" He never even noticed my truck wasn't parked outside.

"Yeah, I guess I should have." Feet go tromping up

the stairs, feet that must be Spencer's.

Shadows pass the crack at the bottom of the door. The click of the heels tell me it's Ella. "He didn't say much about the interview, did he?" she says.

All through dinner—from the paella to the flan—Spencer's answers were short when it came to his interview. With me there, it wasn't the time for him to come clean.

"I know," says Marcus. "Poor guy. He must be worried he won't get in."

I listen harder, hoping they'll say more. Something I can tell Spencer, to put his mind at ease.

"That girl's done him some good," Marcus says.

Ella sighs. "I hope it lasts for a while and doesn't end too badly."

"Who's to say it has to end?"

"Oh, Marcus." Her laughter is soft as Marcus's shadow joins hers. "You're so painfully idealistic."

My throat aches. Ella could be right.

I flip through a world atlas for a few hours, waiting for the house to go quiet and Spencer to join me. Hard as I try, I can't trick myself into believing I'm not heartbroken over Wen. In our lifetimes, we've only had a handful of harsh words between us. Nothing like this.

Now Wen's clinging to the Wanderers while I'm pushing them away. I'm chasing some vague notion of living in the outside world, and he's crushing his. He's held on to these dreams like a kid with a bug in a jar, and now that it's dying in his hands, he'd rather let it go than watch it suffocate.

With my head against the foam pillow, I listen to the noises overhead—faucets running, the heater turning on and off. Soon the house calms to a nearly silent still.

I wake up and feel for Spencer, but the blankets beside me are cold and empty. I collapse against the futon. He never snuck downstairs.

Voices rumble overhead. It isn't morning—it's pitch-black inside the basement, no light streaming through the tiny half window high up on the wall.

I listen closely. There's whispering I can't decipher, only the rhythm of Spencer's voice. There's definitely a rhythm to Spencer: his voice, his walk, the thoughts that dash across his eyes that he doesn't say out loud.

More voices.

Exhaustion overtakes me before I figure anything out.

Spencer's parents go to work early the next morning. He breaks me out of the basement, carrying a plate of warm Pop-Tarts and a jug of orange juice. He kicks off his shoes, and slips between the sheets, leaving some distance between us.

I pick a Pop-Tart off the plate and bite a hunk out of it, scattering crumbs across the blankets. "What's on the agenda today?"

"It's just us and Margaret." He swipes some crumbs onto the floor. "Do you have any kind of plan now?"

There was a time when the wheels of my mind never quit cranking, when plans were as easy and essential as breathing a con into life. I know I can't let Wen leave with them, but where the Wanderers are going, wherever that is, it's no longer somewhere I care to travel.

"No plan at all," I say.

I take a shower in the bathroom across from Spencer's bedroom. I wash my hair with a big handful of shampoo that smells exactly like Spencer, and stay under the steaming hot water until it runs cold.

"Tal," Spencer says through the door. "Are you okay in there?"

I wrap a white towel under my arms and finger-comb my hair, careful not to leave any of my long strands behind as evidence I was here. "You can come in."

Tufts of steam billow past the open door into the hallway. Wearing a grin, he's got an arm tucked behind his back. "I didn't think you were ever going to come out. I want to show you something." He flashes three computer printouts with glossy pictures and sets them on the bathroom counter. "Prague, Florence, and

Portugal. These are brochures for international colleges. If I went to one of these, I could travel by train on the weekends. All over Europe. Wherever I want to go. I'd get it all, then—college and the world, too."

"What about your parents?"

"I talked to them late last night. For a long time. It's not what they wanted, but they're okay with it. They're being . . . supportive."

With one hand holding my towel at my chest, I brush my wet hair over my shoulder and fan the pages out enough to see all the covers at once. "You're doing it. You're really doing it."

"Well, it's a compromise. And Portugal, you know, distancewise, isn't that far from Africa."

"I'm really happy for you, Spencer. I am." But my voice quivers.

He backs up against the cabinet and rests both hands behind him on the edge of the counter. "You don't get it. This wouldn't just be for me. I mean, I have part of senior year left. I'm trapped until graduation. After that, though, I thought, maybe, if you wanted . . ."

The whole world is sitting in my hands. All I have to do is close my fists to make it mine. But there's one person holding me back.

Wen jumped into the Wanderer world with both feet, and I'm no longer straddling the line; I'm a full-fledged markie hiding in the home of a judge and a gallery owner. The spaces between our worlds are only widening. Now I can see my brother, a small boat on the horizon, about to fall off the edge forever.

Spencer sighs and stacks up the brochures. "I don't have to know now. Or anytime soon. It was only a thought."

He leaves me alone in the bathroom, shivering in my towel.

We settle into the couch and camp there all morning while Margaret plays upstairs, intent on creating magic. I hook my legs over the back of the couch and dangle my head over the edge of the cushions.

Spencer leans over me while I hang upside down. Breathing into my wet hair, he says, a little disappointed, "You don't smell like you anymore."

We watch a marathon on the Discovery Channel, and his arm finds its way around me. Maps of far-away places are swirling in my head as I feel a buzzing against my thigh. Spencer reaches into his pocket for his phone.

"Hey, son," Marcus says through the speaker. The volume's turned up, so I make out almost every word. "Weatherman's saying there's a tornado warning."

Spencer sees me craning to hear and shifts the phone

to the ear closest to me. "In November?"

"Yeah, I know. Crazy damn weather we've been having. It touched down in Pike, so there's a good chance it'll be here soon. Take Mags into the basement until the warning is over."

"Oh sure," Spencer says. "But you mean it's a watch, not a warning, right?"

I tilt closer to the phone. A watch is nothing—I've sat beside a scratchy radio with Wen enough times to know. A watch means the atmospheric conditions are right for a tornado to happen. A warning means it's as good as here.

"No, it's a warning," says Marcus. "Don't worry, though. Last time this happened, it only touched down by the lake. Be safe, all right?"

By the lake. By camp. My mind swirls with images of trailers and RVs spinning through the darkening sky, the dream Wen told me about. The dream about the two of us getting separated. Wen is out there alone.

"You have to take me back to camp," I blurt. "I have to make sure Wen's okay."

Spencer snaps his attention from the phone and locks eyes with me. "Now? That's insane. We need to stay here until the warning's over."

I want to think I'm above manipulations now, especially when it comes to Spencer. I want to think I'm a new person, a better person. But Wen needs me to be the old Tal, so that's who I'll be.

Leaping from the couch, I grab on to his shoulders. "Spencer, I won't forgive you if you don't take me out there."

He shakes his head but finally says, "Let's go."

Margaret trudges around the corner, carrying a cape and her stuffed white rabbit.

"Mags." Spencer lowers to the carpet on his knees in front of her and shakes her small shoulders. "Run next door to the Brooks's house, will you? Tell them your parents aren't home, and I told you to wait with them until the storm passes."

He releases her, and she wobbles like a top that's about to fall over, before she takes off out the front door.

CHAPTER 41

THE SKY IS SICKLY GREEN AS WE DRIVE TO THAT SPOT in the woods. We didn't bother with seat belts. Or common sense.

With the wheels sliding around the winding mountain roads, Spencer says, "You realize this is crazy as hell, don't you?" But he doesn't slow his driving as we round the sharp turns.

He ducks between the steering wheel and the visor, watching the sky change colors. "Sirens haven't started yet. We've got some time."

We make it to the edge of the boundary and leap from the car. My feet twitch, but I turn back, and Spencer's frozen, staring at me over the hood. "Tal, I shouldn't go into your camp—"

As he steps to my side, Margaret swings the car door open and plants her feet on the ground.

"Are you kidding me, Mags? I told you to go next door!" says Spencer.

She sinks her hands into her hips and glares up at

him. "You're not the boss of me."

"I'm going to tell Mom and Dad that you didn't listen, and you'll be in big trouble—"

"Look!" yells Margaret.

Owls are flocking from the forest in droves, filling up the yellow sky. Spencer looks my way and watches me like I'm about to shatter.

I rub my palms over my face. "It doesn't mean anything."

But I'm not sure what I believe anymore.

Spencer's attention snaps back to the car, the clearing, the forest. "Hey, where'd she go?"

He flings all the car doors open, and the trunk, too. No Margaret.

"Margaret!" I yell. "Margaret!"

He looks right, then left, and screams into the forest, "Mags! I'm sorry! I'm sorry I was a jerk! Just come on out, and we'll forget about it, okay?"

Tornado sirens wail in the distance from Cedar Falls proper.

Spencer stares toward town. "We only have a few minutes now. I'll find Margaret. You get Wen and we'll . . ."

"There's a low-lying ditch on the other side of camp, halfway between the lake and the interstate."

He nods. "I know the one."

"Meet me there. We'll all wait out the storm

together."

Finally, I'm hit with the urge and the courage to tell him how I really feel. But now isn't the time. "Spencer, be so careful."

"You, too. I'll see you at that ditch."

"You—you better be there."

He forces a small smile. "I'll get there or die trying."

I run the rest of the distance to camp, where Wanderers are hammering stakes into the ground, tying belongings down, and grabbing their children. They know. None of it's going to make an ounce of difference if a tornado decides to come by and pick up their homes.

Other Wanderers migrate to the ditch in herds. Across the expanse of camp, Rona drifts that direction. But I don't see Wen.

I burst through our screen door without knocking. He's not there.

Tumbling outside, I come face-to-face with Sonia.

"You're back?" she says.

"I don't—" I check the road behind her, searching for Wen's dark head. Nothing. "I don't have time for this right now. Wen—I have to find him."

"He's working at that book place again." She blows the hair clear of her mascara-coated lashes. "He didn't even care when Lando said he'd beat him senseless. Wouldn't listen to no one."

All the air I've been storing flows from my chest.

Wen changed his mind—and he's safe. With those sturdy buildings downtown he has to be.

Wen's probably hiding in a storm shelter beside Blanche, holding a flashlight, and riding out the storm with a book. He hasn't given up on wanting more for himself. After everything my brother said, he still won't let go.

The forest rattles, and my jeans thrash against my legs. It's starting. I scan the horizon for Spencer. We said we'd meet at the ditch—that was the plan—but I won't be able to hold up my end of the bargain, not while he's out in the wild because of me.

"I have to find my—my friend."

"That guy you left us for?"

I blink and take a step backward. There's no sense in denying it. Breathless now, I say, "I have to—"

"Go," she says. And I do.

People race around me as I cut through the trailers. I break the line of trees, running to the deepest brush, almost losing myself in the dull greens and browns of the forest.

"Spencer! Margaret!" I cup my hands around my mouth. "Spencer! Margaret!"

Someone touches my shoulder. "Spencer," I whisper. My whole body relaxes as I whip around. But it isn't Spencer. It's Wen.

My chest gets so full I feel like I'll burst. I sob as our

arms wrap around each other. Into his shoulder, I say, "What are you doing here?"

"When we heard about the warning, I had to find you. I knew you'd come for me."

I pull back. "How did you know?"

"I just knew. We always find each other. Always."

"But you should have stayed put!" I knock my fist into his bicep. "You would have been safer!"

"No." Wen smiles. "Fortune favors the bold."

There's a howling sound, and I look straight up, through the branches woven together overhead, at the darkening sky.

"Spencer's out here. Spencer and his little sister, Margaret. . . ." I smear the tears off my cheeks.

"I know. I saw his car, but—"

The wind picks up, throwing leaves around us, stinging at my arms and legs through my clothes. A tree sways to my left and starts to plummet. I squeeze my eyes closed as it crashes to the ground, and when I open them, Wen's covering his head.

He grabs my hand. "The dock by the lake."

"But Spencer and—"

"Tal!" he yells over the wind and sirens. "We have to go! Now!"

We run downhill toward the lake. I search the woods for Spencer, but I stumble and almost trip. As we run, the ground beneath us wavers, and trees start toppling. We run faster and faster. Not once do we lose each other's hands.

We make it to the dock, and Wen throws himself onto his stomach and crawls beneath the dry space beside where the dock meets the water. I follow him, and we wrap our arms around each other, shielding our faces in each other's necks.

A board from the dock above goes flying off into the sky. The sound grows unbearably loud above, like a freight train barreling down.

Spencer is in the woods, and Mags, too, unsheltered and alone because of me. I wish I'd said the words I'd been too damned stubborn to say at the car. Some last-meal, too-little-too-late offering. That I love Spencer. Because I do.

Over the deafening wind, I barely make out Wen's words. "Spencer'll be okay."

Deep down, I know Wen could be horribly wrong. The way I love Spencer and the way I love Wen may be different, but the feelings are equally intense. Maybe we get no more than one great love in our lives, and maybe Wen and I are each other's. This is the way it always was and maybe the way it's supposed to be. Me and my brother, alone in the world.

Boards rip away above us. It could be the wind or

my panic rising, but with my face buried in Wen's chest, I can't catch my breath as I imagine uncharted worlds I'll have to wander for Spencer and me both.

CHAPTER 42

EVEN AFTER THE WORLD ABOVE US GOES STILL, Wen's weight anchors my body to the dirt beneath the dock.

I roll onto my back. Through a section of boards the tornado ripped clean away, I see the gray sky overhead. "I think it's over."

We crawl out, and as he dusts himself off, I scan the forest. Most of it is completely leveled, trees fallen down on each other and some half sunk in lake water. I stand still and stare over the trees, searching for some movement, even a rustle. Spencer couldn't have had time to make it all the way to the ditch.

"Spencer!" I yell. "Spencer!"

He should have heard the words I was too proud to say.

Wen cups his hands around his mouth. "Spencer! You okay, man?" He looks over his shoulder at me, his face softening. "He could be okay."

"His car isn't there anymore." Wen points up the

hill at an area where most of the forest is gone. "Maybe he found his sister and drove out of here."

That day on Main Street, I imagined him there, and I know it's silly, but maybe if I only think vividly enough—about his navy blue suit, his plaid shirts, the way his hair falls onto his forehead—I can imagine him back into my life.

Hollers and screams shatter my thoughts. Wen sprints in front of me, but it's not easy to make our way back to camp. We hop over fallen trees, stumble against splintered stumps, sink into the wet mud from unearthed roots.

We run to the edge of the fallen forest and stop, both Wen and me, at the outer edge of camp. Only half of camp still stands.

Trailers and RVs are destroyed, torn into a million pieces and scattered along the ground. It's hard to tell where every vehicle—every home—began and ended. But our tent trailer's okay, and so's the Chevy.

"The owls," Wen says. "This is what the omens were about."

Only I'm not so sure. If the Falconer—or anyone else—was trying to warn us about something, it wasn't this.

Maybe those owls were showing up to threaten me against betraying my Wanderer life. But maybe, just maybe, the Falconer was telling me I didn't belong anymore—and maybe all those years ago, he was telling Mom, too.

Wanderers pool around one overturned vehicle. My feet carry me farther—it's Sonia and Emil's RV.

Scanning the crowd, I find Rona, Felix, Lando, and Boss. I can't breathe until I see Sonia emerge from the back of the crowd, stumbling closer and bending toward the ground.

A boy is buried beneath the overturned RV, and he's staring at the sky, his eyes wide open and glassy. It takes me a few heartbeats to recognize the boy as Emil. His body is crushed from the chest down.

Sonia pushes forward, all the way to Emil's body. She slumps to her knees, one hand covering her mouth and one on her belly.

Her nails scratch against the metal siding. "Pull him out!"

Lando ambles from behind Boss's wheelchair and says, "He's gone, Sonia. Getting him out's not gonna make a difference."

Lando sets a careful hand against her back.

I shoulder through Wanderers. My eyes meet Lando's.

"She's *my* best friend."

His hand slips away as I slide to the muddy ground onto my knees beside her.

Sonia's soft weeping turns into wails as I crush her

against me.

We squeeze each other until I've lost all sense of where her limbs end and mine begin. There's nothing I can say. She wanted to be the other half of something, and I always wanted to be all of me, but that doesn't mean my heart's not shattered for her.

With her chin digging into my shoulder and her sobs wracking both our bodies, I stare dry-eyed at the unmoving forest.

I catch a flash of silver. High up in one of the few trees that refused to fall is the bumper of Spencer's sedan. Like Emil, somewhere out there, beneath a fallen tree, spread out among winter-cold leaves, might be Spencer.

Rona tries to close Emil's eyes, but they won't stay that way, so she finds a blanket and spreads it over him. She soon pulls Sonia's sobbing body away from me, and Wen hooks an arm under her, lending her support and leading her toward her parents.

"Come inside with us, Tal," says Wen as they trudge by.

My arms feel empty as I stare at that ravaged, unmoving forest. I sink lower into the mud.

There's a rustle from between the fallen trees, and Spencer emerges from the forest with Margaret hanging in the shadows behind him. He focuses on me and lurches forward but looks back at his sister and doesn't move.

He won't walk out here, in the remains of camp, with Wanderers pausing and staring at the woods.

Out here, we're something different.

I am something different.

But Spencer takes two steps and plants his feet in the sunlight.

The mud sucks at the knees of my jeans as I get my legs under me. I try to go to him, but it's as if my whole body has gone to sleep.

He hesitates there, at the edge of the boundary line, the uncertainty before his touch now present in his sad eyes. And I remember that when the Wanderers are watching, he doesn't know if I'm his, if I'm still the girl I am when the lights are low and we're alone in his room.

Until right now I wasn't sure, either.

I set my body in motion, taking careful steps across the debris, never letting my eyes leave his. I meet him halfway.

CHAPTER 43

ALONE, I SIT INSIDE A COFFEE SHOP ON MAIN Street. Through the fogged-up windows, I watch workers rope off the street while I wait for Sonia.

Her cheeks are pink from the cold as she takes a seat across from me. It's been three days since the tornado struck.

I push one of the mugs of tea her way. "How is everything at camp now?"

She drums her fingers on the table. "Nobody can believe all those owls, those omens, were warning us about something like that. About the tornado. About"—her voice cracks—"about Emil."

I reach across the table, but she stills her hand against the Formica, leaving a space between us I don't try to fill.

She empties two packages of sugar into her tea. "You'll be happy to know your plan worked, after all. Horatio's been noticing some of his savings going missing for a while now. He marked a few bills and caught

Lando with them. Everyone came forward then, claiming they had money missing. Turns out, Lando's not that good a liar. He admitted it was all hidden in Boss's RV."

A genuine smile creeps up. "You can't be serious. Does Boss know?"

"Damn straight." Sonia matches my grin. "Boss got his chalkboard and scribbled that it didn't matter if Lando was his son, he wasn't his successor anymore. Not only that, he wasn't welcome at camp. Already packed his bags and hit the road. And Felix took off, you know? He told Boss he was going to tell his parents he didn't want you, after all. That it was fine by him."

I stare out the window, at no particular spot on the sidewalk. "That's great." I actually mean it, though the feeling doesn't shine through. "Who's going to take care of Boss now?"

"Rona. She said she'd be his caregiver until his end. Lando leaving doesn't change anything, does it?"

I try to smile, but my lips don't cooperate.

"You're gonna stay here, Tal, after all that's happened." It's not a question—she knows my mind is made up.

"I can't be a Wanderer anymore."

Streaks of mascara spill down Sonia's cheeks. "You gotta do what you gotta do."

And I do know what I have to do. What I want to do.

My words come out fast as I take her hand. "Stay with me. Here in Cedar Falls. Things have been weird between us, I know, but they don't have to be anymore. Stay, and everything will be okay—I promise you." I look to her belly. "I'll help you with the baby. It'll be the way you always wanted it. We'll get diapers and a crib and even some toys, and your baby'll have the both of us. For always."

Sonia doesn't look up.

"Sonia, stay with me." My voice quivers. "You don't have to go with them now. I'm so, so sorry about Emil—I never would have wanted that to happen to you—but you've got nothing holding you back now."

She cringes. "Tal, it was never because of Emil that I wanted to stay with camp. Staying in one place is never gonna be enough for me."

My chair's legs screech against the floor as I scoot away from her. "We won't stay in one place. Not always." Spencer's maps swirl through my head. I'm not certain we'll see the world, but the hope I have is enough to make me stay. "We'll—we'll see everything."

A sad smile parts her lips. "I need more than the promise of the world. I gotta keep going."

Sonia wants the Wanderer life, and I want something more—something different—than being a Wanderer. And now I understand. So did Mom.

She's out there somewhere, not with camp, not with us, and, for the first time ever, the thought of her making her way through the world alone doesn't anger me.

It isn't always right or pretty what we have to do to end up in that place we belong. Or who we have to leave behind.

Wherever Mom is, I hope she likes her decisions. And I hope Sonia does, too.

We finish our tea without saying anything else. She pushes away from the table, and this is it. We're likely to never see each other again. I move closer to her and open my arms, but she says, "Hugging you is only going to make me cry," so I glue my hands to my sides.

She winds her scarf around and around her neck and breezes onto the sidewalk. Over her shoulder and through the windowpanes, she glances back at me, the weight of her dreamy eyes almost knocking me over.

My voice dies inside my throat as I search for a way to get Sonia to stay behind, wishing for the power to cure the restlessness inside her.

She walks on, and the moment is gone.

My stomach twists as Spencer strolls through the doors, even though I've known for three days he made it out of the forest alive. The tornado ripped a violent path through Cedar Falls, but it left the Sways' home, Marcus's gallery, and, most importantly, Spencer untouched. Margaret took shelter in a drainage pipe, ready to wait out the storm. That's where Spencer found her.

I don't really know how I could have lived with myself if Spencer hadn't found Mags and crawled in beside her, knowing the boy I love—yes, *love*—would have been thrown among drying winter leaves, his great big heart unmoving inside his chest.

"Everything all right?" he asks as I pay the tab.

"No." I weave my fingers between his. "But it will be."

The air is colder since the tornado. The streets are empty, except for a few cars zipping past and even fewer people walking outside. Spencer and I sit on a bench in front of the bookstore, and I press my numb face into his shoulder while he runs his fingers through my hair.

Across the street, I feel someone's eyes on us. I turn, and there's Whitney with her hand lifted and a smirk on her lips. I nod back. We might be friends, after all.

It's hard to think about staying here in Cedar Falls and harder to think about leaving. Even if being a compass was a lie, something out there, or inside me, led me back to Cedar Falls.

I'm not the kind of compass from the markie world, pointing toward true north, and not the kind from the Wanderer world, leading our camp to the luckiest places. Yet there's something inside me. It kept me turning in random circles for ten years and then brought me back to a small clearing of trees in Cedar Falls.

I don't know what I believe in—the stars aligned too serendipitously for nothing magical to be real—but I do believe in possibility. Of what, I don't know. Of magic, of omens, of compasses, of love. Some of it's a little bit true.

Through the bookstore window, Wen glances to me, and he turns the sign on the door from OPEN to CLOSED. Keys jangle as he locks up the bookstore for the day. Only for the day. He'll open the doors for business midmorning tomorrow and help the people of Cedar Falls find stories they can sail away inside.

Blanche Fairchild offered us a cottage she owns, right on the outside of town, but we told her our tent trailer felt too much like home to abandon. So, instead, she's got a patch of land on her property with our name on it, the right size for parking the Chevy and the tent trailer both.

Wen settles into the space on the other side of me. "It's almost time."

Down on Main Street, one block away, I hear the trot of horses and the excitement of town. The yearly Thanksgiving parade is about to start, though I won't be riding down any floats of clouds or soapsuds this year.

For so long, I tried to chase away the invincible wilds living inside my heart. But now I know there's no beating them, that sometimes those wilds send your wheels turning to new, faraway places. And sometimes, those wilds keep your wheels from turning at all.

Sitting between Spencer and Wen, not traveling with the camp and not really settled in Cedar Falls, either, my feet are calm for now, though I don't know for how long. The whole world's out there, all waiting to be seen, and I want to walk to the very edge of it, as far as I can go.

ACKNOWLEDGMENTS

Many wonderful people came into my life to make my dream of getting *Wandering Wild* published into a reality. My deepest gratitude to the following:

My editor, Alison Weiss, who loved this book enough to acquire it twice. Thank you for believing in my words even when I didn't, and for giving me such expert editorial guidance. You made me fall in love with Tal's story again. This book wouldn't exist without you. Yahtzee.

Julie Murphy, my critique partner, and partner in crime. Your unfailing belief in my writing has kept me from leaving this world. Without you, I'd probably be a boring lawyer by now.

Stephanie Garber, I so appreciate your willingness to listen, your prayers, and your advice. We were meant to climb this mountain together. Joanna Rowland, my favorite cheerleader and a wonderful friend—there aren't enough bottles of Runquist to show you the depths of my appreciation. Jennifer Mathieu, your friendship and support over this last year have kept me afloat. Janelle Weiner, for countless hours of talking, and for helping me take my story to another level.

My Fearless Fifteener family, especially Alexis Bass, Virginia Boecker, Kelly Loy Gilbert, Stacey Lee, and

Sabaa Tahir. Even though we didn't share a debut year as we'd planned, you made me feel as if we did. Your talent astounds me and your kindness has meant the world.

Kendare Blake, Katherine Longshore, and (John) Corey Whaley, for lending your beautiful words to praise *Wandering Wild*.

Julie Matysik and everyone at Sky Pony Press for coming to my rescue when I found myself without a publisher. Sarah Brody, for designing this gorgeous cover.

Sarah LaPolla, for your guidance on my early work and for matching *Wandering Wild* with the perfect editor.

My agent, Melissa Sarver White and my Folio Literary family, you can't know what your enthusiasm and your confidence in my writing have meant over the last year.

A special thanks to Sarah Clift, Rose Cooper, Kim Culbertson, Shannon Dittemore, Kristen Held, Jenny Lundquist, Heather Marie, and Valerie Tejeda. You talented writers have given me the kind of community worth even the rockiest days of this journey.

My lifelong friends, Ardeep Johal and Allison Fuller. Ardeep, for sharing your books and making me love them. Allison, for reading my first terrible writings and believing wholeheartedly that I could make a career of this.

And lastly, my parents for going above and beyond to support my dreams of being a published author. Thank you for making your life harder so my life could be better. I love you both so very much.